JESSICA BERRY

First published in Australia in 2024
By Jessica Berry

Text Copyright 2021
By Jessica Berry

National Library of Australia
Cataloguing-in-Publication data:
Berry, Jessica, 2024, author
Wake/ Jessica Berry
author
ISBN 978-0-646-70892-8
Adult Fiction
Fiction_visionary and metaphysical

Design by Jessica Berry

What is it you're looking for?
Are you still going to search for it?
Don't you want to try
going into a dream, into a dream?

-English translation of
Minna Yume no Naka- *Into a dream*
by Kuranosuke Hamaguchi

1.

Loneliness

*I*dea wakes.
At first her awareness is suffused with a sense memory of sweetness, only to sink back into a memory of the heavy and bittersweet anguish of existence. For Idea this heaviness is a daily robe she dons. It falls into its groove as a record needle into vinyl and plays its dirge. She knows it like dirty tracksuit bottoms, is at once repulsed and comforted.

Idea lays in bed and thinks up these metaphors for existential pain, sends them out like torpid notes from the bowstring of a battered cello. She gives it all her attention, feels into the corresponding body sensations, notes how tears rush to her face, how her eyes precipitate their storm. It coalesces, heavy and drab, and she begins to gather up its edges with an intensity of focus. Her 'hands within hands' work into its mass, pulling and shaping, creating edges and herding them to the centre of her chest. Then she pushes, timing the push with her out-breath. All at once a dark thing shlupps from her chest into a concentrated mass hovering above her, and with an intense focus she probes it for a shape.

Is it to be a poem today? Or simply a note? Does it have the semblance of identity? Ah. There it is. That point where wondering becomes certainty.

She waves her hand elegantly, because for Idea; *theatre helps.* The thing obeys her gesture and solidifies into a form. A dark bird emerges, within

1

the centre of its eye a karmic wheel turns. The bird gives a caw and ruffles its feathers. Idea sees the intention of flight in this gesture, and with another gesture of her own quickly seals it in a transparent sphere. Within the sphere the bird shape-shifts to a simple grey gloom, that charcoal grey right before black, and the sphere drops onto the bed, rolling to rest against the mountain ridges of her bedcovers.

Idea pretends she is named for her work. She is one who captures ideas as they are born within her attention and gives them worldly forms. It never feels like it is she who entirely gives the forms however, but some occult entanglement of herself and the thing born within her. This is mere posturing, in fact she is named Idea, simply because it is short for No Idea. She does not remember who she is.

Idea catches a whiff of her own fetid morning breath, and makes a comic sick face, one eye closed, the other staring, her tongue lolling out from the side of her mouth, *gack!* Her bladder sends an urgent signal to her brain, and she heaves her form out of bed, and shrugs into her robe. As she hastens to the toilet en suite she speaks aloud to her bladder,

"Another fine nights work of transforming foods into urine," she tells it. "I'll just go deliver your urgent message to the toilet shall I? You're welcome."

Idea is the definition of lonely, creates friendship for herself from nothing, anything, even her own bladder. *Hah* she puns to herself, *urine vited*, then groans inwardly, *dork.*

Idea lives currently in a reality devoid of any other living soul, devoid of any sort of companionship. *Well. There's Library.*

Idea has often mused on whether she herself is simply a character projected from within the database of Library, deluded with some notion of an extrinsic existence. She suspects she's probably made herself up, mixed together from a batter of stories into some sort of person.

"Oh, I *seem* to be sitting on the toilet... but is there *really* a toilet?"

The toilet is enclosed within an alcove entered through an automatic sliding panel, and when the toilet panel opens the lights glow automatically in an ambience so balanced she rarely notices they exist. Where is she? Currently Idea drifts in the depths of outer space. The ship in which she travels is very well equipped, she thinks of it as 'self-functioning'. The ship is odd, there is no control room, no deck housing a warp drive. Idea speaks to her toilet as it flushes,

"you do you."

She knows that it self-cleans.

This simple automated service initiates a stirring in her bosom, a kind of welling immensity, and she knows it at once; *Oh! simple gratitude.* With a tired gesture she pops it from her chest already encapsulated in a sphere. This one has no form, just a soft glow of pink light with little golden flecks. She yawns and drops it into one capacious pocket of her robe, then rolls the other sphere towards her from the bed and drops that into the other pocket.

Idea makes her way along the down ramp to Library. The entrance panel senses her approach, slides open in perfect timing, and Library chimes its small cooperative tone to salute her arrival. She makes taps on the interface screen and Library displays its home page in what she has dubbed 'basic mode', a screensaver of simple blue and green lines shifting in an allusion to the aurora borealis.

She recalls that; 'aurora borealis', it is something of Earth, and she fears that her home planet has been utterly destroyed. There is a problem with this theory: she can't remember even a tiny detail of what would surely be the single most epic incident in the life of a human. She may be the only human left alive in the universe, but she often mocks her own surmise; *Behold, the narcissist ponders her abject loneliness, comes to solipsistic conclusion. Yep. It's all about me.* Library is a database referencing planet Earth, data right up until the year recorded as 2019 AD, and then nothing. What has happened to Earth? Idea has no idea, but she has a few working theories. Next to the Library interface there is a tube receptacle for the spheres, and she plops them in one after the other. She speaks to Library as she waits for its dialogue box response, "there you go you old monster, a banquet on the spectrum of angst to gratitude."

A tiny rainbow circle rotates on the screen interface in response.

"I'll leave you with that shall I?"

Idea never knows how long Library will take to digest her inputs, so she continues down the spiral ramp into the Library 'reading room' and drops into a battered leather chair.

"Hmmm, what shall I do with my life? Oh, that's riight, guess I'll do some reading..."

Instead, she falls into a reverie on whether she has any agency at all: *the ol destiny vs freedom conundrum.*

Idea's current pet theory is that the ship is somehow 'fueled' with the spheres. This matches the concept of 'feeding' the spheres into Library's 'mouth', but this theory would position her in a very abstract situation indeed. A more practical assessment would be that the ship is simply solar powered. She knows that even though the ship appears to float through the darkness of some unfathomable region of deep space, the light of a billion suns still surely exerts some influence? She can turn off all the lights in the ship, and still be bathed in starlight through the 360-degree windows up on the observation deck. As she sits and ruminates in her armchair, Idea lets out a short, bitter laugh, and says aloud,

"a strong symbol of the authority I am invested with aboard this ship; turning the lights off and on."

Laughing at my own jokes, someone's got to do it.

She does not *really* understand Physics and Math. *Maybe that's why I'm not allowed to drive.* Her brain seems custom built for whimsy and feelings, things she currently thinks of as 'sphere fodder'. She refers to the idea of gravity as 'uppydowny' and to Algebra as 'al-Khwarizmi's folly'. She does not need to understand physics and math, as everything is *done*. The ship flies itself. Idea lounges in the leather armchair and knows its artful homeliness is simply part of the holo-function of the ship. *Hollow function.* It seems like a comfy armchair, but it's all just part of the holo-responsiveness (HR) systems onboard the ship. This supreme responsiveness of the ship ultimately depresses her. She suspects the unchanging view of space on the observation deck is possibly also a hologram. She has a deep longing for what she thinks of as 'really real reality'. She has failed many times to render a sphere from the shape of this longing. 'Really real reality' remains elusive. Sometimes she amuses herself with simply appending more 'reallys' onto it; *maybe if I can capture the essence of 'really, really, really, realest, reality' I'll nail it.* Not so far. With an extended sigh she pulls herself theatrically up and out of the chair and slumps up the spiral ramp to the interface.

"You done yet?"

She knew it was done. She both wants to sink into a kind of 'state of Tao' with the ship and is simultaneously at odds with this. It manifests as what she calls 'the game of intuition'. This game entails sensing the functions of the ship and responding to them seamlessly, a pantomime of its own superb service; *I want to out-butler the butler.* She always knows when Library is done digesting her spheres, but she also pretends she doesn't. Instead of reading the dialogue box immediately, she sinks to sit cross legged on the floor. Idea remembers much about Earth, and still considers herself an Earthling. As she sits, she recalls the early 21st century notion of 'defanging' devices. This entailed 'turning off all notifications' and was ultimately a Band-Aid response created by the initial victims of the early social media apocalypse. Idea likes the idea of de-fanging, it fits in with her notion of Library as a monster. She has turned off all notifications of functions in the ship, bar the Library entrance chime. *I like the entrance chime, it's like there's someone here to say hello to me, even if it is a monster.* Idea stands to look at the information generated in response to inputting the spheres. Library displays an infographic based on the supposed 'data' of her spheres, an output for her input. This is rendered in a jolly vector graphic of a generic genderless body, a kind of motion graphics style animation showing percentage ratings with corresponding colours for her 'thought-scape'. The infographic always includes a probability rating of whether she'll commit suicide that day. Today's reading shows 'likelihood of suicide: low'. Idea gestures over the Library interface, pauses the animation and flips through it in stills instead. She pauses on a category that always amuses her; 'Likelihood of enlightenment' and notes it shows as 'ineffable'. Idea mutters darkly in response, "I'll give you effing ineffable" then continues idly flipping through her readings. Something bumps up against her ankles. She squats down and pats the little vacuum bot on the head

"Hi kitty kitty".

The display on the small circular vacuum shows a basic pixel style animal face, its mouth flicking from an x shape to an open square, Idea thinks of this as 'meowing'. She tells it "enjoy your crumbs little one" and steps aside to let the vac-bot continue on its programmed path. Each level on the ship has a little vacuum and she thinks of these as her 'pets'. She can type questions into Library and receive what she can only assume are reliable answers. Library appears to be a database of a 'curated' collected annals of humanity up to the Library end of records, 2019 AD. Some questions however are deflected. Early on Idea had typed in, with a mixture of whimsy and seriousness,

'Is this ship powered by thought?'

The answer was, "I think therefore I am".

Library contains data from Earth. Idea assumes she is human. Her head appears to be full of human stuff; *but where are all the other humans?* There were questions to which Library gave enigmatic answers and Idea referred to these as 'Things Library Won't Tell Me'. These answers were always in the form of quotes by long-dead human writers. Library monitored her thought-scape through the spheres, and produced the infographics, but it didn't feel like judgement, it felt more like she was perhaps Library's pet project, like she was some kind of human lab rat. The ship self-functioned and Library was the only information interface, the bits she was allowed to access. Idea grimaces to herself, there is a daily feedback loop of questions that runs around and around in her head. *Where is the engine room? How does the ship create the food I eat? How did I get here? Who created the ship? and 'What has happened to Earth?"*

Some days she believes the Earth is fine, and that she has actually been ejected from her home planet. She wonders whether she was some kind of arch villain, and they wiped her memory before sending her into space. *Thing is, I don't feel like an arch villain... but is that what an arch villain would think?* Idea had awakened to her intergalactic sojourn from what she assumes was a 'stasis pod'. There are no records of her time spent in the pod. There are no records of her time before the pod. There are no records of herself previous to awakening in the pod, either in the Library interface or in her poor Swiss- cheesy head. The pod itself appears to have been 'absorbed' by the ship, she cannot find it anywhere on board. The ship does not have any function that measures the passing of time, and Idea is cast adrift from any circadian rhythm. No 'Sun' rises and sets in view of the observation deck, because she is not on a spinning planet orbiting a sun. Idea is more like a sort of asteroid set on 'drift' rather than 'hurtle'. Idea is a mystery unto herself, 'a riddle, wrapped in a mystery, inside an enigma' as Library would say. The thing with the spheres...

This has not always been a thing. After awakening, she went through a period of novel interest in the ship, then slumped very quickly into a profound depression. Depression could not accurately sum it up. It was a claustrophobia of herself, a loneliness that felt like social anxiety, a prison in which she had been sentenced to an eternity of the intrusion of nothing but the monotony of the hamster wheel of her own head. She had lay where she fell, and she lay like a miasma, like a stain. She had no energy left to end her life. She saw a vision of the self- cleaning function of the ship recycling her biology gradually and efficiently, like a colony of AI ants. All she need do was give up the resistance that was *herself*, but the trouble was Idea did not know exactly *who* 'herself' was. She sat in various postures of defeat about the ship, the curved mirror walls reflecting back funhouse versions of her image to mock her. Eventually she had grown bored of this. Into her mind crept the notion that while she believed she existed simply in a state of decay, in fact she was in a torpor of renewal. She saw that she renewed her despair over and over again, that as it began to lift, she added new ballast to drag it down. In this moment creativity dawned. She saw that all this was just notions. The idea of despair, the idea of defeat, the idea of the status of victim.

She saw that all this was an assumption. She felt the lifting of her spirits and stopped fighting it. *After all, why not just let em lift?* There came the knowing that her 'heart within her heart' was stronger than all of her ideas. All at once this epiphany had coalesced into the sense of a shape within her. This shape felt at once like a thought, and like a body sensation, like a 'body thought'. It had struck Idea suddenly as odd that she assumed thoughts seemed to be 'housed' only in her brain. This 'body thought' felt as though it were born within her heart. The shape was not a vision of lightness, but the presence of a black and heavy substance. She felt then the first sensation of 'hands within her hands', and felt within these hands the idea of a blade. She began to carve the dark stuff in crude chops, hacking and breathing raggedly with effort. In time there came a sense of completion, and she saw before her a carving of the organ of her heart, black as though burned, raw and bludgeoned into shape. Her innermost hands gestured, and the form was enclosed within a sphere, this had dropped to the floor of the hallway she lay in with a deep and hollow sound, and rolled, coming to rest some distance from her. Idea had lain then in a wretched state of wonder. She had slowly staggered upright, retrieved the sphere and headed to Library to tinker with it.

What awaited her was downright spooky; the Library interface had changed. Next to the interface screen there was now a receptacle of corresponding shape to the sphere she held in her hands. This had not been there before. Idea had accepted her madness then and realised it did not matter. She had pictured a 'certified mad' swipe card on a lanyard around her neck, an albatross of bureaucracy. A scene of herself had flashed through her mind, a sort of Bladerunner bar scene, a droid bartender wiping a glass,

"So what do you do?"

Herself as the AI Rachael,

"I can't rely on my memories."

So began her daily 'work'. She thought of her spheres as inputs, it was her job to make them and feed them to the ship. Perhaps this was some kind of post apocalypse paradox? Endless space and time alone to create, only no one to share it with. Just the feedback from Library that she would live another day; 'likelihood of suicide: not today'.

Idea has a host of characters inside her head whose lives she imagines as alter-egos. *Who would I be if I wasn't stuck in the enormity of space with no home planet, no memory of my past and no agency for my future?* One of these was MC Hamster. A little hamster that ran around on a wheel to nowhere, her head chock full of delusions of grandeur. She imagined herself at another dystopian sci-fi bar, this time one exclusively for space hamsters.

"Oh, I work in an office by day, but by night I'm a hip hop MC, you may have heard of me?'

Her alter-egos were never superheroes, never what she referred to as 'Protagonists'. She had seen her reflection in the mirror, and she did not return often to look upon it. She knew she appeared to very likely be the much despised middle aged. *I'm many shades of brown and kind of lumpy. Brown hair, brown skin, brown eyes. I'm pretty much a human version of the comfy armchair in Library.* Oh, she does yoga. This was partly what convinced her she had not been ejected from Earth. *What kind of arch villain does yoga?* She has another character she calls 'Armchair Worrier', *I am a powerful worrier for the empire, a soldier to cry on.* She thought of her extended armchair musings as 'workouts' as in; *I'm busy working things out.* Perhaps someday soon a ship full of Protagonists on their mission to save the universe would come across her floating aimlessly through space. She'd flash her 'certified mad' lanyard and they'd grant her a job washing dishes in the galley. Protagonist women had pillowy lips but firm bad asses, not truly bad, but baaaad. These ones looked great in all rubber, and their pert little bosoms defied gravity as they ninja kicked British bad guys in the face. *At least this stopped the baddies going on about their dastardly plans. 'Thanks rubber babe! I couldn't listen to another minute of Evil Nemesis' ranting'.* Idea pictured herself with a little rubber fan flag waving somewhere at the periphery of the heroes and villains. Protagonist men were not born but hewn from rock. They had staff who misted them so that they perma-glistened, and they powered their laptops from their own constant ketosis. They were so purposeful that their bodies were a love poem to action. They crushed their own poop before it left their bodies as dust, they had no time to take a dump. Boring sections of their lives were artfully montaged. Idea had spent many 'days' slumped in her armchair, longing for a montage. At least she has a mystery to work on. *What happened to Earth? What happened to my past? Who am I?"* The kind of math she could manage was 'things that don't add up'. *If I'm not 'a Protagonist' how did I come by this spaceship?*

Early on she'd made a list of passengers it made sense would be onboard this ship.

The President: she simply could not picture a president ejected from Earth without a retinue.

Heiress: If she were an heiress, she imagines she would feel more entitled. *Of course, the ship is self-cleaning, of course I don't have to drive.* She felt more like a prole about to wipe her dirty hands on the white leather in the back of a white-on-white Mercedes.

11

Some kind of Genius: with Precious Knowledge crackling like inspired lightning between her ears: nope.

Future Eve: the last woman alive on Earth, ejected into space with her precious cargo of ova. So where was Adam? This was her favourite theory, *some hope for a future hook up is nice!*

Variation on the arch villain theory: She's done a bad bad thing and she's wiped her own memory of her personal history, so she wouldn't feel bad for her abandoned family or whatnot. This had merit, though surely into the ashes of a wiped memory would be born a similar pattern of self? Was it possible for a budgerigar to arise from the ashes of a Phoenix?

Surely, I would have to be a representative of the 0.1 % of the 1%? Some kind of card-carrying member of the Oligarchy?
Idea simply has no sense of herself as having an important destiny.

Then there was the data available within Library and the 'blank canvas' of the ship itself. It appeared to be an unbranded space. Surely her spaceship was funded by SpaceX? None of the dominant Earth tech giants she remembered appeared to be responsible for her present circumstances. When she watched movies from Library's movie menu it was not accessed as Netflix or YouTube. She could read about these corporations, but none of her data appeared to stem exclusively from them. Library was not Google. She could not go online shopping; she could not download messaging apps. She could download nothing interactive, just the recorded works of the collective imaginations of the (all dead?) inhabitants of Earth. There was no logos on anything, anywhere within the ship. Where was the evidence of 'space travel brought to you by...'? Was it possible that she was so rich that she had taken passage on the only unbranded space left on earth? Earth 2019 was clearly owned by corporations, the playground of a handful of infamous billionaires and (according to some) a shadowy cabal of bankers who drank the blood of children. Earth was made up of tribes of folk who agreed with each other's crackpot theories on 'what the fuck is happening here?' and vehemently opposed each other's niche beliefs. *How did they cultivate such unswerving belief in their narratives? Where are all these 'holders of opinions' now?* She'd read many different theories of impending apocalypse in Library's records, but there was no concrete evidence that any apocalypse had occurred. In 2019 humanity appeared to live in a state of impending doom, but there still seemed to be 7.8 billion very much alive doomsayers eking out their online lives saturated in anxiety.

Situation: Certain Doom, Status: pending.

There were humans busily planting trees and other humans busily cutting them down. The data of Library sketched a portrait of a planet trapped in a misinformation age. There was no recorded evidence that humanity had yet achieved 'manned' space travel, but for a lot of bluster about a plan for making it to Mars, and a rarely noticed side battle over the rights and ethics of mining the moon. All this data (or lack thereof) made it very difficult to make sense of her mystery, as she very much appeared to be travelling through deep space. The Library interface did not have the means to take photographs, she could not download a picture of herself and do a Facebook image search, she could not access Facebook, only engage with it as a record of the times she appeared to have left behind. What hegemony lay behind this spaceship? Still, part of her was pleased that the apparent age of zero privacy included a woman so totally alone and unknown as herself, even if she did have to be floating aimlessly through deep space to find it. Was she so tired of opinions that she simply ghosted on Earths' party? Snuck away under the radar in the simple pursuit of peace and quiet? This felt like her strongest theory thus far.

Idea yawns widely now, and types into Library,
"Am I naught but the creation of the patronising AI of this ship? An anthropomorphic folly?"
Library: "Old Macdonald had a human, AI,AI, oh?"
Idea pokes the screen interface with her index finger,
"haha, tres amuse."
She throws a hand across her brow,
"I'm leaving you forever! The dining pod AI and I have fallen in love! Goodbye!"
The screen interface only flickers mutely through the stock images on its screen saver in reply.

The dining pod. Idea has very mixed feelings about it. It could never be true that she had fallen in love with it, as it was equally untrue that Library was capable of jealousy. The dining pod simply makes her squeamish. *What am I actually eating?* Early on she had asked Library if she was eating her own recycled poop. Library had this time answered her with a straightforward: "no."
The dining pod contained a little nook for one person to eat in, an introverts' booth at a diner. There was no prep bench or sink as there was no cooking, just a 3D printer that printed out a small selection of food shapes in a limited selection of colours. It was ghastly. Idea often

thought *whoever invented this ship is a monster!* And then prayed it wasn't herself. She gestures over the printer interface and prints 'fruit salad'. This was her most colourful dish. The food printer had two 'flavour options': savoury and sweet. Idea thinks again whether the ship had been created by a child savant. She places her hand to her belly. It is pooched, and she feels a touch memory in her finger of the stretch marks above her pubis, the scars of a deflated balloon. A thought occurs to her, and she is suprised by its vehemence; *this body has borne a child.* Inside her heart within a heart she traces similar scars, her heart had once been full, and now it sagged, empty. *Where is the child?*

So passes Idea's 'life'. She is stuck in an anti-montage, someone has edited together all the mundane bits and set them in a loop. Nothing grows, no process goes through its transformation to the soulful notes of a guitar. This life was pure ennui. Sometimes at 'night' Idea dreamed. Her dreams were things of light. The dappled light of Earth's sun, the dappled dance of light and shadow. She dreamed of the shapes and tiny flutters of leaves. Of figures silhouetted and limned in gold. Of the slow gradient from dusk to night, the august return of the sun at dawn. She dreamed simply of touch, of hands held, shoulders squeezed, cheeks kissed. In Ideas' dreams she had company, she was loved and gave love. There was the face of a child, the swell to bursting feel of her heart. There were trees, and flowers, and a multiplicity of flavours and scents. The trees glowed with the light of gods, the colours of flowers seemed to leap forward in an airy ink, painted in holy strokes. She dreamed she rode a bicycle, felt the deep satisfaction of powering her vehicle with her own rhythm. These sense impressions ebbed and flowed to her as on a tide, each wave carrying a simple joy. There was the boisterous bark of a happy dog, and the up-turned and fluffy belly of a fat cat. She drank in this nourishment all unknown to the attendance of her waking mind. Her dreams dripped the nectar of connection as from a mothers' breast, and she surfaced into the waking place wrapped in the soft tissue of gratitude. Then, her mind would remember, and those golden offerings would flee, dissipating in a mist of forgetting. Sometimes Idea dreamed she knew who she was. It felt like a given, like an 'ah, of course'. She woke from these dreams with a sense of profound loss. Her hands within hands would set to work, attempting to perfectly transcribe this sad story of loss and despair into a sphere of surpassing poignancy. No matter what dark spheres she fed into the Library receptacle her likelihood of suicide rating always read as 'low'. *Is Library attempting to keep me alive? And yet my presence on board the ship seems passive and non-essential.*

She felt purpose in the creation of the spheres, thought of it as 'her work'. She suspected her human nature was just addicted to finding meaning in the morass of her days.

Punctuating waking and dreaming was deep sleep.

Who was Idea then?

2.

Tokyo, Earth, 2038

Haruki Mori is half Japanese, named by his white Australian mother for her favourite Japanese author. He thinks of Murakami as his patron saint, and half expects some day to find himself at the bottom of a well, with only an early eighties telephone. He would pick up the receiver and hear the voice of his ex-wife, telling him over and over again 'I'm leaving you'. He would then awake uncannily back in his apartment and cook a spaghetti dinner while listening to soulful jazz, or perhaps a Rossini overture (Amongst all this Murakami daydreaming he still had a preference not to find himself inseminating his ex-wife in a dream). He'd grown up in Australia, with his taciturn Japanese father and his erudite mother. He spent his childhood and adolescence steadfastly molding himself into the dried husk that was his roughly sketched approximation of the Australian male. Not until his thirties had Japan knocked on his heart's door in the petite form of his (now ex) wife, he had allowed it entrance ruefully. They had moved to Japan just two years ago, his wife had been missing it. She could not put her finger on exactly what it was she missed, but Haruki now understands. In his childhood he had struggled to relate to his father, and was shocked to find that the country that had baked his fathers' clay awoke in himself a poignancy he'd thought held under water and drowned by the sunburnt hands of his childhood bullies. The couple had been duly vaccinated, health transport stamped and deemed fit to transfer their officially inspected bacteria from the biome of Oz to the petri dish of Japan. Haruki is tall for a Japanese man, but average height for an Australian man. His hair is quite long, and rather messy. His clothes often look as though he recalled he should put some on before leaving the house. His face is open, could be described as child-like, although he is in fact in his early middle age. He has the eyes of a dreamer, wide open to the world, and yet far away within his own. Just now he strolls and thinks to himself; *God the Earth is a suffocating straight-jacket of human bureaucracy. The fucking ticky-boxy life. Did we really evolve to be lab rats, repeatedly pawing our little dopamine levers?* He takes a bite of the yakitori[1] skewer he's just purchased from a mask and glove clad street vendor. The pandemic is long vaccinated and absorbed into history, but there's a lingering social code around it in Japan, thus there's still street vendors, but they all wear masks and gloves as both a symbol of social responsibility, and even this long post-madness, by dint of a lingering lockdown anxiety. Earth 2038 has many new social rules to navigate, but Haruki chews happily as he strolls to the nearby park, and sits down on his usual park bench, giving thanks for the simple pleasures still available to him. He shivers a little in the brisk winter air, shrinks his neck down slightly into his down coat and congratulates himself on his purchase of sheep-skin lined boots. It still snows sometimes in winter in Japan. Winter has seemed very long this year to Haruki. On the other end of his bench is a cat asleep under an open newspaper. He waves at the cat,

"Konban wa Hoboneko-san."[2]

1   *barbequed chicken skewer*

2   *"Good evening Mr Hobo-cat"*

18

He shares this same bench each evening he has work with a vagrant feline he's dubbed 'Hoboneko'. Hoboneko has not deigned thus far to openly acknowledge his existence. Haruki understands cats however and saw that Hoboneko was 'happy' to see him by a subtle flick of his tail, or by a lazy ear flick in his direction. Sometimes Hoboneko would simply roll off the bench and stalk away, tail in the air, displaying his testicles proudly like Christmas baubles. At this Haruki would always mutter,

"Merry Christmas to you too mate."

He thinks to himself, *Man I love cats, the bloody royal insouciance of them!* Haruki sits on his daily bench and ponders. He suffers from a broken heart. His wife left him a year ago, and since then Haruki moves about his life like a thought bubble untethered from its thinker. He has been gut punched right in the Trust, and he had felt he had been Abandoned by Life. *Yet now, I drift, like the plastic bag in a suburban parking lot.* Briefly Haruki chuckles as he pictures his own sad face badly photoshopped onto the bag.

Happily, of late what was a festering arrowhead of abandonment has begun to slowly transform into a sense of freedom. Haruki muses about this; *Maybe it's my orphan superpowers emerging?* His parents are still very much alive, yet he feels himself orphaned by 'The Dream'. The Dream was that life that followed expectations, that purpose-filled ticking of the boxes that apparently *mattered*. He senses also that his 'heart within a heart' still functions, albeit while still in pieces. He is somehow able to find the beauty in his drifting plastic bag-ness. Hoboneko returns to his napping place on the other end of the bench and rolls himself upside down, contemplating the park from a fresh perspective.

"You know Hoboneks, you are so right, I need to look at this in a new way. I need to collect all my heart pieces and kintsukuroi[3] them back together. But what gold do I use?"

Hoboneko shifts fluidly into 'playing the cello', one toe pointing in the perpendicular, assiduously licking his baubles.

"Oh, I get it, you are suggesting I work with what I've got."

A mother ushers her little boy past, looking askance at him with a very Japanese mixture of concern and politeness. Haruki bobs his head in a mini bow, and murmurs,

"sumimasen, Nekochan wa totemo kawaii desu ne?"[4]

The mother bobs her head politely in return and lets out a soft little "kawaii ne."[5]

As she passes the little boy looks back curiously at him, one arm held aloft limply by his mother. Haruki switches to internal dialogue only, pulls off a little piece of chicken from his yakitori skewer and places it next to Hoboneko. The cat takes it with alacrity and turns to eat it with his back to him.

When he was recently moved to Japan from Australia with his wife, he had worked at 'Big Camera' in the IT section. After she left, he felt like a rug had been pulled out from under him, and everything he knew was swept aside. He could not face any aspect of his old life, so he had moved from Osaka to Tokyo and spent a period of time barely able to get out of bed, let alone leave his apartment. His cat Totoro had happened into his life at this point, and in the love that grew between them began his slow restoration. He had recently obtained a curious new casual job, one that he felt fit perfectly with his re-birth into an untethered life, and one that was quite fitting to the themes beloved by his namesake.

---

3   Japanese ceramic art of re-joining broken pottery using gold
4   "excuse me, but the dear cat is very cute don't you think?"
5   "Cute, eh"

Haruki had met his current employer in a little tucked away downstairs bar. His feet had walked him in there randomly, part of this odd new untethered life was accepting that kind of thing. She was a regal looking Russian octogenarian, and his first impression had been of her as a Cheshire cat. She seemed to look at him with a curious mixture of restraint and avarice.

"Forgive me" she had said in English with a strong Russian accent, "It always fascinates me when a person looks Japanese but is clearly in the possession of a western inner mythology."

Haruki had grinned but rolled his eyes at her, thinking her pompous. By now he was used to being regularly outed as 'not Japanese'.

He'd told her "Sure, but really it's just my height that gives it away." Her eyes had sparked a little at this.

"Touché. But really, I simply wanted to employ a conversational opener, and it has satisfied my ploy."

They got chatting, and she turned out to be a fascinating individual, even for all her obvious narcissism. He thought that rather than being born by mortals in the usual way, she had sprung into being as a ready-made octogenarian from the dark corner of the bar they sat within. A portal keeper. He'd put on a creaky witch voice in his head at the time, 'This way seeker, descend with me into the strange, hehehe'.

Her name was Varvara Kuznetsov, job description 'Narrative designer', though she bombastically referred to herself as 'The Architect of dreams'. She was part of the team of five self- described geniuses who created Mortech Lab, the company Haruki now works for. Mor stood for Morpheus and Mor stood for 'more than this'. Haruki had thought how they didn't mention that it also stood for mort, as in death. Mortech Lab specialised in 'immersion pods'. This was fairly new tech, but also a fairly obvious evolution of aspects of the VR (Virtual

Reality) scene. It was currently viewed as fringe tech, as it was definitely an extreme lifestyle choice. It found its natural resting place in Japan, as the phenomena of Hikikomori (post- modern hermits) had been around since the advent of the post-modern era. Hikikomori were life renunciates, generally because of a deep sense of shame and failure. They were originally thought of in the popular mind as social parasites, left to the sole responsibility of their parents, but its members had grown, flourishing particularly in pandemic year 2020 when lockdowns had triggered an almost total online life. Many people emerged up and out into the light once the most intensive lockdowns were over, but many also never came out again. Mortech immersion pods catered to the niche market of wealthy renunciates. This had struck Haruki as odd, but apparently there were those left still unsated by their privileged lifestyles. Even these wealthy elite were apparently not immune to the tawdry depressions of the masses. Like everyone else on the planet, it seemed even the rich felt tossed about by the suffocating social rules that flourished as a response to the pandemic years. Haruki felt catering to these oligarchs was nothing new as capitalism was simply created to funnel all the privilege upward and keep it there. He thought he'd probably never had a job that didn't predominantly benefit the rich. Haruki also knew Mortech had the support and endorsement of one of the richest tech celebrities in the world: Vish Bakshi, CEO of the American tech giant Mitech, 'Celebrity Tech Guru' himself. Vish Bakshi was also busy funneling his trillions into preparations and projections on mining the asteroid belt.

The principle behind the Mortech 'experiment' was that the human brain could construct any reality, even if denied life in the 'real world'. It was not necessary to live in 'the world', the human brain would work cooperatively to create a reality from whatever repetitive materials and parameters one fed it. Ms Kuznetsov assisted Mortechs' clients design a custom 'reverie' in which to spend their days. She seemed to Haruki to have a vast library-like knowledge of narrative tropes inhabiting her genius noggin, and nothing surprised her. Haruki regularly felt paralysed by her tendency to accurately predict the behavioural patterns of humans, including his own. He had begun of late to think of her as a creepy oracle who one found out later had actually written the plot behind your fate. She seemed cynical and tired. After all, how could life surprise one who knew how every story panned out? A Mortech reverie honed and refined patterns fed into the 'sleeping' mind of the pod occupant, training their brains to accept their tailor-made constructed fantasy as real life. Haruki thought of it as cheat's heaven. *Why wait for the afterlife to collect your winnings? Why not have at the elysian fields right now?* He privately thought of the clients as vampires, and the immersion pods as the coffins in which they shut out the light. Mortech currently housed 7 experimental pods, client privacy assured. Only two members of the Mortech Five knew of the client's past, or the content of their current reveries. These were known as 'The Architect' and 'The Gamer'. Haruki was just a 'pod monitor'. Though the position was officially called a 'pod technician', he knew nothing worthwhile but how to set in motion the emergency protocols, should something go awry with any of the pod occupants. He felt a mixture of pity and revulsion for most of the pod occupants, though he cared for them in his capacity as 'monitor' to the letter. It seemed there were still mundane jobs available for humans in this post-AI life, and broken-hearted untethered Haruki was grateful for the luxury of minimum effort in exchange for survival coins. All but one pod, simply titled Occupant XE. Varvara had recently let slip something personal about OccXE, referring to the inhabitant of the pod as her 'guinea pig'. Haruki had raised a concerned eyebrow at her, and she had replied,

"don't worry, my principled friend. This 'arrangement' has the full consent of the occupant."

She called OccXE a 'charity case'. Apparently, Kuznetsov herself was one of the wealthy elite who desired to 'get away from it all' permanently, but she felt it prudent to test the pod on a willing lab rat first.

"Perhaps I may go senile naturally, but I wouldn't want to foist it upon myself through ballsing up the apex of my life's work."

Haruki recalled how he had enjoyed the sound of her thick Russian uttering of 'ballsing up', but the thought of her going senile seemed very unlikely. Haruki thought about Occupant XE far more than he liked to admit even to himself. 'OccXE' perturbed him. In regard to the pod occupants, he had the working poor's distaste for the oligarchy and felt any mishaps occurring within this 'experimental phase' would probably serve them right. But Varvara's reference to OccXE as a guinea pig set fire to a latent urge to heroism within him that left him embarrassed. He realised he was projecting, but he had begun to get a more and more urgent sense that OccXE needed rescuing. He had glimpsed into the shady corners of his psyche and noted a growing story told to himself about this particular pod as a kind of 'snow white's coffin' and Varvara Kuznetsov definitely fit the witch trope. Thinking of himself as the handsome prince came with more difficulty, and much squeamishness.

This batch of seven pod occupants were Mortech's first, and it was considered an experimental phase. Before entering the pod, clients had their 'personal narrative tapes' 'adjusted', by the process of some new-tech type of hypnotism. They relinquished the stored history of their 'identity memory construct' and went in like narrative infants to their new reality, all the better to seamlessly believe themselves to be the heroes of their particular reverie. After his Mortech induction Haruki had pictured a tanned yet sagging oligarch slipping off his silken bathing robe and descending in to the Mortech pool for baptism. The tech was intricate, and infant was really the wrong word to describe the change wrought on their identities. Pod occupants kept the basic working files of an adult, they just relinquished their life story up to now, and simply donned a new mask. Apparently, the human brain will construct a working narrative for itself from the barest of threads. There were the stories of coma patients living rich lives within while without their bodies reposed in a vegetative state, the profoundly blind whose brains reconstructed for them a working visual world. It seemed to Haruki a little too steeped in turn of the millennium 'new agey' vibes, all that 'manifest your dream reality' hype. The ending of Haruki's marriage had kicked him in the arse so thoroughly that he no longer believed in life as a kind of project towards an ideal. Haruki had done his darnedest to be the perfect husband to his beautiful wife, but she'd left him anyway. She'd left him for a woman. She'd left him for a life in the bondage and kink scene and was now a dominatrix. This was her truth. She had told him she married the idea of him as a perfect loving husband, with the idea of herself as the perfect loving wife, but that it wasn't her truth. She had neglected to share her process toward discovering her truth with him, so to him it had hit him like a bolt from the blue. In retrospect he could unpick all the little unravelling threads, all the little red flags. At the time he was so deep in the hallucination of his own daydream that he'd failed to notice things falling apart. He'd blamed himself at first, that he had done it all wrong, but all along it had simply been a made-up dream, what he was supposed to do with his life. He actually thanked his wife for choosing her truth. Well, he thanked her now, after coming out the other side of being an utter wreck.

Haruki enters the Mortech lab by allowing the security interface to scan his retina and dons his Tyvek overalls and hairnet. He thinks privately all this is pure theatre to make it all seem more 'sciencey', *but I guess dust and mildew getting in the doodads is not ideal.* His job is basically babysitting.

He was drilled in all the emergency protocols, and if a pod occupant was somehow in trouble, he would know about it. He was continually amazed at the trust the Mortech Five placed in their own creations, but then he was not an agent of design in this scenario, only a tool in their hands. Of the 'Mortech Five' Haruki only engaged with Kuznetsov, and one other pod babysitter, also of her personal selection. The five principal geniuses behind Mortech each had their exclusive employees, some kind of privacy thing, *some kind of battle of the narcissists thing.* It wasn't too badly paid considering how little he actually did, though more boring (if that's possible) than his retail positions. He had studied IT and dabbled a little in making blockchain revenue in the VR realms, but the way this acquired knowledge had manifested as an occupation thus far left a little something to be desired. Here he was, somehow middle aged, divorced, living in a tiny apartment with a cat and still earning barely above award. Haruki sighs to himself and grins wryly, *Haruki-kun, that's a sad story of loss and despair.* Of late he has been gradually noticing that very often, the workings of his mind are simply repeating patterns experienced as narratives. As he goes about his boring job, he re-affirms his current life-creed to himself: *This is the untethered life, I'm determined to live moment by moment, deep in the flow, making no assumptions. Or is that also an assumption?*

Haruki thinks about OccXe and falls into a Murakami-esque reverie.

26

He sees himself enter a bare stage before a spot lit telephone table holding a mint green rotary dial phone atop it. He walks to it and picks up the receiver,

"Hello, is that OccXE?"

The voice on the phone says

"No, it's Hitomi, your ex-wife."

Haruki replaces the receiver and exits the reverie, imagines a thought bubble disintegrating above him. *Man, this job is boring, but lucky it appears I'm reasonably self-entertaining.* Haruki does a lap of the pods. As always, the lab is dark around the edges, and the pods each emit their own LED night light glow. The pods are white, smooth molded plastic, with a cool blue LED strip around the middle of each. The letter code of each occupant is light projected in a retro-futuristic stencil typeface to the floor, and nothing mars the smooth surfaces of the identical pods. Haruki can see a vague reflection of himself in the surface of the pod but seen as though through a diffusion lens. Haruki is both amused and a little disturbed by the perpetual sense of something paranormal about to happen, some kind of jump- scare imminent amidst all the purring High Tech. He chuckles to himself, *but there's absolutely nothing happening, it's all only in their heads.* He finishes his lap and goes over to the staff interface.

He types in: "As usual, everything is hunky dory. All occupants peacefully pooping pants, right on schedule".

His finger hovers above Enter, then he deletes it, and types in the string of letters and code numbers he is supposed to. Mortech is scrupulous about privacy. Privacy is still a mutable concept in the year 2038, so Haruki mock applauds Mortech's sincerity. His private suspicion is that it is simply part of their branding. He allows himself a sardonic inner remark, *Yep, Celebrity Tech Guru Mr Bakshi is all about privacy.*

*Maybe he's teeing up a little something or other reverie for himself with
Varvara as we speak?*

The pod occupants desired a life apart from not only the dirty masses,
but also the filthy rich they formerly rubbed shoulders with. Haruki felt
pretty squeamish about the experience he imagined on the inside of the
pod. Mortech guaranteed the state of the art self-cleaning functionality
of the pods, yet he knew it was a glorified high tech pooping of one's
own pants. He couldn't help but picture the bed sores and the fat cheese.
Haruki rubs his eyes and stretches. He goes within himself in search of
silence. The Mortech lab always puts him in a cynical mood.

Why am I working here?

Later, Haruki and his co-worker Fujioka Hiro drink sake at their
favourite little late-night place under the bridge next to his local train
station. Fujioka-san is short and tubby with a round merry face, on
this night he wears a turtle-neck jumper depicting a cartoon bear that
Haruki is certain no western man would ever wear. He is in his mid-
thirties and lives de-facto with his 25 year old girlfriend Momo. His
girlfriend has an elaborate hamster village made up of interconnecting
tubes running around the ceiling of their lounge room. Haruki calls
the hamster village inhabitants 'The Sims' and he and Fujioka toss
around a few in-jokes about them before getting on to their favourite
topic; Mortech conspiracy theories. They had both signed written
contracts that they would never speak of Mortech Lab or the work they
undertook at Mortech lab to any Mortech outsiders, and this adds to
the 'forbidden mystique' vibes that make it their favourite topic. *The*

first rule of Mortech is: you do not talk about Mortech. It's last drinks in the bar and Haruki looks around and determines no one is within earshot as the bar slowly empties. He leans towards Fujioka,

"Do you ever think about how gross the vampires must really be inside the pods? High tech my arse."

Fujioka looks thoughtful and gazes into his sake like it's a crystal ball.

"I'll bet they've gotta crack open those coffins and swab the babies down manually sometimes?"

Haruki nods several times in rapid succession, just like he was a native Japanese,

"So desu ne..."[6]

At Mortech Haruki had clocked out as Fujioka clocked in, and their relationship had been at nodding level for months. Then Fujioka changed shifts and Haruki was currently on nodding terms with a new worker. Haruki missed him for a bit, until the day they ran into each other at the konbini[7] around the corner from Haruki's apartment. It turned out they live in the same neighbourhood, and now they met for drinks at odd hours, always feeling a little furtive, like they were breaking the rules in hanging out. Fujioka raises an eyebrow at Haruki and wiggles his fingers,

"I can't picture the witch swabbing anything down, I'm sure she never removes those many bejeweled rings she wears."

Haruki has raised his sake to his lips to take a sip and he snorts,

"No there's got to be secret swabbers! Nothing's *really* self- cleaning in this world... yet."

Earth 2038 is the tech equivalent of 'fake it til you make it'. After 2020 everything began to shift into the service-based life. This gave the

---

6   *a way of showing agreement in Japan*

7   *Open all hours convenience stores found everywhere in Japan*

illusion to first world city dwellers around the globe that everything was done, and that humans were free to swan about like celebrities, with the sole function of 'creating content' for the tech giants. At least these days people got a few 'bit coins' for posting content on the socials, at least it wasn't only the 'influencers' who made coin. Haruki privately called them 'viral influenzas'. The truth was that most of the billions were still working crappy jobs and spending their 'bits' on ephemeral consumer junk. Sure, carbon emissions were reported as 'down' but no information seemed 'verifiable' anymore. Life seemed to have become almost purely propaganda. The world governments had a tacitly united 'Benevolent patriarch' type face on things, dubbed 'The Great Reset'. The past decade was one dominated by conspiracy theories that gave birth to online cults, everyone still puddled about in their own echo chambers. At least they could get out and about these days, but the pandemic lockdowns had irrevocably shifted life on Earth for urban humans. Haruki thought it was hard to know what 'really real reality' was anymore, the online life felt to him like he was drowning in information that was nothing more than skewed opinions. He was old enough to actually fondly remember 'the before times' and felt quite sorry for the children born into this current era of what he considered straight up insanity. Haruki and Fujioka had nicknamed Mortech Lab 'Uncanny Valley.' They both knew they would never know what really went on in the uncanny valley. Neither of them really wanted to know. Haruki had old fashioned notions of leaving Mortech and finding 'meaningful work', but he wondered to himself *the world was so abstract now, what even is meaningful work?* He stays on at Mortech as though he is waiting for some mythical train to arrive, *'the loop train to Destinyville'*. On the macro scale Earth 2038 also felt like this. This populist notion that they were on track to building a 'Golden Age'

seemed to him hollow. He knew there were still anti UN 'freedom rallies' going on around the globe, though it was hard to access unbiased media about the freedom movement that wasn't pro-UN propagandist. Haruki often chuckled wryly to himself over his old fashioned notion that there could even be unbiased media. *Life seems comfortable enough?* Haruki had not shared his private feelings for OccXE with anyone but his cat Totoro. Totoro's opinion was always something like 'you should scratch my belly, feed me, never leave so I can stay on your lap.' *Kind of off topic.* He hesitated now over whether to discuss it with Fujioka. He did not know whether Varvara had slipped any back story about OccXE to anyone else. He also felt pretty embarrassed about his notions of heroism. He felt like these notions were simply symptoms of a broken heart adrift in a meaningless world. He suspected he was suffering some sort of 'narrative malaise' that led to ideas of him having a destiny, or more likely craving a destiny. His recent trauma had rendered him but a mote of dust, and did dust have grandiose narcissisms? For now, he zips his lips, and they move onto to discuss and joke about other hot topics of the day before getting kicked out onto the street by the bar staff. Fujioka and Haruki bid their goodnights, "Oyasuminasai."[8] "Mata ne?"[9]
Haruki collects his bicycle and begins a slow and thoughtful cycle back to his apartment.

---

8 *"Good night"*

9 *"see you later, hey?"*

3.

Solipsism

Idea lies at the bottom of a deep well.

She can feel that her body is broken in many places. She can see far above her the twinkle of stars in a night sky, and somehow these distant lights give silvered outlines to her form. She swivels her eyes and is drawn to look at her stomach, sees that it is a portal of darkness. She understands that though she cannot move her body at all, her eyes can zoom in and further in toward the darkness of her belly. *There is something in there.* She zooms her vision telescopically closer to this dot of light and it is revealed that it is herself, lying broken at the bottom of a dark well. The image squeezes in on itself and she enters the black hole of her own stomach again and again in a timeless loop, a Mandelbrot set of her broken body abandoned in darkness. Her throat feels painful and dry, but she finds eventually that she can use her voice, and rasps out,

"Am I dead?"

The well echoes back at her "Dead, dead, dead."

She wakes with a gasp and her dream recollections tatter to shreds, ribbons of darkness evanescing to light. Her room usually senses she is awake and shifts into an auto ambient light, but this time her room is profoundly dark in the way that only a deep space bedroom can be. Her eyes go through the process of trying to adjust to the dark and she sees ghostly forms begin to emerge in her field of vision.

She pinches herself, "ow!' I'm either awake or that was some high-tech VR pinch pain."

Where is the light? The auto function is supposed to be movement sensitive. Idea flaps her arms in an attempt to activate the light. *Nothing.* She rolls tentatively out of her sleep shelf and probes in the direction she believes is the door. *There's no door.* She reaches the wall and gropes along it, thinking *eventually I'll activate the toilet panel at least?* As she gropes, she fights a rising panic, she feels her heart beating faster.

A shout escapes her mouth, "I'm trapped!"

As her heart begins to pound within her chest she stops, breathes out. *This could strike me as amusing.* She lays on her back on the floor with her limbs upright dead bug style.

"Damn right I'm trapped, trapped within my room, within a ship, within deep space. Trapped within trapped within trapped."

Her bladder stirs, becomes immediately urgent, and she smacks the ground.

"Who invited you? I still have some sense of dignity! I do not want to lie in a puddle of my own urine."

She gets up onto her hands and knees, the sensor light winks on and the ensuite door panel slides open. She shakes her finger at the light.

"Got a sense of humour now do ya?"

She realises she is in some kind of delusional relationship with the ship. She marvels at the human minds' capacity to create relationship from illusion, to create agency from automation. As she pees, she has an 'epeephany'. She sees a parallel in the functioning of her own body with the functioning of the ship. She does not have to instruct her bladder on the finer points of brewing a wee. She does not have to tell her lungs to breathe. She does not even know where her thoughts actually spring from. Humans classically viewed themselves as the authors of their own thoughts, but she realises she's not entirely sold on this.

"Hmmm, it seems I'm just along for the ride in more ways than one. Thing is, who or what am I without my body? Who is this one who's 'along for the ride'?"

Idea raises her hands to begin the making of a sphere, then drops them back to her sides.

"I will not stoop to creating art with my pants down in an intergalactic ensuite."

This notion of who I really am, I'll let it be for now, status pending. Is this avoidance? No matter. I already appear to be deep in space avoiding the entire planet of my origin.

Idea shuffles back to bed, pulls the covers up to her neck and attempts to get back to sleep. Apparently her brain does not get the memo, because she continues with pondering instead. *Library though.* She feels into her gruff affection for the database, and sees that she feels it in the same way she experiences some kind of relationship with herself inside herself. *I am adrift in space, profoundly alone and yet my mind just makes up friends for me. Friends? More like self-reference points, ways of assuring myself I still exist.* Idea puffs out a sharp breath and swings out of bed. The lights come on this time as they are supposed to.

"Damn it! It's a recipe for solipsism! The relentless voyage of the space narcissist on the SS Solipsist."

She sings in a faux operatic voice "me, me, me, I, I, I."

Then pauses. *Where am I going? Oh. The observation deck.*

A walkway proceeds from the circular deck that includes her bedroom and the dining pod and terminates as a centre point platform of two crossed ramps. One ramp leads down to Library, and the other goes up to the observation deck. Idea follows the curving ramp upward to the obs. deck. As she walks the lights anticipate her, and she knows they dim behind her as she exits a space. The entrance to the obs. deck is a large stately archway. Whoever designed the ship was to be admired. For all her grumbling Idea was definitely an aesthete, and she jokingly thought of herself as 'an Olympic aesthete'. Designed as a dome with a full 360 view of space, the observation deck never failed to draw a gasp from her. *No doubt about it. Deep space is awe inspiring. Even if it is a hologram.* She particularly loved the moment when her eyes shifted to a greater depth perception of the stars, she called this phenomena 'chandeliering'. However, despite these manifold depths, it was evident the view was unchanging. It was impossible to get a sense that she travelled at all. She knew of course that 'landmarks' were few and far between in deep space. The obs deck was both what made her sum up that she was travelling through deep space, and also a prime source of doubt that she was even in outer space at all. Since waking aboard the ship her sense of the uncanny was palpable. Idea in fact trusts nothing. She feels like a Truman. *But am I just being paranoid? How would I know?* Idea takes a seat on one of the long white couches that run around the base of the dome window. Though the aesthetic on the obs. deck can be described as epic, sometimes Idea thinks, *how bout a planet?* She draws her legs up to sit cross legged facing Space and falls again to pondering Library. *Library is my touchstone to Earth, but Library appears to be a closed information loop.* She thinks again about the anomaly of the spheres, *I'm certain the Library receptacle for the spheres did not exist before that first sphere I made. What does this mean? What kind of AI is Library? Is it even AI?* She makes a crazy face at her reflection in the window. *What if I'm trapped in a dream? Are the phenomena of the spheres proof?* Idea winks at herself and spins around on her bottom, stopping to stretch out her legs in front of her. *If this is all a dream, can I 'go lucid?'* Although Idea does not remember her past with any sense of identity, she still has memories as though she has a past. She remembers in this moment that she has had lucid dreams before. She adds this to her narrative, *I'm someone who can lucid dream.* Her mind is flooded in response to this thought with moving images of lucid dreams she has dreamed before in a kind of sample reel. Idea is distrustful. *Are these MY memories?* She feels like the ship is gaslighting her, *but am I simply gaslighting myself?* She sticks out her tongue, speaks out loud, "Huh, well there's literally no one here to judge me but myself. Operation 'slip the Solipsist' it is. Cue montage. This is the bit where Idea studies, experiments and works towards Lucid dreaming an SOS signal function into existence. Or an engine room. Or a control panel. Or a cockpit. Heck even a decent meal would help."

Idea lays on her back on the floor and gazes up at endless space through the dome window. She feels a niggling sense of immortality in this moment. "A view like this gives one delusions of grandeur. Am I an eternal soul? Am I the kind of immortal that is ironically dead and just doesn't realise it?" The problem with lucid dreaming is that she currently struggles to remember any dreams at all. Each time she wakes she feels their vestiges but cannot form these into cogent memories. *Is this evidence that this is ALL a dream? But surely dreams are the place in which anything is possible, even waking up from them?*

Idea falls asleep on the floor of the observation deck, in an apparently dreamless sleep.

While she is in deep sleep, where is she? Who is she?

Eventually she wakes and strolls back down the ramp to the dining pod, and prints herself a 'blue, salty' breakfast. She carries this with her down the ramp to Library.

She gestures over the interface panel to bring up the keyboard and types in, "Library. Am I dreaming that I am floating through space?"

There is the rainbow ball for a moment, and then the answer pops up on screen in its usual dialogue box.

"All that I see or seem is but a dream within a dream."

"Well. I guess I expected Descartes from you, but Ok, I'll take that as a yes."

'Things Library won't tell me' seemed to be direct answers to direct questions about 'the really real reality' of the situation she finds herself in. Idea takes her plate to the comfy chair and ponders whether this is proof she is dreaming. Finally, she makes a loud raspberry sound and shouts out to no one in particular,

"Bloody confirmation bias!"

In the dream there is the sea. Idea both stands on the shore and at once sees herself standing on the shore. The quality of light is the softening lilac and apricot gradient of twilight. The lulling music of the ebb and flow of the waves harmonises with the ebb and flow of her own breath. She hears her own laughter, and now finds that she is running while giggling, that she runs with a small child, and the child's face shines up at her in an openness of love. There is a joyful bark, and a large and merry chocolate dog lopes past with his tongue streaming out the side of his mouth. These three, in love with everything, collapse in the wash of the shore, wet and gritty with sand and weak with laughter. Then it is night, the same sea, the same music of the ebb and flow of the waves and her breath. The moon rises above the sea, set in its midnight cloth, spangled with an embroidery of stars. The sea is calm, the light of the moon shows its silver ladder. There is the sense of wholeness, of home. She can feel that her skin is imbued with the sense memory of herself holding her child in her lap, like a chick in his nest, warm with sleep. The child is not here, but he is *here*, her skin knows. The seashell of her ear knows the warm huff of the breath of the dog, the sound of his lolling tongue, the memory of its wetness, at once gross and wonderful, because it is *his* breath, and *his* silly tongue. The dog is not here, but her ear knows he is *here*. If the play of light and shadow were music, the fade of light from the moon is played as a soft adagio, the gentlest bleeding of the last drops of colour from the world. Now she is formless, but for the song of the sea, so timeless that it has never needed patience.

Idea surfaces. She is slumped in the Library armchair. Both hands are cupped around her lower belly. She feels very calm, as though she had been gently rocked in a mothers' arms, held safe and warm. Her mind begins to slowly boot up, to restore its pages, but this peace lingers, and for a moment there are no problems to solve. Then the clockwork of her cognition starts its tick-tocking and time comes to exist for her once again. Her first thought is of her hands at her belly. It strikes her as strange that she has assumed her scars are the result of a child burgeoning in her belly, *after all could I have been simply very overweight in the past?* Thought number two takes over, and simply remarks 'no.' Her belly knows. *But where is the child? Where is Earth?* Idea touches her face and is astonished to find it wet with tears; she has no memory of their arrival. Then, she feels that feeling in her chest, an imminent sphere. She becomes completely alert to it, like she is the embodiment of listening. Her hands gather there, waiting to receive whatever comes to be born. A shape delivers itself into her hands. Keeping her eyes closed, her hands investigate it like the sensitive hands of a blind person, smoothing over and over its cool spiral shape. There is a lip, and it dips down into a hollow. Her hands bring the shape to her ear, she listens, and she hears the song of the sea. Idea raises her arms up as though offering the object up to the sun and opens her eyes. It is a large seashell, spiraling, creamy white with brown flecks, its inner mouth a sweet coral pink. Idea softly draws a sphere around the shell as though it is a child she tucks into bed. In a trance she ascends the ramp to Library interface, but she feels reluctant to drop the shell into the receptacle. She brings the sphere of the shell to her bosom, it feels infinitely precious to her, it seems an atrocity to drop it into the sphere receptacle. Idea slips the sphere in her pocket instead and leaves Library. Her feet walk her to the centre point between the two ramps. She sits down crossed legged and gently places the seashell sphere in her lap.

"I have come to suspect that I am dead."

4.

Projection

aruki's cat Totoro had entered his life stage left as his wife exited stage right. Haruki believes that Totoro saved him from drowning in despair, and Totoro accepts Haruki's love (bordering on worship) with the magnanimous equanimity of his kind. Totoro is very like his namesake, grey and fat, with a magnificent white belly. He also shares the same pleasing combination of mystical wisdom and down-to-earth-ness of the beloved Miyazaki character he is named for. Totoro enters and exits Haruki's life as he pleases through his bedroom window, and Haruki often daydreams about Toto's life out in the back alleys and fence-tops of Tokyo. He paints small, charming vignettes of these daydreams in gouache, and smiles often to himself about Totoro's mystery life. He loves that Totoro is 'his own man' and that he came to be with Haruki because he chose to. The trauma of the end of his marriage wrought a catharsis of assumptions about life to burn in its wreckage. Haruki sees that we humans live lives anchored in viral ideals that we agonise over measuring up to, and police each other into adhering to. Haruki takes Totoro as his sensei in the Tao; *Totoro has the right idea about a life well lived. Trouble is, someone has to work to buy the cat biscuits, and I'm that someone. The untethered life is all well and good as a theory, but how does work fit in?* Haruki sees that he must not make an ideal of the untethered life as some kind of lifestyle, *I'm pretty sure the wind doesn't blow because its making a lifestyle choice. Probably work just 'works'. It seems to keep showing up.*

Haruki lays on his back on the floor of his kitchen with Totoro generously dolloped atop his chest. He lays in front of a small blow heater wearing only his socks and underpants, these ones have a tiny hole that sometimes catches his penis, but he does not throw them out. From this position he can still see the clock on the microwave. It is signaling its tyranny, sternly reminding him that he has to get ready for work. He and Totoro blink at each other tenderly instead. Totoro gazes his love directly into Haruki's eyes, then looks politely away. Then, he pauses and rolls over to lick his butt. Haruki takes great joy in the incongruent flexibility of this fattest boy. His ample belly spills forth splendidly while an elegant toe stretches perpendicular to the ceiling. Haruki falls into the pleasant imagining of a dance company made up of Totoro's and then groans aloud as he recalls the time.

"Noooooo!"

Totoro looks over his shoulder at him with an expression of distaste and pours himself like a liquid over the side of Haruki's chest, spills his form as a puddle to the floor, and looks upside down at the offending microwave.

"Yes buddy, we humans invented this thing called work. Is there no end to our madness?"

Totoro trots over to the cat food bowl.

"Yes my friend, one of us must buy the biscuits."

Totoro looks pointedly into the half full bowl in response and curls himself coquettishly around the sack of biscuits, his tail a perfect fluffy question mark. Haruki rises to his feet and pulls a comic concerned anime face, imagining the little hash symbol and bead of sweat at his brow. He absent-mindedly pours out a few cat biscuits, then gets ready for work and leaves the apartment. Totoro comes out onto the landing and looks down at him as he descends the flights of stairs, but when Haruki looks up, he looks away, and delicately licks his paw and washes his face.

"Totoro-sama, suki-da! Mata ne?"[10]

Later, at Mortech, Haruki goes through the motions, and thinks of his job as a ritual dance, the arcane appeasing of some bureaucratic god. He looks up at the camera in the corner and thinks *are you appeased by my devotions tiny god?* He knows the cameras are there to monitor the safety of the pod occupants, but he can't help but respond like he's being watched himself. *I certainly am.* Earth 2038 has a nostalgia about what privacy was like, back when there were non performative spaces to inhabit. Haruki feels retro even looking at the camera and knowing it's there, *wah, I'm so 90s right now.* He checks the interface read-outs of each pod and wonders why there's not an AI doing his job instead. *There's an AI producing the readouts, the pod occupant is in the thrall of a reverie maintained by an AI, so why is there a real live dude doing this bit?* Haruki smirks to himself, *aw, thinks he's better than AI, cute.* Eventually he gets to OccXE and can't help giving the pod a friendly pat. He thinks of the pods generally as glorified coffins, but OccXE seems to him more like the cocoon of a butterfly. *Why am I so wack about OccXE?* His bias toward OccXE perturbs him. He has tried to dismiss it as an old fashioned socialist-leftist bias against the 1%, but it feels deeper than that. He smirks again, *the socialist left ARE the 1% these days.* He wants to live his life in the flow of intuition, but instead

---

10   *"Esteemed Totoro, I like it! See you later hey?"*

keeps exposing his own bias and second guessing himself. He feels connected to OccXE in the strangest way but doesn't want to expose his tenderness to the watchful eye of the Mortech surveillance system. Haruki resolves to talk about it with someone, as keeping it inside has made it into an obsessive crush. *But who?*

On the train home from work Haruki continues to consider who to tell about *the thing with OccXE*. He has signed the declaration of privacy not to talk about it, so really he should only talk about it with Fujioka, but he feels too close. He has friends. Some he has even kept from what he thinks of as 'the before times,' that mythical era he recalls existed before the end of his marriage. His friends are an eclectic bunch of Japanese natives and foreign ex-pats like himself. He also still has friends and family back in Australia. He could definitely talk to his mother about the OccXE thing, but she just doesn't feel right for this one. She tries her best to upgrade her relationship with Haruki to the latest operating system, but sometimes he thinks she's simply a little outdated in her ways of thinking of him. Haruki feels like a person who has been destroyed and reborn, but reborn with his essential essence intact. His mother knows him for his essence, but also carries so many memories of the many Haruki's of old. He reflects that he is also probably the same for her. Haruki talks to himself as he crosses the road from the train station over to the little place he frequents after work. He likes the place as he doesn't feel obliged to always drink alcohol there, it's a bar but not a bar, more like a night cafe. Its name is 'Tsuki'[11] and the noren over the entrance are indigo blue with rabbit moon motifs. They serve Ochazuke[12] for a homely touch, and Haruki orders a bowl and

---

11   *moon*

12   *leftover rice with green tea poured over it, and various savoury condiments added*

slides into one of his preferred booth seats at the back. He has a moment where his mind becomes silent, and he ceases talking to himself. He is one with Tsuki, the wood of the table is himself, the soft breeze ruffles the noren as though it is his own hair. Then he notices this oneness and the spell is broken. His ochazuke arrives and he looks around at who's at Tsuki tonight. He knows Fujioka won't be here. There's the comfortable mix of regulars and newbs as usual and he exchanges a few nods with those he is on nodding terms with, including the bar owner, who is in tonight. He's never progressed beyond the nod with the owner but he loves the owner of Tsuki cafe as an extension of his love for Tsuki the place. The owner is post retirement age, but loves to pop in and enjoy the place still, and he's got a mellow and comfortable vibe. There's a tiny corner seat with one chair only, and Haruki thinks of it as 'the writers' chair'. He imagines the solitary writers narrowing their eyes at each other, all thinking of the spot as their private and personal territory. *I would love to sit in it myself, but I think of myself as merely an observer of writers, what's the word? Oh yes, a 'reader', hah.* This night there's an interesting looking man sitting there that he hasn't seen before, and Haruki observes him as subtly as he can in his peripheral vision. He is short and sturdy and probably somewhere in his fifties. He wears the kind of puffy vest that Canadians universally favour. He has a wonderful silver sponge of hair, tightly curled and emerging as an ebullient froth from the top of his head. His skin is a beautiful warm brown, and his well-formed black eyebrows are currently gathered in the centre of his brow. True to form for the writers' chair, he bends and scribbles in a notebook, and pauses now and then to chew the end of his pencil. Haruki has the sensation of tasting the unmistakable taste of a pencil himself and falls into a reverie about empathy. He looks up, and the man has slid into the booth across from him.

He speaks in English with a strong Portuguese accent.

"Very presumptuous I know, but I subtly observed you 'subtly' observing me, so I thought I'd come over and break the fourth wall."

Haruki grins and points at his chest, "Haruki."

The man mirrors the point to his own chest in return, "Felipe."

Felipe says, "I hazarded a guess that you are from an English speaking country, though you wear the Japanese disguise very well."

"Yes it's that sign over my head saying 'not Japanese-Japanese' that everyone reads. I must have forgot I put it there."

Haruki mock searches the space above his head.

Felipe laughs with pleasure and a Tsuki staff member looks over with a solicitous face. Felipe points at Haruki's bowl of ochazuke with a smile and the worker nods affirmative. Haruki and Felipe fall to chatting and getting along famously in the way of strangers destined to meet in an alignment of stars. Haruki senses in Felipe a rare quality of peace and spaciousness, and Haruki realises he feels more comfortable with him than he has felt with any human in a long time. He gets a sudden urge to tell him all about Mortech Lab, and more importantly, about OccXE. He realises he really takes his privacy declaration seriously, and inwardly curses his ethics.

Felipe raises a perfect quizzical brow, "your face is a complex blend just now?"

"I've got something weighing on me, but you're right, it's complex. I was about to take advantage of you in your capacity as kind stranger."

Felipe smiles warmly and gives Haruki a wink, "Well, let's have at it, I've got nothing but a lonely Airbnb to return to this night."

Haruki squirms, *how to talk about this without talking about it?* He puffs out his cheeks, lets out a slow breath.

" Do you remember that movie from back in the day called 'Her'?"

Felipe grins "Sure, the one where he wants to bang his AI, but she runs off with the AI Alan Watts instead?"

"That's the one."

"You have an AI that you want to bang?"

Haruki winces, "no... but it is sort of similar in a not similar way."

"ok."

"I've developed feelings for someone I've never met. It's an idea of someone. I realise it as countless layers of projection, but there's this sort of intuitive certainty about it that keeps arguing with my rational mind."

Felipe tells him, "It sounds like you are pretty across it then. What if it is just as you say, a bunch of projection with a sweet nugget of truth at its core?"

Haruki replies, "a sweet nugget of truth?"

Felipe leans back and extends his legs under the table, then puts his arms behind his head and tilts his head back, miming with one hand as though taking a drag on a cigarette and expelling a smoke ring,

"a truth nugget."

Haruki crosses his ankles and cradles his chin in his hand, giving in to silence.

"It is as it is. You are right."

Felipe gives a warm chuckle, "my friend, 'It is as it is' is the right answer to all things."

"It *is* the answer, the one we always forget."

He snaps his fingers, feeling suddenly unburdened.

"Felipe, are you just a magnificent stranger, blessing me for one night only?"

Felipe holds up one hand, starts ticking things off on his fingers

"Well, you know I have an email address, a phone number, social media."

The two laugh and hold up hands for a double high five.

"Well met Felipe, well met."

That night Haruki cycles home, grateful for his gloves in the fresh winters' night, with a beautiful zen-like assurance.

It is as it is.

Idea has become very nearly convinced that she is dead, but she does not know how the dead should behave. *Should I be all 'self-aware', and drop the entire farce of engaging with Library in any way? Or is the dance of the dead just this, some delusion cooked up by a bodiless wraith? If my body is dead, then why not my mind?* It is a conundrum, but Idea finds that she is ok with conundrums in deep space with an AI that is possibly not an AI, and the phenomena of conceptual spheres emerging from her chest. Things were weird. Idea begins to perceive that with each sphere leaving her body, it has felt like a small catharsis, like a birth through her chest cavity, from within her 'chest within her chest'. With each sphere leaving her she has felt lighter, more buoyant, floats about now like an untethered balloon. She muses, *maybe I'm not dead, but dying.* A memory enters her mind of anecdotes about near-death experiences where things lose all sense of time. *So, where's my dead grandma waiting at the end of a tunnel and whatnot? I'm dying, but in denial. Has my brain cooked up a narrative to explain something happening that I actually can't cope with, but its half cooked?* More and more Idea can *almost* remember her dreams. They tease at her, ineffable/effable. They are taste memories, very much part of her but seemingly inaccessible to her conscious mind. She drifts about the ship, letting go of all routine, all manufactured rhythms. She no longer visits Library. She makes no more spheres. Slowly she also begins to stop thinking, more and more she becomes surprised to find she still exists. It is a dullness however, nothing like the dream of ego death, more like the trance of the undead. Time passes somewhere else.

Varvara Kuznetsov sits stubbornly in the cold on a bench in a little park she favours and hears the voice of what she thinks of as her inner victim. It asks what it often asks of late; *why am I still alive?*

At her feet sits a small, scruffy brown dog with soft upright triangular ears. At odds with his humble facade, Varvara has dubbed him Hermes, and occasionally calls him Herpes in a type of dry playfulness. Hermes is profoundly happy in the manner of the profoundly stupid. She does not love him, unless loyalty can be considered love.

She tells him often, "you are the last Hermes."

In her eighty-plus years she has had seven little dogs called Hermes, all varying degrees of gormless. Hermes of the profound stupidity sits placidly at the end of his leash. She feels his simple emotions through this tether. At times he was full of nervous tension, tightly wound with the desire to chase and investigate. Other times he was sleepy and torpid. Sometimes he licked his little useless balls and got a tiny purposeless boner. Hermes did not argue with life, he was deep in the Tao, but he suffered from a misplaced adoration of his owner. Granted some of the Hermes were better than others, this last Hermes was like a summary of all Hermes before him. Varvara looks Hermes in the eye, and Hermes smiles a dog smile in return, with shiny eyes and tongue lolling. As she continues to gaze at him, over long, he cocks his head to one side and emits a little whine.

"You are right to fear me, tiny dog. Correct. Well done."

Hermes licks his chops and circles about for a bit before settling in the exact orientation in which he began his circling.

Varvara nods, "Also correct. You illustrate the point of pointlessness most pointedly."

For one as vacuous as he, he makes valid points.

Varvara could be said to be 'Russian', but this was as meaningless to her as being identified as 'white'. Her life felt to her many lifetimes long. Her inner victim was so tired. *Victim. If only you could get your wish and simply die and be done once and for all with this load of bullshit called life.* Her inner victim did not die, only went dormant. She barely tolerated its inner incursions and felt a sense of disgust whenever it rose its head. She never spoke of her past; it was profoundly irritating to have assumptions made about herself. *If anyone were to make assumptions about me, surely it should be myself? Humans are so disgustingly intertwined with each other, so needy, so avoidant, so pathological, and I am one of them.* Varvara longs for the time when she can enter an immersion pod herself and her neediness becomes something she no longer knows. *And yet. And yet.* Yes, it had to be admitted, she was frightened. Her dream of ultimate agency included the possibility of herself at the mercy of her own invention, an invention that would no longer have her able to intervene. *Why must life be so fucking ironic?* A butterfly drifts past, she throws her sandwich at it with a shout and the sandwich drops broken to the ground. Hermes trots over and strains at the length of his leash to eat it, at once both choking on his collar and swallowing the food in great gulps.

"Indeed, this is how things are in life. Right again Hermes. Right again". She allows herself a throaty cackle and disturbs a flock of teenagers preening in her periphery. Varvara gives them an evil smile and triumphs in their immediate scurry out of her space. Varvara is well aware that very often other people think of her as a 'witch', yet she is unperturbed, and finds this gives her the space to be as difficult as she pleases. It has never been her desire to be pleasing. Hermes finishes the sandwich and comes to sit on her feet. Varvara finds this persistent habit of his most irritating and lifts her feet just high enough to tip him off. Hermes takes the hint and moves aside a small distance to lie submissively at (rather than on) her feet. He rests his head on his paws and looks up at her with suitable contrition. Varvara becomes as still as stone, her gnarled hands rest atop her cane, and she thinks on her employee, Haruki Mori. Mori-san was entirely too sentimental for her tastes, a whimsical man. She hates all men but abhors whimsical men especially. She had employed him because she had met him in the same bar in which she met the woman currently known as Occupant XE and felt an immediate chime of intuitive connection between them. Occupant XE was a woman whom life had destroyed, one mired in a profound morass of victimhood brought on by a personal tragedy she was unable to emotionally incorporate. Mori was currently in a state of disassociation bought on by the shock of the bursting of his particular dream bubble. She felt them as pieces on a board, uncertain as yet how play would proceed.

The reverie currently being enjoyed by OccXE was one she wrote for herself, an ode to solitude. As she did not like the thought of becoming a victim to her own creation, she had seen that it was expedient to test it first upon a consenting subject, the woman was perfect for this purpose. She had felt a kinship with OccXE, in that she was her opposite. Varvara controlled all aspects of her life such that it was an artform, whereas OccXE was adrift like a floating piece of ash after a fire. Varvara sat in life as a spider in its web and felt her intuitions like the tremors of her silken threads. She feels one such tremor now, and knows that she must make her way to Mortech Lab. Nothing surprises her, but she finds with pleasure that it seems she is yet intrigued by the unfolding story of her life. She stands slowly and regally and thinks to herself *it seems there's juice in the old husk yet.*

That evening toward the end of Haruki's shift Varvara emerges from the darkness at the rim of the lab, the sound of her walking cane preceding her in sharp echoes. Haruki keeps his back to her and makes a wry grin to himself; *oof! there's my jump scare.* Actually, he enjoyed reveling in her theatrics. He knows she plays with him as a cat plays with its kill, and lets it be. The truth is, he cannot help but feel compassion for her. Her monstrous act is so thorough, so seemingly seamless, that it has to be a sham. *What would melt her icy heart?* He does not yet know, but he is interested to find out. He doesn't mind if he just hears about it, he doesn't have attachment to doing the deed himself. In stories witches were generally either transformed through mercy or burned in hell, most often the latter. He always preferred transformational myths, he liked it when everyone ended up free of guilt. *But how will she toy with me this day?* He turns to face her, hand to his chest, and acts surprised to see her, sketching her a hasty bow even though she is not Japanese.

"Varvara-sama! Konban-wa."[13]

"Mori-san, I see you have been polishing the pod of our dear OccupantXE most tenderly. Oh? you thought yourself subtle? I have a subtle eye." ____

13   *"Respected Vavara! Good evening"*

He replies obediently, "Yes Varvara-sama. Very tenderly."

Haruki felt the usual awkwardness of using her first name with the traditional honorific, but she insisted on it.

"Since you told me OccXE is your guinea pig I have felt protective. I think of OccXE as 'her' and even sometimes as 'Snow White.'"

There. Let her be caught in her own web.

Varvara arches a thin brow and chuckles throatily.

"Well, well, Mori-san, more astute than I gave you credit for I see."

Haruki feels the back of his knees become sweaty despite the perfect climate inside the lab, and the silence grows overly long as he waits for her to throw him another bread crumb. He appeases his nerves with a comic image of himself as a pigeon, one wearing the same old worn out underpants.

The old serpent speaks, "so, you wish to be a hero, yes? Life has you beaten, and you wish to rise up in compassionate triumph?"

Haruki remains stubbornly authentic in response to her goading, "I do believe in kindness."

"Believe me Mori-san, this is a kindness. You see, Occupant XE has already been rescued, her heroine stands before you. What fun, when the witch can also be a kind of heroine, no?"

Haruki stares at the folds of paper-thin skin at her neck, and swallows. Two beads of sweat trickle from either armpit. He folds over at the waist in an involuntary bow.

"You reassure me, Varvara-sama, doumo arigato gozaimasu."[14]

"What tyranny will you fight against now my dear Mori-san? Did you watch the footage of the latest marches against the global elite in Berlin? But of course, you will never see that kind of social uprising here in Japan. What to do?"

---

14 *"Respected Vavara, thank you very much"*

"Sensei-sama[15], you are also very astute. But perhaps you mistake me for an activist? Am I not too busy feeling sorry for myself?"

"Oh, very good. Yes, one point to you. I am indeed one who loves immodest self-deprecation. But let us talk more of your little crush, our dear Occupant XE. I will reward you with a little tidbit. You are correct in your assumption that she is a *she*. I wonder if it was some latent patriarchal sentiment in you that led to this understanding, or simply old fashioned unmet romantic notions?"

Haruki resolves to keep on with meeting this arch play with simple honesty.

"Truth tell I've been sifting through all the possible projections it could be, but there's this nagging intuition about her. I've felt a little tortured that my feelings may be simply manufactured responses to my conditioning. My preference is to trust my intuition."

Varvara looks him in the eye, and Haruki feels it as though her gaze is a force penetrating his soul.

"It is very pleasing that my lab rat is self-aware. This makes the experiment so much more interesting. You will report back to me on this topic Mori-san."

She releases him from her gaze and taps away to view the readouts of the other pods. Haruki sketches an air bow at her back

"Hai! Sama! Ganbarimasu!"[16]

After work Haruki heads straight home, answering his phone messages on the train. *There's one from Felipe, the bloody champ.* Haruki pauses to feel gratitude for friendship, and his heart swells. He sees a beautiful image in his mind of warm honey light dripping from his heart into a golden chalice, and then overflowing this chalice into his body. It's an

---

15   *Respected teacher*

16   *"Hai! Sama! Ganbarimasu: Yes! Esteemed one! I'll do my best"*

old favourite meditation of his. *Man! I am so very attached to images.*
Haruki broods for a moment on being attached to being attached and
feels a wry chuckle within.

He answers Felipe's text, adding the horrified face emoji,

"My boss totally makes me want to wee my pants."

Felipe answers back immediately, "Tell me more. Tsuki's?"

Well, why not?

Haruki swishes through the noren at Tsuki's in anticipation of a
swell time. Felipe is not yet arrived, but he sees Fujioka sitting in their
favourite booth.

Fujioka grins and raises his sake glass, "kampai!"[17]

Haruki hastens over and slides in to face him.

"What's happening, watashi no tomodachi?"[18]

Fujioka and Haruki talk in an eclectic patchwork of English and
Japanese. Fujioka is determined to improve his English and Haruki still
struggles with fluency in Japanese.

"Good news my friend, another friend is coming to meet us tonight,
and he only speaks English or Portuguese."

Fujioka pulls a comic frightened face and wipes imaginary sweat from
his brow,

"So desu yo! Ganbaru!"[19]

"Ganbate![20] Also, we have to talk about Varvara-sama."

"Oof. Varvara-sama. I am tiny, frightened man"

Fujioka mock quivers.

Haruki groans, "she's got me in her claws! She's a fucking genius for
chrissakes. I can't best her at her own game. My only hope is to attempt

17 *"Cheers"*
18 *"my friend"*
19 *"Right! I'll do my best"*
20 *"Do your best!"*

to surprise her."

"Haruki-kun, I think this woman is unsurpriseable. Just lay down and allow her to slash open your soft belly."

Haruki makes a mock horrified face, then sees Felipe enter, and waves him over. After introductions Felipe slides into the booth. He raps the tabletop with his knuckles,

"What's cooking?"

"Fujioka and I work together; we are commiserating over our mutual terror of our boss."

"Ah, the old boss problem. You see; this is why I am my own boss."

Haruki says, "Oh! Felipe! In all our bonding chat we never spoke of work. I'm impressed."

"Indeed, this forms the foundation of what I believe is destined to be a true friendship."

Felipe and Haruki beam at each other and Fujioka groans.

"You two! You know in English they say, 'get a room', no?"

Felipe laughs with delight, but Haruki slumps internally as his mind stubbornly turns his attention back to what he thinks of as 'the Varvara problem'.

"Seriously guys. You've gotta help me with handling Varvara."

Felipe assumes a thoughtful pose,

"So. You are on a first name basis with this difficult boss?"

Fujioka gives a little shudder,

"She insists on us calling her 'Varvara-sama'. I am a Japanese man, this 'Varvara-sama' is a strange business. Sumimasen[21], but she is one oddball gaijin[22]." Haruki knows Fujioka's use of the term gaijin signifies his deep discomfort with their boss.

---

21 *Excuse me*

22 *foreigner*

Felipe nods, and holds up one finger,

"Ok, but let's discuss this, is there any such thing as a truly evil human? Surely evil acts are the result of humans in the service of an evil ideology? So what's her ideology?"

Fujioka and Haruki lean in, this is getting good.

"That's the thing, she's not truly evil. We can't talk specifics about our work, but it's ostensibly a service with lasting happiness as its motivating factor."

Fujioka looks at Haruki with a skeptical gaze, then looks pointedly at Felipe and points his thumb at Haruki.

"Mori-san, always trying to see the best in others, our boss is the original majo, witch-lady. Felipe-san, have you seen 'Spirited Away'?"

"Indeed Fujioka-san, I've seen all of Miyazaki's works, you see, this is why I am in Japan! I am a visual artist! Japan is a mecca for my kind. But you know in the end, the witch in Spirited away is seen with compassion. Chihiro can't help but use her pure heart to transform everyone around her, a common motif in Miyazaki-sensei's work."

Fujioka raises his sake glass in salute,

"So desu yo[23]. Haruki-kun[24] must transform her with his pure heart."

Haruki looks wistful and replies, "Haruki-kun has only a partially completed kintsukuroi[25] heart... I'm not strong enough."

Felipe says, "There's the pure heart of a child yes, but this is a kind of pre-ego. What about post-ego? One who survives a broken heart intact is purified perhaps? It's only those who don't come through that stay embittered I believe. This is the poisoned heart. Perhaps your Varvara-sama is broken-hearted? This is a classic witch motif, the heart

---

23   *"So it is"*

24   *adding 'kun' to a male name implies affection and closeness*

25   *gold repair*

of ice."

"Felipe, you are definitely on point, but Varvara is a genius, and an expert on narrative. She knows every trope back to front and believes we humans are nothing but identities as constructions of viral myths. It's highly likely she has created the witch mask as an identity to throw people off perceiving her true purpose. She's too wily for me, the old fox! I'm just a whimsical man. This is why my wife left me for a dominatrix." Haruki laughs and blushes at once, endearingly ruffling up the back of his hair with his hand.

Felipe looks to Fujioka, "This is true?"

Fujioka nods with a serious face "True story".

The three men each take a sip of sake and sit back to reflect. Haruki raises his glass.

"As for my ex-wife, it's her truth, I wish her all the best."

Fujioka and Felipe raise their glasses to Haruki, and Felipe says, "To the pure of heart."

That night Haruki stumbles into his apartment, he has had a little more sake than he planned. Totoro is out. Night time is 'business time' for Totoro so Haruki is not surprised. Haruki considers splashing his face with water and brushing his teeth, but staggers to his bed to lay face down. The light of the full moon streams into his room through the window and spotlights his open mouth squished to one side; Haruki has fallen instantly asleep. After an interval that is unmeasured by his mind Haruki begins to dream, the moonlight highlights the rapid eye movement beneath his eyelids. He groans and rolls onto his back, and there is a small damp patch where his face once was. Still fast asleep, his arm throws one hand over his eyes to shut out the moonlight. Totoro appears briefly at the window and disappears just as quickly. A crow caws in the tree outside his window, an incongruous sound at night. Within Haruki's mind there is a nightmare at play. He dreams he is trapped alive in a coffin; he screams and bashes at the lid, overwhelmed with panic and claustrophobia. On his bed in his apartment his body begins to sweat, his head turns from side to side, he emits a low moan from his lips. In the dream he screams until his throat is hoarse, until he becomes silent. In the coffin there is only profound darkness. Haruki's mind intrudes now on his sense of panic and inserts a lucid thought, *how do I know I'm in a coffin?* In a rush Haruki wakes. His body is damp with sweat and Totoro is standing on his chest, sniffing the salt. Haruki takes a moment to properly return to full waking consciousness and Totoro curls his claws softly but decisively into his chest.

"Ow! Buddy! Jesus!"

Totoro leaps off his chest to the floor in one bound and trots out of the room. Haruki places his hand to his freshly clawed chest and registers his nightmare. Then, he rolls over and returns to sleep. In the morning all this is forgotten, the only thing left behind is his stinking breath. Haruki goes to the bathroom and splashes his face and brushes his teeth.

Varvara sits in her house in her customary chair and hears the voice of her victim intrude into her thoughts once more, *please, all I want is death. Make it stop.* She remains unmoved by this voice, has not cried in twenty years, and only then with efficiency rather than release. Tears form an orderly queue at the portal of her eyes and immediately dry up before falling. There is only a sharp sting and a red rim to indicate their presence. Varvara barely sleeps any more, is plagued with wakefulness.

Hermes sleeps much of the time, whining and trotting out his dreams. Varvara watches him sleep and wonders about the old saying 'ignorance is bliss.' She is well aware she is probably burdened by her genius, straightjacketed by her knowing. She does not know how not to know. She reflects on her employee Mori-san. He pleases her, it pleases her to go up on the ladder from contempt to intrigue. For a moment she almost stops thinking, she is almost rendered catatonic with the immensity of what she calls 'The Pattern'. Her life's obsession has been seeing into the intricacy of the interweaving of the narrative threads of human life. At times she teeters on the brink of dropping into a state of 'all-knowing', and she calls this greater knowing 'The Pattern'. Varvara does not know that she is trapped completely in the cold prison of her egoic mind. Varvara's tender and fragile heart is locked deep inside her, safely hidden behind her mania for control.

She intuits this risky brink of surrender and quells it with a practiced inner hand; *no! this is the folly of those addicted to transcendent experience, I will not allow it.* She understands that she is profoundly alone. Her body is full of pain, her hands arthritic. The pain keeps her awake. *Surrender is so distasteful.* When her body finally does surrender to deep sleep she awakes vaguely disgusted. It is night still, dark and implacable. She allows herself a soft groan as she rises from her chair, walking slowly and painfully to the kitchen sink to fill a glass of water. She watches the glass fill and then pours it out again. Softly she tells herself, *it's all meaningless. Empty.* Outside the kitchen window a crow caws in the night. Varvara recalls the old belief that a crow cawing in the night signifies impending death. She throws the empty glass at the window and screams "Fucking superstition!"

The window shatters, admitting the cold night air, and Hermes comes cowering into the room as though it was his own fault. He looks at

Varvara with his small brown apostrophe eyebrows raised and cocks his head to one side with a small whine. He licks his lips and then sneezes with a little whuffing sound, and his eyes seem to roll around a little with the sneeze.

"Yes Hermes, Chaos. Observe and learn."

Hermes goes over to the door and scratches to be let out. Varvara mourns the window a little, as it was the last made of old fashioned breakable glass in her home.

5.

Claustrophobia

Idea lays on her back on the reflective centre platform between the up and down ramps of the ship. She is sensing what it is that senses her experience.

If I am dead, what is this sense of 'existence' that still seems apparent? She pinches her arm. It hurts. She slaps her face. It hurts. She brushes her cheek tenderly where she smacked it, this tickles. She puts her hands away, those instruments of sensation, and attempts to track what it is that senses by other means. She is sensing the sensing. *WHO is sensing the sensing?* An image of herself with her hands over her eyes turning around to a tap on the shoulder comes into her mind, the self inside the image turns around to a self with her hands over her eyes who turns to a tap on the shoulder. The word 'recursion' floats by as a thought. *Who is thinking?* Abstract parameters are felt in her sensing, a notion of penumbra. Her mind has an endless supply of words, images and sensations it seems, they billow up like smoke from an incense stick. *Surely death would just be nothing? Like actual nothing.* For a moment Idea is miffed, *I better not be in a bloody coma!* She smacks the metal of the platform, and it rings in a clanging bell tone. It offends her that her experience could be nothing but some hackneyed old chestnut. The face of a laughing child enters her thought stream. The face is familiar, and dear. *It is the child. It's the child who is dead.* Idea sits up quickly, her head spins a little. *The child is dead.* This is a truth nugget. *I had a child, and the child is dead. Where is the child?* Her hand goes to her belly, tears stream out of her eyes. Her heart feels tight, her hand goes to her chest. *I can't breathe. I'm not dead, I am dying. My heart will kill me. Someone is squeezing my heart.* Idea begins to hyperventilate; her eyes roll back and begin to flutter in a kind of REM. She draws in breath after ragged breath, her chest heaving. She squeezes her eyes tightly shut. She suddenly feels claustrophobic. *I am in a coffin.* She bashes her arms against the ceiling of the coffin and there is the very real sensation of her arms hitting something hard and decidedly tangible above her, she screams for help until her throat is hoarse. She opens her eyes. She lies on the centre platform between the two ramps. There is nothing for her arms to hit. Sweat trickles down her back, her head throbs in a dull migraine. *What the fuck was that?* Idea leaps to her feet and runs up the ramp to the observation deck. Then she turns and runs back down and across to her room and the door opens silently to admit her. She turns away from the panel and runs across to the centre platform and down the ramp to the library, the door opens and one of the vacuum bots emerges. She pauses and crouches down beside it, blocking its momentum. She lifts it up and peers closely at its pixel face.

"Why do I presume this is the face of a cat?"

She starts to cry again and gently places the vac-bot back on its pre-programmed journey.

"Why did I think it was a cat?"

Her hand goes back to her chest. She has not made a sphere for some time. Idea stands and goes into Library. There is the customary chime, the interface activates and ripples its ribbons of light. Then she sees it, there is no longer a receptacle for the spheres.

Varvara enters the Mortech lab, and the early morning shift worker bows in her direction.

"Nakamura-san, you may leave now. You will still receive full pay, don't be concerned."

Nakamura is a slight young woman, a student completing her physics degree at Tokyo University. She works all the early morning shifts. Nakamura bows several small bows in succession and leaves, Varvara notes her eyes were slightly rounded with a little of the whites showing. It amuses Varvara how easily intimidated people are. *The world is a theatre, humans spouting the same old lines at each other, the same old stories playing out over and over again.* She taps her cane and lingers by the pod of each occupant, resting her palm atop each one and feeling something akin to the quality of loyalty she has extended to the succession of Hermes. She has done perfect work with each of these clients. Their readouts show the predictable patterns of those who are simply dreaming. Naturally each client comes into a state of wakefulness, but their brains simply interpret these waking events as dreams. The neatness of this folly pleases Varvara. She approaches the pod of OccupantXE and notes that her readout shows an unusual level of agitation in her dreaming, she appears to be more wakeful more often. Varvara muses, *in this particular reverie there is little opportunity for danger, no possibility of sexy experiences. It has been designed to keep anxiety at a minimum. How typical of the human mind to create fear where there is nothing to fear.*

A figure emerges from the shadows, much as she likes to emerge at her staff from out of the gloom.

"Tanaka sensei. You old monster. The guilt is keeping you awake?"
she toys with him; he is in fact a stickler for correct behaviour.

Tanaka is old, but not as ancient as herself. He has the face of a snake;
all his features are unusually narrowed. It is nonetheless an elegant face,
a minimalist face.

"Ah. 'The Architect'. Ohayou gozaimasu."[26]

The Mortech Five meet rarely these days, the testing period proceeds
with tranquility. Their great minds have turned to other matters. Only
Varvara remains restless. *What is Tanaka up to?*

Tanaka places a flat palm to the top of the pod,

"Occupant XE. Your particular project. How fares she?"

"Today's reading shows she is agitated, unusually wakeful. I designed
this reverie to exclude anxiety of all kinds. It seems she manufactures
anxiety for herself nonetheless."

If it is possible for Tanaka's eyes to narrow further, they do.

"Indeed."

The two speak in Japanese. Varvara is a polyglot, fluent in many
languages. How else can she call herself an expert on narrative if her
knowledge is not of the universal human tropes?

"OccupantSN is in the midst of a most stimulating reverie, yet his
readouts remain predictable. I wonder what can be afoot in the mind of
my dear guinea pig?"

He inclines his head,

"I am sure you already know. Nothing gets past you, The Architect."

The two know nothing of each other's personal life and are therefore
free to not suffer the usual small talk. This is their version of small
talk. The air quality is tense. They are like cats about to strike. After an

---

26 *"Good morning"*

extended silence Tanaka bows and leaves the room. Tanaka's particular expertise is the intricate cocktail of drugs tailored to each occupant. The Five call him 'The Anesthetist'. Although Varvara considers herself the Morpheus of Mortech, each member of the Mortech Five is a crucial player. None of the Five are naturally team players. Nonetheless a quality of tense neutrality is maintained, as each member bows to the greater purpose of the project. Varvara muses on tragedy. It is a strong pattern. It is of course inevitable that Occupant XE remains in the thrall of her particular trauma. Varvara shakes her head.

"Hope. It seems I actually had hope." She feels pleased that she has noticed herself caught out in this most basic human pattern.

At her gesture, the keyboard made of light appears in the hologram of wood that permeates the Library facade. Idea types in

"Idea. Daily readout. Sphere history."

A page appears with information entries addressing the topics within the sentence she typed. She pulls at her bottom lip and types,

"Idea. Likelihood of suicide"

Again various entries appear. Idea jabs at the keyboard image with hard fingers,

"What happened to the spheres?"

Library provides a page of possible relevant entries.

Idea screeches in frustration and bangs her hand against the wall.

"What the actual fuck!?"

Idea kicks the interface with petulance. She covers her face with her hands and drops to the floor, drawing her knees into her chest with her arms. She begins to rock, pulling at her bottom lip. She looks up, narrowing her eyes. "No." She gets to her feet. "No!"

She leaves Library and goes to the dining pod.

"I refuse. I refuse to let whatever the fuck is this motherfucker of a scenario be such a motherfucking motherfucktard."

She slaps the table for emphasis. She goes to the food printer and taps all the buttons randomly. It prints out a grey goop. She sticks her finger in the goop, she forms the goop into the shape of a mountain, she slaps the goop aside.

She tastes the goop on her fingers.

"huh. Umami."

She walks slowly back to the chair and slumps bonelessly in it, then sits up straight. *Ok. So, the spheres are no longer a thing. I am most likely NOT dead. The child is dead.*

Her hand goes to her belly, and she stops halfway, then she shakes out both her hands. Little bits of grey goo splatter off her fingers. In the background the function of the ship disappears the goo. *Things are not normal. We know this. Who is this WE? There is no we!*

Idea is still certain she is not really mad. *I find myself within a mad scenario. The child died, so perhaps I AM mad. Mad with grief.* She gets up and stalks to the bathroom and looks in the mirror. The same face as usual appears there, but of course in reverse. *Same brown eyes. Same brown hair, brown skin. A brown woman. Who the fuck am I?* A face enters her thought stream. It is the face of an extremely old white woman. The eyes are so blue they are almost transparent. The eyes seem almost kind and yet deeply frightening, unfathomable. She sees this face overlay her own momentarily, then shakes it off with a shudder. Idea washes her hands and face and brushes her teeth. She puts on pajamas and gets into bed, at first laying on her back and then rolling on to her side, her hands under her face. Her hands smell salty. She begins to cry. Tears roll silently down her cheeks at first, and then she lets herself cry in earnest, great heaving sobs. She lets it empty her, she moans like a cow giving birth. Snot streams from her nose and she lets it run into her mouth and then wipes it with her pajama sleeve. She cries all of it, until she is nothing but a husk. At last, in this empty space she is surprised to notice that she feels good. *I am at peace. It is not meaningless. It is probably some kind of grace.*

Slowly she falls asleep and does not dream.

In the morning she showers, dresses and neatly ties back her hair. As she passes the little vac bot she nods to it politely. She eats a yellow meal in the shape of a pancake and makes her way to the centre platform of the ship. Idea goes through a number of yoga sun salutes and then sits quite naturally in a simple meditative pose. *This is to be noted. My body has past programming.* This done she makes her way up to the observation deck to check on it. The observation deck is unchanged, simply a 360 degree view of the profound depths of outer space, as usual. Idea begins to map the view; her work will be noting every shape and pattern.

She is seeking discrepancies.

Hermes has been dismissed by his human with the label 'stupid'. He could also quite fairly, from another perspective, be called 'sensei'. Hermes is a master of reading body language. He sits at his master's feet at her customary park bench and quivers a little. To all appearances his human seems an old woman taking an innocent nap, but he knows the roll of her eyes behind her parchment lids signifies something more arcane. He whines a little and rolls his eyes to look at the cat seated sphinx style two benches down. This cat is the denizen of this park and smells strongly of 'bakeneko'.[27] He can smell the similarity between this cat and his human, it is the whiff of the unpredictable. He hides his tenacity skillfully behind the safety of the mask of the idiot, it causes these dangerous entities to narrow their eyes and look away, dismissing him as a being of non-consequence. He rolls his eyes back to his person, and he senses the subtle tension in his leash, his umbilical tether to her. His leash carries messages to his body that he does not need to assess with his mind, he simply knows, and knows simply.

Varvara's eyes spring open. She has been in a state of deep processing, the intricate fibres of the inter-webbing of her mind thrum and glow. She looks down at Hermes and follows his eyes as he rolls them to the park cat two benches down. She and the cat narrow eyes at each other. The face of Tanaka floats into her minds' eye, with the same narrowed eyes as the cat. Varvara smells a rat, and she is delighted to understand it is herself. She knows now that she has been played, so intent on her own game of lab rat that she has not noticed Tanaka's own game of cat and mouse. Varvara celebrates every instance of surprise she experiences. She knows so much that she longs to not know. She knows of her own longing to not know. Unknown to her, Hermes is her mascot in this capacity, he who knows without knowing. Her mind flashes through her encounter with Tanaka earlier that day, a reprise of the deep processing she has just surfaced from. *Tanaka has been meddling with the dosing of Occupant XE, of this I am now certain. It seems XE will wake, and soon. Tanaka means to foil my experiment.* Her mind moves to consider the shadow player in their mutual game, *Hades*. She feels nauseous as usual at the pomposity of the name but acknowledges that the nickname is

---

27 *demon, monster or spirit cat*

most certainly apt. Hades is the Mortech moniker for Vish Bakshi, the American tech celebrity with a considerable investment interest in the success of the Mortech experiment. Hades is one of those people of power with a public face, who conceal all trace of their true identity and intent. Hades may not just be acting as an individual but could represent a group interest. She has hidden her lack of knowledge of Hades behind a wall of disdain, but of course she knows this about herself. The Mortech Five have expressed mutual distaste for Hades, but the funding cannot be denied, and as yet the contract with him has revealed no sinister intent. She thinks again of Tanaka and detects a glowing thread between him and Hades. Is Tanaka in the midst of a plan to either foil or further the interests of Hades? She recalls that the youngest member of the Five, 'The Gamer', had dubbed him Hades. She had been forced to work closely with this child, *this Pokemon enthusiast*. The Five know so little of each other, a team of privacy obsessed genius' united only in their vision for the project. The identity 'narrative adjustment' was the bone of contention among them, and it seemed this idiom could shift to become the spanner in the works. Tanaka did not believe the narrative identity could be successfully subdued, he asserted that it would arise and destroy the fabric of the reverie with the seed of disbelief. Varvara's assessment was that whether it was subdued sufficiently or not was beside the point, her assertion was that it would be simply co-opted by the reverie, if the reverie was correctly tailored to the client. The key was to weave the reverie skillfully around the core desire framework of the client's operating identity, and this she had done for each of the trial occupants, bar OccupantXE. Tanaka had been against her trial of OccupantXE from the beginning, he did not understand her penchant for controlled chaos, dismissed it as a vanity, an eccentricity. Yet he had agreed, and she was surprised that he would taint the trial with meddling, she had trusted he had sufficient belief the trial would prove his assertions by failing naturally. Meddling in the experiment went against the scientific method, she knew he held the method holy, and thus, the likelihood of outside pressure from Hades to explain his actions. *Curiouser and curiouser.* Hermes sees his human's hand go to her pocket, and he salivates, ready to receive the treat he knows is impending.

Lately Haruki has been feeling claustrophobic. He has certainly suffered various forms of anxiety over the years, but this was new. He now takes the stairs instead of the lifts, and suffers an uncomfortable peripheral sense that he is 'trapped'. His chest feels tight, and he takes the train to the seaside town of Chigasaki in an attempt to find relief. As an Australian, the ocean is part of his identity. Standing in this liminal zone watching the transition of twilight has always brought him a small measure of comfort. On this visit he stands in the ebb and flow of the tide with his trouser legs rolled up and watches the colours bleed from the sky. The feeling of the sea in Japan is very different from the character of the ocean in Australia. There's much about Australian 'culture' that he doesn't miss in the least, but the ancient land itself definitely has a claim on his heart. Haruki feels the tightness in his chest and attempts to forgive its presence. His mind circles through solutions, all in the theme of escape. He wonders once more why he stays at Mortech, he wonders if the tightness in his chest is a manifestation of the claws of Varvara. People like Varvara live complex lives, and Haruki desires simplicity. Haruki genuinely loved his wife, but concludes she ultimately found him lacking, *boring*. In the past his anxiety had led him to hide in small places, even the conceptual cave under his bedcover was sufficient as a child. He feels a conflict in his desire to hide in a small place and this new feeling of claustrophobia. *Why do I stay at Mortech?* Despite Felipe's zen assertions, it is clear his feelings for OccXE are simply a projection implanted by the manipulative Varvara. The strange thing is he feels tremendous empathy for Varvara, she feels to him more and more like a tight wall of pain he can feel in his body, and this makes him sorry for her despite her witch act. Standing slouched with his hands in his pockets Haruki kicks at the water and curses his empathy. He feels both lonely and the concurrent desire to remain alone. He closes his eyes and tunes the rhythm of his breath to the rhythm of the tide, hoping he will simply fade to nothingness, disappear and be done with it. He fades out a little, the problem solving cycle continues in his surface consciousness while some deeper part of him is simply under the waves, down in the dark. From this deeper place he observes his mind continuing to throw up symbols, words, images and tiny movies in a frantic attempt to explain and problem-solve the uncomfortable feeling in his body. Slowly, very slowly he begins to be ok about it. *Maybe not knowing the answer is ok?* As the twilight shifts him into silhouette he begins to cry. The tears sting his eyes. Some tears are sweet and soft, not these. These tears are sharp and acidic, they hurt. These salty tears slide off his nose and onto his shirt. He bends forward and his nose drips his own salt into the salt of the sea. He prays sincerely for death, *I can't go on here on Earth, it's too much for me.* He starts to tip forward slightly, *why not just fall into the sea? But I can't take my own life, it's too violent.* He has trouble breathing, his shoulders shudder. He thinks of Totoro and his parents, feels the threads of their connection like tethers. *Trapped!* Eventually the tears come to an end, the tightness feels ragged and raw, and he walks away from the sea, his face swollen and sticky. It's a bit of a walk back to the train station and he walks hunched into himself and salty all the way. He boards the train and returns home, but it's late and Totoro is out. He eats leftover plain rice and plays computer games until he feels empty, and then goes to bed.

His dreams aren't worth remembering, but he wakes the next day returned to a gently humorous mood. He cuddles Totoro and gives him as many snacks as he wants, despite his (actually wonderful) fatness. Haruki gives a limp fist shake at the sky and thinks *ok life, you win, as usual.* Later he goes for his pre-work yakitori and takes it to his park bench to see if Hoboneko is around. He has come out without his coat today, and he notices the green buds swelling on the trees, ready to unfurl their greenery into the slowly dawning warmth of Spring. In Japan Spring is in his name, Haru. There's no sign of Hobo, but he is shocked to see Varvara with a small dog on a leash two benches down from his customary bench. He stands rigidly in a state of fight or flight. The little dog stands up and wags his tail with a soft question in his direction, and Varvara looks over. She says nothing but keeps gazing at him speculatively. Haruki waves awkwardly with his yakitori hand, puts his other hand in his pocket and drops to the bench. *I'm not sure what's the right thing to do here.*

Varvara stands and walks over with her dog, looming despite her small stature.

"Mori-san. You know this park also? Wonderful gingko trees around here."

Haruki rallies, "Gingko! Yes. I did not know you also favoured this park. It's not far from the lab though, so it makes sense."

"Indeed. You are en route to your shift?"

Haruki waves his yakitori and looks sheepish. The little dog licks his lips and whines a little.

"Hermes, contain yourself. Hermes is also 'a man of the Tao' you know Haruki. You too would quite likely get along."

Haruki shrugs and grins lopsidedly, decides to take the intended insult as a compliment. Haruki squints up at her,

"I'm a wanna-be man of the Tao."

He bows to Hermes, murmurs "sensei" and gives him a little wink. Hermes sits fatly at Varvara's feet and rolls his eyes at a sarareman[28] that hurries by. There is an uncomfortable silence. Haruki looks up at Varvara's face and is surprised to see the ghost of an expression he has not witnessed there before, something that looked a lot like vulnerability. She covers it quickly and her customary mask returns.

"Well then Mori-san, I wouldn't want you to get in trouble with your boss for tardiness. I'll bid you good day."

Haruki bows at her retreating back and nervously tousles the back of his hair. *Look at me auto-bowing like a Japanese man, Dad would be proud.* He sees Hoboneko approaching his bench and sketches him a bow also. Hoboneko sits straight up like a statue with his tail curled around his feet and regards Haruki for a moment with an unblinking stare, then turns politely away and begins to groom. Haruki bows again and turns away marveling. *Huh. Hoboneko actually directly acknowledged my existence. What does that signify?* He stands, narrowly avoids bumping into a person on the path and hastens down the stairs to the train station with his hands in his pockets and his head leaning forward.

---

28   *Katakana form of 'Salary-man'*
    the Japanese name for workaholic office workers

Varvara walks out of sight of Mori-san and puts her hand to her heart. She feels tenderness. The same maternal tenderness she apparently feels for OccupantXE. She looks down at Hermes and thinks her remarks at him. *Well, well Hermes. A further crack in the icy heart. For what purpose?* Hermes sits up straight and holds up one trembling paw for a moment before sitting back expectantly. She speaks aloud to him now, *old women muttering to their dogs is de riguer after all.*

"Perhaps a sign of my impending death? Smote by a bolt of grace and cracked open?"

Her hands tremble and she feels a tightness in her chest. Varvara has led a life of non-stop strategy, a high stakes chess match with the rest of humanity and life itself against her in the opposing chair. She struggles to believe in authentic kindness in both herself and others. *Humans are nothing but manipulators, gaping holes with hungry mouths.* Hermes is smiling up at her with wet shining eyes. *Idiot.* She looks at him and acknowledges that he has a certain appeal, would likely be termed 'cute'. She is struck by the desire to scatter the chess pieces from the board. It's not the first time she's had this impulse. *Would would it be like to just be an old lady? Feeding morsels to her little dog and doting on children in the park?* Her whole body is stiff with pain, she clenches her teeth against it and puts out a hand to hold the fence in front of her. *Weakness! Why am I so weak? It's the victim, so needy, so disgusting.* She feels bile rise in her throat and hastens away. Hermes chokes mildly as he is reluctantly pulled along, puffing. His short legs are all out of proportion with his roundness, his body the result of years of ancestral breeding that render him defenceless, a folly of humans.

Tanaka's first name, Yoshitaro, is rarely used. It sits, dusty, in official documents and his childhood. His home is majestic in its minimalism, impeccable. He thinks occasionally with fondness of his long dead wife, though his romantic preference has always been for men. His face is the ultimate poker face, but this is simply the result of the collision of narrow featured ancestors. Tanaka has come to accept people read into his closed features many stories that are not actually written there. Tanaka is clean and spare, and his hands are cool and deft. His mind is as uncluttered as his home. This mind turns to pondering Varvara. *A woman of great passion, masquerading as one who is made of ice.* She does not trust him, and indeed this is warranted, but he simply wants to save her from herself. Ordinarily it has been his creed to accord others the privacy and respect to create and fall into their own self-made traps. Curious to himself is the understanding that he also desires to rescue occupantXE, whom he has never met. Varvara is a typical narcissist, reading her own motivations into the actions of others. Tanaka has great respect for his work, he is never sloppy and formulates the correct dosing of his clients with great integrity. For all his controlled grace he allows intuitive inspiration to work through him, he trusts implicitly the clarity of his own mind. He understands his actions regarding the dosing of occupant XE stem from this clarity. He has made attempts to speak openly with Varvara, but she does not know how to respond to him as an ally. He sits in his low mid-century leather chair with the highest quality headphones perfectly fitted over his well-proportioned, tidy ears. He allows the surge of symphonic elegance within their hemispheres to render him as a dust mote, adrift and yet one with its beauty. *As for Hades, I can certainly trust that creature of avarice to destroy himself in the end. This pattern is already set in motion I fear.*

6.

Awakening

ach day Idea applies herself to her work.

She has a notion that if she can find some sort of glitch in the ship, she can wangle it into some sort of portal to freedom. She is certain that despite the semblance of a static experience, she is yet in a liminal zone. She does not know why or how she is inspired to this notion but is sincere in her desire for understanding. She lies on her back on the observation deck and allows the visible span of deep space to chandelier. The observation deck is spacious and open, but she has a deep body sense of confinement. *Odd*. Idea has a curious notion that if she stares at the openness of space and concurrently attentively notices the trapped feeling of her body, somehow they will cancel each other and create an opening. It is a strange notion, but what can she do but follow the inspiration that occurs most strongly to her?

Idea punctuates her work of deep focus with short breaks of loose focus. She moves her body, she eats, sleeps, experiences routine body functioning. Her mind also revolves through its routine patterns in these breaks, but she simply relaxes the intensity of her concentration. She does not know how long she undertakes this process, she has no sense of time.

As she lies on her back letting her gaze be commandeered by the emptiness of dark space, her body mines and releases subterranean emotions and traumas. Idea is unfettered in this work by a social conscience, she is free to abandon herself to catharsis. As she unfurls into emptiness her reverie becomes a reverence. In this requiem she hears an angelic toning, she experiences her body as though it is being recreated layer by translucent layer. In this lucid state her body sleeps and surfaces, sleeps and surfaces, yet her attention remains awake. Finally, a palpable fear looms into focus. Idea feels the sensation of infinite falling, and her mind begins to clutch at objects of stability. *The child. My body. Thoughts. Assumptions. Ideas. Death.* Her heart begins to feel crushed by gravity, she believes in this moment her heart will kill her, squeezed indefatigably by an unseen hand. In this terror her sense of self begins to run about, masks are donned and fall away as her body trembles and sweats, moans escape her lips. She is deep in this nightmare, yet somewhere a lucid flame notices.

Who notices?

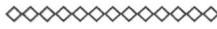

It is 1.11am, Tanaka walks calmly into the lab, nodding with complicity to the staff member who is working. That night's shift worker bows and withdraws into the gloom at the edge of the lab, this event has been pre-arranged, set smoothly into motion by a deft hand, the hand of Tanaka. He passes all the pod occupants without glancing at their readouts, his motion is implacable and direct, he moves as an an arrow of focus to the pod of Occupant XE. Swiftly his narrow eyes take in the information available on the interface. He gestures over the screen, brings up a luminous keyboard, types a series of commands into the dark control panel visible now in the interface. He looks up and looks carefully around the lab. All is quiet, peaceful, still. The time has come for Occupant XE to wake.

The metaphor that she is a meteor entering the atmosphere of a planet at speed occurs to Idea. She mentally pulls the release cord of a conceptual parachute and lurches into a state of relief. Slowly the calamity of the fight/flight reflex abates, it is as though she is drifting toward an eventual landing in the ocean, a lone shuttle pod ejected from an obliterated ship. *It's the strangest thing, this sense that I am in a tiny, enclosed space.* This story of the shuttle pod told to her brain by her mind seems so real. She opens her eyes to darkness, only now realising that they were tightly shut, her hands stretch out to feel her perimeter, coming into touch sensation of a cool, hard surface. There is a sense of climate, around her body a sense of warmth, *but there, up above, it's a little cooler. I don't know where I am. This does not make sense.* It seems she no longer lies on the floor of the observation deck. Her heart begins anew to thud, and she feels a surge of apprehension, her pores release an alarming chemical profile to her nostrils. Then, in a slow and soft gradient, ambient light dawns. She blinks as her pupils adjust and raises her palms to regard them. Her skin is puckered as though she has been too long in a bath. She can smell the sharp tang of disinfectant. Her mouth and throat are dry, she runs her tongue across her lips, and notes they are chapped. It seems she is in a dim and shiny plastic coffin, there is a slim strip of LED light running around the perimeter. As she begins to shift there is a rustling sound and she sees that she wears a kind of paper nappy. Her hand goes to her belly, to her breasts, to her arms, there is an emollient lubricant gel slicking across the surface of her body. She is now viscerally alert. She hears a muted huff, has a sudden sense of decompression. Above her a lid lifts and opens in a smooth hydraulic arc. The light that meets her gaze is dim, neutral, medical, professional. Absurdly she curses, *Fuck!* But her voice is in her head only, all that actually emerges is a rasp. An austere face appears above her and gives a subtle nod. She sees that it is the face of an older Japanese man. His face seems stern, implacable. He looks over his shoulder and a young Japanese women appears. She bows gently to Idea. Idea nods several times and understands that she has urinated in her nappy.

Tanaka shifts to the interface and keys in a command to release a light but effective dose of a mild tranquiliser of his own creation. He leaves Nakamura to present a gentle face on the situation to the newly awakened occupant. He notes the readout, the tranquiliser begins to take effect. Nakamura looks over at him and they share an understanding nod. XE has closed her eyes. Her readout shows she has gently re- entered sleep, this time one that could be considered normal. Nakamura has a medibot next to her, and it assists her to deftly remove all the now unnecessary contact points and fluid tubes from XE. She tears open packets of alcohol wipes and gently swabs the lubricant gels from her skin. When these tasks are complete Tanaka lifts her into a seated position and Nakamura slips her into a hospital gown. XE is thereafter removed swiftly and professionally from the lab to a safe place in anticipation of the initiation of her recovery protocols.

On the morning of his next shift at work Haruki receives a brief and impersonal email informing him that his casual position of employment at Mortech Lab has been terminated. There is no telephone contact at Mortech, only email communication. Haruki types in a hurried response, "wtf ???" and almost hits send. His hand hovers above the keyboard and shifts instead to the back of his head. He goes slack jawed and stews. He happens to have opened his email on his desktop, and he gives one slow rotation in his swivel chair. Totoro jumps up onto his computer keyboard and his considerable girth adds an additional emphatic string of vowels and consonants into the body of the email, then somehow the entire screen shifts into a sideways view. Haruki snorts in a mixture of frustration and enjoyment and gives a mock stern, "Toto!"

Totoro remains unperturbed, he falls into a more fulsome sprawl across the keyboard and offers up his fluffy white belly, his ears flatten out under his now upside down head and he stretches his forepaws out full in one direction, his back paws splaying open comically like the front and back covers of a book. Haruki's hand goes by instinct into the verdant fluff of Totoro's belly, he rests his elbow on the table and cradles his chin in his hand. His hand goes to his pocket for his phone, and he searches Fujioka's number, but as he searches the number it rings. It's Fujioka. He answers immediately.

"Hiro! I was just about to call you! I got an email just now from Mortech."

"Whaat? You got one too. Then we've both been 'terminated'."

Fujioka suggests, "Tsuki asap, yes?"

Haruki responds with, "I'm there."

Varvara reads the email from Tanaka a second time. Like the man it is short, clear, direct and formal. An innocuous invitation to dinner two days hence. For Varvara it is very far from innocuous, rather it reads as a declaration of war. The Mortech Five do not invite each other to dinner. *What has Tanaka done?* She smells a checkmate. Her instinct is to destroy, to ravage, to become as Kali and eat the nearest soul. At her feet is the ubiquitous Hermes. He quivers a little and prepares his fluttering soul for its imminent annihilation, he will not fight this. He looks at her instead with liquid eyes of devotion, an exhausted deer pinned under the implacable paw of a hungry tiger. Varvara is stilled in his gaze, her rage empties unspent, the serpent descends back into its coils. *It is too typical to rage, too easy to spend the rage on the innocent. I refuse to be victim to this pattern. I am the narrator, I am The Architect, not some fool player.* She types an elegant acceptance to Tanaka.
The game is afoot.

That morning at the private entrance used by the Mortech Five Varvara's retina scan is refused. Her heart begins to pump, and she quells it with an icy inner stare. Among the Five there are no allies, each genius dwells within a walled fortress. *Yet this refusal at the door is unthinkable. I am the originating principle of Mortech, this is a nonsense.* Varvara sits within her coils and seethes. *What is my move?* She taps a small distance away from the door, the sound of her walking stick is a hollow reverberation in the empty underground carpark that houses the entrance door. *This calls for an elegant chaos.* She must not fetch Hermes, she must go somewhere she has never been. Like the cat who views life upside down for part of each day, she must upend her perspectives. She has become complacent within her own habits. *I must be destroyed and then resurrected more powerful.* In the dark private underground carpark Varvara becomes stilled. She allows her thoughts to ebb away and wills her focus to emptiness. All her senses become muted and yet more alert. An image of a dark and deep inner abyss arises, she dismisses it. *This hoary thought chestnut I have seen before.* The deeper she sinks into the nothing the more theatrical the mind's performance becomes, throwing out image after image to catch her and lure her away. She is implacable now, she is as the centre of a black hole. She stands ancient and stooped at the door as though made of stone, to come to life only to ask a riddle of any seeking entrance. Into this silence a new actor enters the stage. Varvara does not see him, in his current form he is rarely seen, he is The Mathematician. The Mathematician is a chameleon, able to assume any form needed to deflect attention. People forget him instantly, he leaves no trace. This is his preference, he is a master of shadows, a master also of light. His touch on Mortech is intrinsic, and yet forgotten even by the four others. His architecture is transparent as hegemony and goes unheralded. He regards Varvara. Her eyes are open and yet unseeing, she is frozen in place, a basilisk turned to stone by her own inner gaze. The Mathematician is intrigued, he loves a puzzle game. Usually, Varvara is a storm of masks over a cold fury, a willfully dampened passion. *This stillness is very interesting.* He waits, tasting her stillness for himself, assuming her form fully and easily into his own inherent emptiness. If any were to gaze upon this scene they would witness two ancients facing each other, still and folded over their canes, a Gemini tableaux. The Mathematician created the retina scan for Mortech, a unique form of a now common technology. He steps lightly now to the side of Varvara, who remains unaware of his presence. The others do not know that for him the scan is unnecessary. He pauses in the now illuminated portal and understands that it is necessary to leave the door open, just long enough. This shapeless one disappears into the lab, intent on his own enigmatic errands. The light from the open door spills over Varvara, dawns across her as across an ancient mountain. She stirs. Her eyes clear, she returns to motion, all clocks resume their ticking. She turns to the open door and smiles a serpent smile. Her process has yielded fruit. She has no memory of The Mathematician, he is one who can only be referenced in ones' periphery, and then forgotten.

Varvara enters the lab, regal, taking her time, hurrying for none. She taps up the hallway on a direct route to the nest of dreamers, oblivious in their cocoons. Nakamura is on duty. She gives her usual bow, but Varvara detects the faint aura of an anxiety she can't hide. Varvara knows that Nakamura is a minion of Tanaka. She resists the urge to play cat and mouse with the young student, but begins a theatre of restraint, tapping and pausing among the pod occupants as though her whole body does not strain toward the pod of Occupant XE. It is arduous, Varvara feels the strain of her age, her arthritic knuckles swell upon the duck's head of her cane. Nakamura plays her part well, discreet as ever. Varvara goes to the desk interface used by the pod monitor staff. She enters her code and is denied access. She enters Mori's code and is denied access. Fujioka Hiro's code also denied. She shows no outward response to Nakamura, Nakamura remains silent. She clicks back to the home page and makes her way to the pod of occupant XE. As she has already assumed, it is empty. The screen interface shows no data. She raises one age spotted and be-ringed hand and summons Nakamura.

"Nakamura-san. How does this pod come to be empty?" Nakamura bows in her peripheral vision.

"Gomen-nasai[29], Varvara-sama. I know only that it is empty."

Varvara lets out a short ironic huff.

"You are dismissed."

"Gomen-nasai, I am under instruction not to leave you alone in this lab."

"Indeed. Under the authority of whom?"

"I received a staff email with this instruction."

"Oh, very good. Artfully evaded. So neatly tied up that its signature can only be that of Tanaka."

Nakamura bows again, "sumimasen[30] Varvara-sama. I have nothing to give you, gomen nasai."

Varvara's grip on her cane tightens. She feels the customary throb of the rings she cannot remove due to her arthritic knuckles. She refuses to have them cut off. They are her reminder, the pain keeps her alert.

"Nakamura-san. Withdraw."

She nods to herself. *It is time to talk to Hades, that human stain has an unmistakable stench.*

Idea dreams. The dream is a cascade of sensory impression only. There is the sensation of humidity, an image of a vivid green tree snake, the whir of crickets. She feels that she is running, on her feet the sensation of

---

29   *sorry (with respect)*

30   *excuse me*

flip-flops flapping against the soles of her feet. The hair is raised on her arms despite the sense of humidity, she has that feeling of vulnerability at the nape of her neck. She stops running and turns, is caught in a loop of turning. Then it is night, overhead a fat moon rides the heavens, wisps of cloud rush across its face. Suddenly the sky opens, and she sees fat raindrops falling, the turgid drops burst against her face, she feels the cling of drenched clothing on her skin. The point of perception shifts, and she sees herself as a child in front of her, small and brown, bedraggled brown hair about her round face. She opens her hands, and a firefly flies up and out of them, backlit for a moment against the orb of the moon. There is the sense of hallways. Flickering light. Curtains stirred in a soft breeze. There is the ever present smell of green. Idea surfaces. She can still smell the moisture, yet the sheet under her hand is crisp, dry and cool. For a moment she can't feel her legs, then her whole body is subsumed with an aching heaviness. Every part of her is a dull pain. She struggles to open her eyes, they are gritty with sleep. She lays on her back. Turns her head to the side and opens her eyes, raising a hand to rub at the grit. The Japanese man is there. She remembers him and regards him like a puzzle she is in the midst of tinkering with. She opens her lips to speak, and her throat swallows her voice. The man has a cool glass of water ready, she sees the droplets of condensation on the glass in sharp relief, she sits up gingerly, takes the glass, and sips. It is coconut water. She pauses to reflect, realising she remembers coconuts. Greedily she slurps it down in a rush, wetting her chin and neck and the front of the white cotton pajamas she appears to be wearing. The man places his palm flat against his chest and bows very slightly, tells her "Tanaka."

Idea checks herself internally, then points to her head, pauses, then shakes her head and points to her chest, and tells him,

"I have no idea."

She wonders if the expression on Tanaka's face is a smile. It does not resemble a smile, but nonetheless she intuits the feeling of a smile. Her voice is croaky with disuse. Her hand goes to her head, feels that her hair is just a soft fuzz.

Tanaka speaks, "Inside the pod, we kept the hair shaved from your body. You were due to be shaved. I assume you will prefer to keep your hair now?"

For a moment Idea is lost in the old dream. *In the mirrors on board the ship, I had long hair.* She does not answer Tanaka, is silent for some time. Tanaka waits, he seems infinitely patient. She realises that for some reason she trusts him.

"You are my rescuer? Inside the dream, I expected someone different."

Tanaka makes a spare bow,

"Your rescuer? So it seems."

Idea looks about the room, notes its austere details. Muses to herself, *can coolness be described as warmth?*

She peers at Tanaka.

"I've had only myself to talk to for a time."

He asks her, "what do you remember?"

Idea pauses to assess. *I remember the spaceship. Library. The spheres. Waking up. But what WAS all that? Was it really only a dream? It was so vivid.*

She asks, "have I been dreaming?"

Tanaka's voice is as austere as the room,

"yes. It can be called this."

He pauses, then pours her another glass of coconut water from a slim glass jug. She nods in agreement,

"Electrolytes. I know about those."

Tanaka steeples his hands, regards her face,

"Interesting."

He gestures at the window in front of her bed. Outside her window she sees a traditional Zen garden, there is a soft confetti of white blossom petals over the green moss. *Pretty.* She smiles at Tanaka, blushes a little, and asks him

"I'm on Earth?"

Tanaka gestures at the garden.

"Please. Enjoy this at your leisure, the blossom trees are flowering. It is a precious time of year in our garden."

Idea realises they are speaking English, and understands that she does not speak Japanese.

"Tanaka, I'm realising that I know a lot about Earth. I took this for granted during my 'dream'. I mean, I had Library as a reference. But I had no memory of an experience of Earth's destruction."

She tinkers at her puzzle, in the way that she did within the 'dream'.

Tanaka is very still.

"Library? Earth's destruction?"

Idea studies him. His face is all narrowness, as though drawn with single lines.

"Oh. I guess I was assuming you had some kind of hand in the dream. Even though you are my rescuer."

He leans back slightly, "It can be said that I rescued you, but I was also complicit in the situation you have lately escaped. In this you have intuited the truth. However, please understand that I am unaware of the content of your reverie. I have arranged for you to meet The Architect of your reverie. Later, if you wish it so, The Hypnotist. When you are ready."

Idea feels a small frisson of fear and hugs her arms around her chest,

"The Architect? The Hypnotist?"

"Yes. You consented to experience a pre-designed reverie under the auspices of our company Mortech Lab. I have the paperwork that you signed. You also consented to have important aspects of your identity 'adjusted', so this signature may mean nothing to you at this time."

He studies her face for a moment,

"The Hypnotist is confident the adjustment is reversible. I must tell you I have some reservations about this. I am sorry that you find yourself in this position."

Idea asks him, "I consented to all this?"

"Yes."

"Well. I'm in a position such that I must believe everything you say."

"This is true, but please be assured that what I am telling you is most deifinitively true. Of course, you are free to think whatever you may."

He bows within his chair, his tone is light, cool and neutral.

Idea feels into it for a moment and senses no trickery from the man.

"So, this Architect? I have already met her?"

"Indeed. You and she made this arrangement without the concurrent agreement of the rest of the directors of Mortech. Varvara is her own force of nature. I allowed her to have her game for a time, but your plight weighed on my sense of ethics. I have a strong sense of order, the habit of restoring balance. I also have a strong ethic of non-interference. It interests me that I felt so strongly about this."

" Varvara?"

Idea sees an image in her mind of a woman of advanced age, arthritic fingers festooned with rings.

"Huh. I think I kind of remember her."

"It will be intriguing to discover the new pattern of your memory. Your sense of self. Varvara sees you as her own experiment, she will be possessive. She is also an agent of her own chaos, in this way it will be of interest to see how she responds."

"Ohhh. You've crossed a battle-axe?"

Tanaka leans back in his wooden chair.

"This is how she will understand what has transpired."

"So, you say I consented to this?"

"Yes."

"Then why the question of ethics?"

"It is my view that when you agreed to this, experiment you were under considerable emotional duress, the other pod occupants have had their reveries designed under thorough consultation with Varvara. In your case you were something of a 'charity case', if you'll excuse the expression. It is one of those English expressions, 'to kill two birds with one stone'. You were testing Varvaras' own reverie. One she has personally designed for herself. She wanted to test it before submitting herself to it. She deemed you perfect for her purposes. As for The Hypnotist, he was easily swayed to her cause as he is one who enjoys all experiments, regardless of questions of ethics."

Ideas' hand goes to her hair, slowly rubs across the soft new fuzz, like peach fur. She gets distracted by this for a moment, then recalls Tanaka's presence.

"I think I'm going to be very strange for a while. Hopefully not forever?"

Tanaka stands and bows again.

"So. It is enough for now. Please rest. Enjoy the garden. Chester will bring you some food."

Idea feels suddenly exposed,

"Chester?"

Tanaka bows this time only very slightly from the neck.

"Chester is very kind. Very safe. I believe you will like him. It is ok with you that he comes?"

Idea feels herself nodding yes and Tanaka leaves her. Idea throws back her bed cover and swings her legs to get out of bed. Her feet touch the floor and are flooded with pain, an explosion of pins and needles. She stumbles over in an attempt to stand on her numb feet and falls onto the rug next to her bed.

"Fuck!"

A pair of shoes come into view, brown shiny brogues of an excellent cut and construction. She looks up. Her visitor is a man, probably in his fifties, but glowing with good health. He is tall, lithe and muscular, and his head is abundant with a luxuriant mop of black curls. His skin is a beautiful tan olive, his lips wide and generous, he has a determined twinkle in his eyes. Idea holds up an invalid's hand,

"little help?"

Chester. He puts a food tray on the table by the window and then stoops to help her. *He smells good.* Idea realises she has not smelt this kind of wonderful man-smell in a while and is suddenly overwhelmingly pleased the Earth was not destroyed. She laughs out loud and rolls her eyes as Chester helps her to the table. She squints up at him and puts a hand over her eyes.

"Wow. The patient is very weird. Did Tanaka warn you?"

Chester smiles generously, chuckles warmly.

"He bid me only to be kind."

His voice is warm, mellifluous. Idea feels a blush creeping up her neck and hitting her face in full bloom.

He holds his hand over his heart, does a little bow, saying

"Chester Kask. At your service."

Wait. His accent. She narrows her eyes at him.

"German? Kind of ?"

He deepens his bow, makes it more theatrical,

"Estonian."

"Wow. I don't know for sure, but I'm pretty sure I've never met an Estonian."

"Japan brings many bees to her extremely well-made honey."

He holds out his hand for her to shake,

"I'm a shoemaker. Of course, I spent a lot of time in Italy, but Japan is a mecca for all artisans. I made my pilgrimage a few years ago, and met Tanaka..."

Idea hears in his pause that he and Tanaka are a 'thing', and marvels. For a few moments she is speechless, then smiles at him.

"I noticed your shoes. From down on the rug. Yours?" Chester seats himself across from her.

"No, Scarvattis." He says it like they are also a thing. Idea does not know Scarvatti's shoes it seems.

Chester laughs and gives a sheepish grin.

"They are very expensive, and very exclusive. Monica is a colleague of mine."

Idea taps her temple saying "Sandwich short of a picnic."

Chester suddenly looks earnest.

"Please. Eat a little. You've really been through something. I'm actually surprised you're so chipper."

His accent is very pleasant. *Chester is very pleasant.* Idea allows herself to enjoy him, she has been alone for an unknown time, but it feels like aeons. The food is a bento tray of artfully prepared morsels, Idea is simply pleased it was not extruded by a 3D printer. Chester stands and pushes in his chair like a schoolboy.

"I'll leave you to it."

Idea feels suddenly like crying, her face collapses inward. *Chester is leaving.* She feels bereft. Her hand goes to her heart, clutching her pajama shirt.

Chester looks horrified, exclaiming

"I'm so sorry! You are tired."

Idea hastily brushes away her tears,

"No. It's fine. I feel like I haven't had company in the longest time. Sorry."

Chester sits again.

"Well. Let's 'hang out'. A favourite English saying of mine."

Idea picks up her chopsticks. *I know how to use these.* She stores this morsel of information to ponder later and falls to eating. Savouring. *Real food! Handsome company.*

7.

Unraveling

Haruki, Fujioka and Felipe sit, heads together, in their usual booth.

Felipe stacks the coasters into a card house, Haruki twirls a coaster up on one corner. Fujioka texts his girlfriend under the table, and Haruki spies on the screen. *She wants him to buy hamster chow on his way home, cute.* Today Fujioka's wearing a loose cotton shirt depicting the retro character Gudetama in various classic apathetic poses. By now they've chatted the whole 'job loss' situation out. There's that conversational pause that happens, and each man thinks his private thoughts. Both Haruki and Fujioka have very limited savings. Fujioka is embarrassed but relieved that he lives in his girlfriend's apartment, safe for the moment. Felipe wants to help but feels at a loss. For a moment Haruki feels overwhelmed with anxiety, he has started thinking he'll have to spend a little time making Ethereum, *more like unobtanium,* in one of the VR dominions, then feels the usual nausea at the thought. He focuses instead on the flood of abandonment that hits him in the chest and finds that he is standing before he knows why. Felipe stands also and holds his arms open,

"my friend."

Haruki doesn't take the hug but sits back down in the booth.

Felipe sits back down, feels around in his pocket, brings out a joint, and lays it on the table. Haruki picks it up and puts it inside the house of cards, upsetting the house in the process, the coasters cover the joint in a haphazard pile. Felipe smiles, shrugs, philosophical.

Haruki says, "we'll have to go smoke that with Cho."

Felipe answers with a questioning smile; he has not yet met Cho. Fujioka nods agreement and the three pay their bills and leave Tsuki.

Cho Jeong is a performance artist who lives in a tall thin industrial building in Asakusa. You enter through an alleyway, and get judged by the cat that haunts the alley on the way in. Cho is tiny like a child, but with a raucous demeanour. She often expresses her frustration and sense of oppression by Japanese culture but ends up seeming quintessentially Tokyo although she is ethnically Korean. She buzzes the trio up and they enter her studio to the scene of her constructing a giant joint. She is clad in a canary yellow, slightly translucent zip up type of boiler-suit, magenta underwear is visible beneath. Her head is shaved, and she's sporting her own interpretation on the latest 'ethno-tribal' face paint.

Haruki holds up Felipe's tiny blunt.

Cho smirks as she licks the long length of her own paper construction, "mine is bigger than yours!"

She snorts at her own joke and holds her beautifully made joint aloft, "Camberwell carrot."

Felipe holds out a hand for a high five,

"I love that movie!"

Cho smacks away his hand and wrestles him to the ground, mock punching him in the gut. She perches on his stomach and draws a penis shaped lighter from a capacious pocket. She takes her time lighting the 'carrot', replaces the lighter in her pocket and points down at him, asking Haruki "who's he?" Felipe holds a hand out for the joint and she pokes her tongue out at him at the same time as winking. Haruki lays down on the floor next to Felipe. He lifts Felipe's hand and gestures for Cho to give him her hand. She rolls her eyes and gives him a limp hand. He places it in Felipe's and mimes them shaking, chanting

"rock, paper, scissors,"

he chuckles and winks at Felipe, points at Cho,

"Scissors" then back to Felipe "meet Paper."

Fujioka chuckles and lays down with them,

"I'm Rock!"

Cho dives into Hiro's soft, generous stomach, tickling him and shouting,

"No! You are jelly!"

She leaps up, pirouettes and bows to Felipe,

"Cho. You can call me Cho. It's my name"

Felipe holds his palms together in prayer form, inclines his head with respect,

"Felipe."

Haruki gets up on an elbow and looks at his friends, feeling love in his heart, and then feeling kind of shy. Cho reaches out her tiny hand and pulls him up with her to sit on the giant banana shaped couch, passing him the joint.

"Mori-san you beautiful man. Take this."

Felipe sits up cross legged across from them and Fujioka sits on the heart shaped swivel stool, gently twirling himself around. Haruki passes the joint to Felipe and picks up a toy from the table, a vintage Mario chibi figurine, then he puts it back. Cho looks into his face,

"Haruki-kun. What's up?"

Fujioka spins round to face Cho, tells her,

"Mori-san and I just got fired. Effective immediately."

"Ehhhh? So desu ne? From that spooky job you can't talk about? Well.

Good riddance."

She crosses her legs and feels around in her many pockets, brings out a small wooden puzzle and presses it into Haruki's hand, "a gift for the newly unemployed."

Haruki begins to tinker with it and looks around the studio,

"Cho. You are on your own?"

There were usually randoms floating about the studio, leftovers from the many parties she hosted and frequented.

"Yah. I kicked em all out. Started watching satsangs on my phone instead."

"Whaaaat?"

Cho nods seriously.

"Yep, I want to become enlightened."

Fujioka chuckles,

"Stage one. party. Stage two, become enlightened."

He points at Felipe, "ask this guy about ayahuasca."

Cho bounces on the couch cross legged,

"ehh? I thought that stuff got banned by the 'shamans' waay back."

Felipe nods,

"you are right, too many tech execs from Silicon Valley stinking up the jungle back in the day. But I am from Brazil. I have friends, and respect for culture. So, I have had some experiences."

The intercom buzzes. Cho looks around at the trio and grins.

"A little party before we get enlightened? Fujioka Hiro, call your garufurendo[31]. Time to party."

In no time the studio is full. Antics ensue. Haruki sits on a hot pink bouncy exercise ball like a google staffer from the early 2000s. He is chatting to a pretty blonde American woman and she's giving all the

---

31   *katakana version of the English word girlfriend*

signs that she thinks he's cute. He's surprised. It's hard to feel cute when you are middle aged and in the midst of re-assembling a kintsukuroi heart. He thinks suddenly of Occupant XE and feels immediately sorrowful. *How will I know what happens to her now?* His hand goes to his heart, feeling the loss. The American pauses in her chatting and gently bounces her own lime green ball a little closer,

"Hey. You ok?"

Haruki smells her scent. She smells good, natural. It has been so long since he's been with a woman. *I really genuinely loved my wife, yet it felt like she left me quite easily. Getting involved with someone new will most likely turn out messy.* He imagines sleeping with this woman, some happy times, and then a newly broken heart at the end. Maybe hers. Caused by himself. *Better not to begin.* The buoyancy of his exercise ball is at odds with the sinking of his mood. He sits on the floor and rolls the ball away. The woman does the same, coming even closer. Now he can smell the alcohol on her breath. She brings out a bottle of sake and two plastic cups from her bag, holds them up with a question. Haruki decides to let go. Embrace what this moment brings, *take this waltz.* Occupant XE slips quietly out of his consciousness.

In the morning he wakes up to a horrific hangover. His first thought is of Totoro, *he will be hungry.* Haruki believes Totoro sends him psychic emails, this morning's 'message' is simply his miffed face, his little serious mouth, puffed out square cheeks and whiskers standing straight out either side. Haruki gets up with a groan and sees that he is on the top floor in a room full of futons. The room is empty, but the American is passed out next to him. He groans again, *Fuck!* He sneaks downstairs to the kitchen, telling himself he'll fetch her some water. Felipe sits in the kitchen with Cho, draped in one of her translucent pink kimonos.

Cho ladles miso broth into two handmade ceramic cups. She reaches for a third cup, fills it with miso, and hands it to Haruki, then brings the other cups to the table.

"Haruki-kun. You have had a bender. Come and commiserate with your friends."

Cho and Felipe look at each other with a light in their eyes. Haruki gets it. *Actually, they are a good match.* Cho takes Haruki's hand and also Felipe's,

"Felipe-san is going to come stay with me for a while. He's extending his trip."

Haruki nods. He's glad. His head hurts. He remembers the American. *Um... her name is Amber. That's right.* His hand goes to the back of his head, and he looks rueful. Felipe's eyes go to the ceiling, and he chuckles, "I noticed you enjoying the company of that American woman?"

Cho chuckles.

"Americans are rare in Japan these days. Hard for them to get the health passport. At least you know she's healthy?"

Cho and Felipe look at each and burst out laughing.

Cho rubs Haruki's back,

"friends must tease friends."

Haruki feels a little grim. He has not had a one-night stand since his early twenties, he's pretty certain that's what this is. He sips at his miso, gathering the resolve to go be respectful to Amber. Amber saves him the trouble by entering the kitchen at that moment.

Felipe nods at her, offers a friendly "Hi."

Amber looks disheveled and embarrassed. She goes over to Cho and does a funny little bow, saying,

"Cho-san. Thanks so much for having me."

She clutches her bag to her chest and looks over at Haruki. Haruki gets up. *I'll do the right thing.* He hugs Cho and Felipe and goes downstairs with Amber. They go get coffee and then part on good terms, very likely never to see each other again, though they add each other on the socials. Haruki makes his way back to his apartment with a banging headache, ready to appease his furry friend. Totoro is absent. Haruki showers and gets into his most comfortable clothes. He shakes a few cat biscuits hopefully into Totoro's bowl, but he does not appear. Haruki has a box of treats his mother posted him from Australia. He selects a big bag of chips and takes them to his bed, eating handful after handful in a trance, staring empty eyed at nothing, trying not to think, watching his thoughts go round and round on predictable tracks. Eventually he rolls over and falls asleep, the chip bag slips off the bed and a few chips spill across the floor. In the morning Totoro is curled up in the nook behind his knees, one paw stretched possessively toward him.

"Buddy! I'm so happy to see you!"

Totoro uncurls to offer up his belly and Haruki moves to rest his face against its warm fur.

"Hey buddy. I love your tummy. Also, I got fired."

Totoro purrs deeply, stands up and bumps his head against the side of Haruki's face, claws rhythmically for a while on the quilt, then jumps from the bed and trots into the kitchen to his food bowl and meows loudly, his tail an exclamation mark. Haruki follows, shakes biscuits from the sack and squats next to him. Totoro practically inhales the biscuits whole, completely ignoring Haruki now. Haruki sits cross legged next to him with his back against the fridge and thinks of Occupant XE.

Is she ok?

Kobayashi Kenji pulls his takushi[32] smoothly into place at the address requested of him. On his hands are immaculate white gloves, over his face a custom-made white cotton mask, and his head sports the customary hat. Draped over the backs of all the seats are handmade cotton doilies. Kobayashi is technically a retired untenshu[33], working for many years in the past around the temples of Kyoto. He works now for a select clientele in Tokyo, those who appreciate his mastery. Varvara is one of his principle clients and he is attuned to her needs in the most subtle ways. On this day Varvara shows her customary outward control, but he can sense that within her churns a barely concealed tempest. The neighbourhood is pleasant, an enclave of the elite. The street entrance of their destination lies behind a high stone wall, with a single nondescript gate for pedestrian entrance. He has not been directed to the entrance for vehicles. Kobayashi glances unobtrusively in his rear vision mirror at his client in the back seat, he responds to the body language of his clients seamlessly and will move to open her door for her when she is ready. She is yet unready.

Varvara is speechless with rage. She is not only enraged by the situation, but also by her own rage. Her body is a concerto of pain, each part of her adding its own note to the whole. She has lived with pain for so many years now that she knows no other state; the cessation of her pain would deafen her with its silence. *I must attend this farce orchestrated by Tanaka,*

32   *Katakana form of the English word taxi*

33   *taxi driver*

there is no question of that. Varvara curses her passion, what she needs is coolness, effortlessness, equanimity. What she wants is destruction, chaos, conflagration. She has no thought for Kobayashi, he is but an extension of her will. Varvara seethes. *Men! I am infinitely tired of their myriad forms of posturing.* This thought soothes her infinitesimally, her hatred of men is an old place of comfort, a rightness. *Men are children, never growing out of their need to be placated, catered to. All this exposure and talk of male privilege for so long, and yet it remains transparent to the lot of them.* Kobayashi is not 'men', he is but a symbol of her own agency. Of the Mortech Five she is the only woman. For a moment Varvara enjoys a wry inner chuckle, *I also hate women.* In this way she becomes ready, and Kobayashi moves fluidly to open her door. She does not refuse the gloved hand he offers her, this is correct protocol. He does not desire to be insulted with thanks, and so he leaves her consciousness immediately after his service is complete. Varvara taps toward the nondescript gate. *How very Tanaka. No garish display for that one.* As she arrives the gate opens to reveal a very handsome man, all tumbling curls and lightly tanned, oozing natural appeal, *some sort of freshly baked loaf.* His cologne is himself, the fragrance of a perfect specimen of male beauty. *Why is he here?* He holds out his elegantly carved hand, revealing the tenacious fingers of an artisan. He smiles with generosity, "Konbanwa[34] madam, Chester Kask."

Varvara expostulates, "Chester? Preposterous. You are some sort of Eastern European. What sort of nonsense is this 'Chester'?"

He suns himself like some sort of pampered Lord's hound, all fucking whimsy and good nature and twinkling of eyes, like some mug of cocoa held in cold hands while it snows outside a cabin. Chester bows with easy grace,

---

34 *"Good evening"*

"I'm the welcoming party, pleased to meet you. Indeed, you are astute. I'm Estonian. And you are Russian?"

Varvara decides to throw him a morsel for a good boy,

"In name only."

She internally dismisses him and takes in the garden that is revealed by her entrance. *It is exquisite. I would expect nothing less.* As they proceed up the path the Chester prattles inconsequentials, it is not necessary for her to reply, he is a wind-up toy only. Varvara admires Tanaka's elegant home, the aesthetic equivalent of a zephyr cooling a fevered brow. Her brow is cooled, and she feels gratitude, for why not? She enjoys art as her right, as much as the next denizen of the 1%. Inside the house Tanaka bows very formally, ridiculously attired in a long white apron. *Of course, his hobbies include mastery of sashimi preparation.* Chester stewards her toward a seat on the brown leather lounge, the kitchen is in view of the spacious seating area. Jazz plays at a perfect volume for ambient chatter, the music system is invisible, and the jazz floats as though generated by an essential oil diffuser. Varvara has been tense with the threat of being touched by Chester, she knows his kind, but as she watches him interact with Tanaka she understands that they are lovers. This pleases her. *I have always felt men should fuck only men, stick with their own kind and render themselves obsolete. But why this display of intimacy?* Tanaka has breached a wall that lays between the Mortech Five for good reason. Tanaka has the good sense not to fill the air with social chatter, Varvara feels yet more soothed by congratulating herself on a worthy opponent. *Perhaps all is well, sometimes the game appears lost but is only in the process of some aspect of the greater pattern.* She smirks at her own infantile anger, *squalling like a babe refused candy,* and settles into her coils to play this one out.

Idea enters the room, sees the octogenarian seated on the leather lounge, and Chester and Tanaka at work in the kitchen, enjoying each other in their shared hobby. She feels like she is floating, as though all this is some new dream. *Am I still alone on the ship, eternally mired in deep space? It's like the end of that Kubrick movie, some strange fabrication of reality by a fractured psyche.* Then she shivers, gives herself a little pinch on the back of her hand. *I intend to be done with the SS Solipsist.* As she remains unnoticed she takes a moment to regard the Russian. What she feels toward her is gratitude. *Intriguing.* Tanaka has painted the old woman as a sort of surly badger defending its den. She notes that she definitely feels dangerous, yet there's some poignancy to her, an air of tragedy. She feels the infinite loneliness of the reverie she has lately woken from, and feels a pang of intimacy for its architect, a shared trauma. Idea understands that she must not sit close by Varvara just yet and takes the Eames next to her instead. For a moment they simply regard each other. Memories tease at the fringes of Idea's knowing. Varvara exudes the stillness of a sleeping crocodile, for now well fed, its hunger appeased.

"What do you call yourself, child?"

Idea pauses, considering, then tells her, "Idea."

"Wonderful! This name 'Idea' is wonderful. Do you desire the name of your past identity? I have it. There is also Lennox, among the Mortech Five we call him 'The Hypnotist'. He holds apparent 'keys' to your past identity."

Idea shakes her head,

"Perhaps someday? Not now. I still feel pretty overwhelmed. But thank you."

Varvara gives an elegant nod of accord,

"Yes. This is correct. Too easy. Too fast. You appear to remember me?

Intriguing."

Idea nods slowly, "Yes."

Varvara lifts one swollen hand, her finger pointing toward the kitchen, "This duo. They treat you well of course. You are in respite. In your own time we will talk of your experience. For now, I will allow Tanaka this folly."

Again, Idea nods, feels gratitude towards this enigmatic woman. *Assumptions must not be made about her.*

Tanaka bows at the women and gestures to the large wooden table adjacent to the kitchen. 'Idea' offers her hand and Varvara accepts it. Her mood has improved exponentially, she is now enjoying herself immensely. She suddenly has the absurd desire for Hermes to be here with her. *Of course, there are no pets in this home, no need, Tanaka has Chester. And now Idea.* Varvara sees that the experiment continues in a new form. *I will not waste energy in opposition.* She mentally embraces Tanaka as a colleague, lets the mental title 'opponent' drop. *I will not do as expected.*

As he adds the final touches to the meal Tanaka muses, *as expected, Varvara is gracious, regal, armoured by her own coils.* All come to sit at table, and the staff melt out of the shadows to perform impeccable service. Tanaka notes that Idea feels some sympathy for the old badger and chuckles to himself. *Stockholm syndrome?* Chester glows his customary golden hue, and Tanaka feels a quiet gratitude for his existence. *The love of my life, what a surprise.* He basks in the quiet joy of food skillfully prepared, of balance restored, a feeling of a stage of completion to this concatenation. He thinks of Nakamura, of her enjoying her well-earned bonus, bringing a modicum of comfort to the necessary austerities of the student life. He rests in his customary role of observer, speaks little, only when necessary. Tanaka feels blessed by silence, by spaciousness. He is not unlike the sharp edge of one of his perfectly made sashimi knives. An image of the face of his dear long-dead wife comes into his mind. Theirs was a childless union, her womb barren. She knew before they married of his preference for men romantically, yet he was willing to provide her with the means for children. *A very sad thing for her. A wonderful woman.* He gazes unobtrusively at Idea. *She is strong.* He is confident she will recover well. He likes her. The evening proceeds smoothly, he enjoys Varvara, she is in fine form. *Arch and acerbic as ever.* He sees that if she was perturbed by his actions, she chooses not to show it. *Perhaps the Five can deepen our relationships after all? Forge a true allegiance? Retain the correct professional distance of course, but become more allied? This will be of service to the work.* Varvara chooses that moment to bring up Hades. *Ah.*

"Tanaka-sensei. You should know I spoke with Hades two days past. I suspected his paw also in the machinations to wrest OccupantXE from my clutches. He swears I am incorrect. This creature is a stain, why must we suffer him?"

Tanaka inclines his head,

"Hades performs an intrinsic function as you know. But let us not speak of work. You and I shall have our conference, please, do not be perturbed."

Varvara inclines her own ancient mien in response. Equanimity reigns. In time they come to sit together in the lounge. The evening is pleasant, Varvara's untenshu waits in anticipation of his service. Tanaka sees that Idea tires and he becomes instantly solicitous. He nods in his subtle way at Chester. Chester understands and twinkles over in her direction.

"Idea my dear. We must not tire you out. Shall we play a little cards together before you retire?"

Idea nods, understands she is the child in this play, and succumbs to it. Chester bows at Varvara, and they take their leave. Idea looks back at Varvara and Varvara gives her a knowing smile. *So. We will meet again.* Tanaka offers Varvara a meeting in room 7 the next day, assuring her the suspension of her codes was temporary only.

Varvara accedes, and allows Tanaka to escort her personally to the gate in the high wall. After the gate is shut behind her Tanaka looks up. Overhead the moon has begun to wane, she casts her gaze over his exquisite garden, and he bows formally to her.

A fortnight passes. Haruki does not visit Tsuki, he can't afford to spend extraneous money now. He does not resent Felipe his burgeoning romance with Cho and thinks pleasantly of Hiro-kun and Momo in their nest with the furry citizens of Sims City to pass their time. After all, he has Totoro. He calls his parents back in Australia, paints a little, games a bit, sorts the books on his e-reader, requests samples only of new books because he can't afford to actually buy any new ones. He drifts in a mild depressive malaise, stands with his trousers rolled up in the ebb and flow of the sea. He considers taking a train somewhere to stay with friends, then remembers he can't afford that either. One day he recalls Hoboneko, and decides that he might go pay him a visit. To his embarrassment his mother takes pity on him and secretly deposits a little pocket money in his account. *I can buy a yakitori and go shoot the (one-sided) breeze with the ol' Hoboneko. Por que no?* When Haruki arrives at the park Hoboneko is there as usual, he keeps his back to Haruki, but flicks his tail side to side, Haruki takes it as a kind of high five from a buddy. He feels suddenly at peace, and his fixation on the burden of financial anxiety quietly drops away. He simply sits, and watches the black butterflies of Tokyo drift by, feeling gratitude there are still butterflies somewhere in this world, then tries not to get maudlin about the absurdity of the continuing misinformation age he lives in. *Just focus on the now.* Instead, his mind drifts to thoughts of 'The Singularity'. Haruki chuckles to himself, *wasn't that supposed to have happened by now? Maybe it did happen, and no one noticed.* He's always been comfortable hanging out solo, he finds his own mind entertaining. *Friends are great, but humans in general are kind of problematic.* Of course, he's also a human and this has always been a little upsetting for him. *Wouldn't it be better to be anything else? But only a human would have a thought like that anyway.* Hoboneko sits up then like an icon of a cat, his tail curls around his feet, one ear flicks to the right. Haruki looks in that direction and is horrified to see Varvara approaching with her little dog. His armpits let out a hot trickle of sweat, his heart begins to pound, and there's a rushing sound in his ears. *I do kind of want to see her though.* She takes the bench two down from him and appears to expect him to approach her. Hoboneko crouches like a loaf of bread, both ears pointing towards her, he stares at the little dog and flicks his tail side to side. Haruki asks himself, *what's the little guys name again? Odysseus?* Haruki looks back at Hoboneko, the cat slowly closes his eyes, yet his ears remained pointed at the dog, like the horns of a minotaur. Haruki makes a decision, taps his palms once against his thighs and gets up, goes over to Varvara, squats down and lets her little dog lick his palm, then tickles him behind the ears. He drops all formality. After all, she is no longer his boss.

"Hi. What's this guys' name again?"

Varvara looks at Haruki, her expression is unreadable.

"It is Hermes."

Haruki snaps his fingers and gives a chuckle,

"He needs some little winged sandals then, no?"

Varvara sniffs,

"Costuming a dog is a folly of the highest order. I would never debase Hermes in this way."

Hermes sits with his little back legs splayed out slightly around his small fat tummy, his eyes are shiny, he rolls them over to Hoboneko, whines a little. Haruki points at the park cat, smiles awkwardly,

"I call him Hoboneko..."

Varvara looks over at the cat,

"An evil beast. I doff my cap. He is busy intimidating Hermes as usual I see."

Their old uncomfortable banter is restored. Haruki pauses, waits for Varvara to fill him in. She extends the torture, regards him in a twin gaze of Hoboneko to Hermes. Abruptly she closes her eyes. Haruki puts his hands deep in his pockets. *The old dragon can't have fallen asleep?* He moves to slink away, and Varvara speaks.

"You'll be wondering about the welfare of our dear occupantXE?"

Haruki rubs the back of his head, nods, and then pushes his hands even deeper in his pockets and finds himself tapping the edge of her bench with his foot like an awkward teenager.

"You were dismissed from Mortech by my colleague Tanaka. It was not of my doing."

Haruki takes his hands out of his pockets and finds that he has the puzzle Cho gave him in his fist, so he tinkers with it, telling Varvara,

"I never met any of the other directors at Mortech."

Varvara nods,

"Of course, we each had our own minions. Fujioka and yourself were mine. All in service to client privacy, you understand. You signed the paperwork. Your position was casual."

Haruki feels courageous as he solves stage one of the puzzle.

"I understand that I was unfairly dismissed."

"Indeed. You seek compensation? Whimsical men like yourself struggle with financial security."

Haruki hears the usual disdain in her use of whimsical. She's gaslighting him. He suddenly feels infinitely free, he turns his back on her, drops down to the ground in front of her, lounges back on his elbows and gazes nonchantly away from her at the park, as though he's suddenly picnicking in the middle of the walkway. He looks back over his shoulder at Varvara, imagines her as an ancient raven, sees her ruffle her midnight feathers. He sees Hermes as a caterpillar on a leash at her feet, mindlessly chewing through leaf after leaf, complacent with the knowledge that one day she will eat him. Her beak clacks, a caw emerges,

"Mori-san. I see that you are in the thrall of idle imaginings."

He points to himself, winks at her.

"Me? Nah. Unemployed."

Varvara begins to take umbrage at this wink, then drops it, and narrows her eyes instead.

"Occupant XE has awoken. In the end Tanaka was her prince, it was he who bestowed the kiss that broke the spell. She lives with him just now. Jealous?"

Haruki pictures Tanaka; imagining him as a kind of grizzled detective. He lifts occupant XE over one shoulder out of the pod while chain smoking with his other hand. XE is decked out in full princess regalia, her long blond plait lays coiled inside the pod like a golden snake.

Flowers drop out of her hair to the cold and shiny concrete floor, reflected perfectly, doubled like the moon in a still pond. Varvara snaps her fingers again, "Mori-san. I see that you need to get a new job. Your mind has gone on holiday from reality."

Haruki tosses the remaining interlocking puzzle pieces up and down in his palm and puts the solved piece back in his pocket.

"Just like the Mortech vampires. But I don't need to lay pooping in my nappy in a glorified coffin."

Varvara's wrinkle-puckered lips curve very slightly upward at their corners, "Mori-san. I am willing to make you an offer of future employment."

Haruki twists out of his slouch and sits cross legged in front of her.

"I'm done with Mortech."

"Yes. I would take you into private employ. I see that you enjoy play-acting, this role would require you to go undercover. To act as an intermediary between myself and the woman who was Occupant XE. Oh, I have her trust it seems. But you and she are about the same age. I think you could glean some insight that would remain beyond my reach."

Haruki doesn't look up, remains as though fascinated with his puzzle.

"More lab rat duties?"

"Correct."

"You say we are around the same age?"

"Yes. She is not a virginal princess in need of rescuing after all. Though Tanaka provided an escape from her coffin, she had consented to be placed within it."

Haruki stands up, puts the puzzle back in his pocket. "I never wanted to play your sick game."

Hermes whines a little, stands up and gives a tentative half wag of his tail. Varvara puts her hand in her pocket, withdraws a slim gold case, pops its lid and proffers him a card, offering it to him between her index and middle fingers.

"My private contact. You are likely to change your mind."

Haruki ignores the card, places his palms together and gives her a little bow, adds one also for Hermes.

"Sayonara, Varvara-sama."

He puts his hands back in his pockets and walks nonchalantly away, wonders whether he should add a whistle, then dismisses it. *Nah. Too much.*

Varvara watches him walk away, Returns the card to its case and the case to her pocket. She taps her other pocket and withdraws a treat for Hermes. He sits up, licking his chops. Varvara throws the treat just out of his reach, and he strains at his leash, choking himself on his collar. She watches this for a time, then grows suddenly tired, and stands up, allowing Hermes to waddle over to the snack and gobble it up.

"I grow tired of this samsara Hermes. Perhaps it is time for me to enter my own coffin."

Hermes whines, sits, and looks up at her with his small apostrophe eyebrows raised in a question.

"You are right Hermes. I won't leave this place until you have left it before me. I am a sentimental old fool after all."

She taps slowly away. Downstairs from the park Kobayashi naps under his untenshu cap. He will become instantly alert when he hears the tapping of Varvara's walking stick.

Later that evening Varvara sits in her armchair within her home. She did not visit the lab that day, though she has regained full access. She does not visit Idea. Instead, she contemplates ways of ending her life. She does not often permit herself this kind of indulgence. *Suicide is so tawdry, the respite of the feeble. Yet I am so tired.* She drags her inner scrutiny from the cycling of her thoughts and drops into a rare, blessed state of deep sleep. She has not slept so in some time, the pain prevents her from proper rest. Generally, she blacks out, sleep finally forced upon her mind by her body. It is not sweet, more like a tranquiliser shot. Now a timeless nothingness fills her, holds her in its spell, bathes her in emptiness. Finally, she begins to dream, it has also been some time since she has dreamed. Her sleeping face betrays a vulnerability usually steadfastly hidden from the world outside.

No, I don't want to remember.

Varvara is not Russian. The name Varvara Kuznetsov is an artifice, a mask worn so long it almost perfectly fits her face. In her dream she sees a child. Somewhere Varvara's vigilance is watchful but rendered impotent by the veil of dreaming. *No.* The child has her knees hugged to her chest, arms wrapped tightly around them. It is curious that she can see her, she knows in fact the child was in total darkness, her face dirty and stained with tears, her sniveling quiet, unheeded even by the rats. She feels the thin beating of the child's heart in her own chest. Her ribs are visible through her almost translucently white skin. The child is locked in a secret underground hiding place, placed there by her mother, deep in the woods of Czechoslovakia. The hiding place had been hastily dug, the child is filthy with fresh earth. She has been here for some time. She is just four years old. The child does not know what has happened to her family, or her friends in the village. Varvara knows they are all lost, long dead. In her chair in her sleeping body Varvara's heart begins to pump in arrhythmia. She has disowned this child. *Why this memory now?* Varvara is not in her eighties. In fact, she is 103 years old, her post-war birth date an invention. The child in the dream is herself, it is 1939 in the midst of the Nazi invasion of Czechoslovakia. Varvara's sleeping body struggles in her chair. Hermes jumps up into her forbidden lap, gently licks the back of her hand. Her sleeping lips turn white with rage. She believed she had burned this child from her memory. Varvara despises all victims, turns a deaf ear on the endless caterwauling of war victims. The child does not look Jewish, no, just seems a small, blonde, blue- eyed Czechoslovakian child, she could have been a Jugend poster child. Later, there was rape, *no, please, I don't want to remember.* For now, the child, the child who is herself, rocks back and forth in her darkness. The child no longer prays for help, for her mother, now she curses God, investing the curse with all the considerable passion of a small child blindly enraged by her abandonment. This child was born of a human mother, suckled on the warm heart's milk of her breast. The mother of Varvara Kuznetsov was Abandonment, her midwife senseless violence. Varvara denounces all Gods, spits on faith. The pain in her body is the sclerosis of her inability to forgive. Though she believed it denied access, the violence of Varvara's birth lives on inside her. Who would this child born of a human mother otherwise have been? *It does not matter.* Her name is long buried, along with any notions of a kinder fate. Varvara's dreaming mind finally releases her from this memory, moves on to more mundane storytelling, an inconsequential interweaving of nonsense. Finally, the solicitations of Hermes bring her awake, and he leaps from her lap to cower at her feet, his paws comically cover his nose, his bottom quivers upright in the air. Varvara pays him no heed. She can taste the smell of the dirt of the hiding place on her tongue. She remembers. Slowly she rises and makes her way painfully, yet directly to the garage. There is a toolbox, she takes the small bolt cutters from it, and sets about cutting the rings from her fingers. She does not have the strength left in her hands to cut them. She collapses next to the toolbox and sobs, her body wracked, the moans escaping her lips like the groans of a birthing mother. She has shut the garage door on Hermes, he whines and scratches for admittance, but she heeds him not. Varvara weeps now the unshed tears of a lifetime, desires urgently to be destroyed by them, but finally the storm abates. She thinks absurdly of Kobayashi, but there is no one to come and find her, the child broke her way out of the hole alone.

She does not leave the house. She does not respond to emails. She has informed no one of her address. She has decided to die. Her ephemeral economies continue to debit and credit their digits, it will take some time before her death is discovered in this way. She still stoops to feed Hermes. Finally, his food runs out. She opens her door and ushers him outside, apologises to him in her mind only, *I can no longer remain loyal.* He shivers, uncomprehending. She shuts the door on him. He whines and scratches at it. She shouts at him from the other side.

"Go! You are banished."

Hermes lays down with his head on his paws and watches the door, sleeping fitfully, for two days. Finally, he leaves and makes his way to the park, the Bakeneko will tell him what to do.

Idea sits on a park bench by a cat. The air is definitely a little warmer now, the fragrance of a humid summer to come stills the air. There is a cat at the park who sleeps on a sheet of newspaper. This is not the first time she has visited this park, and she muses *I wonder who refreshes the newspaper for him?* She's taken to riding the trains around Tokyo, and stops sometimes at this park, not far from a train station. Privately she calls the cat 'Sarareman' and imagines their park bench as a seat on the train, he and her engaged in their own private thoughts, but serene with that companionship of strangers that occurs at times, some unspoken kinship. A little dog appears from out of the garden across from them and approaches. He's one of those small scruffy terriers, this one has round and shiny eyes and he looks morose. He approaches the cat and crawls under the park bench beneath him. He whines a little, and his little body quivers. The Sarareman yawns hugely, somehow his entire face disappearing at the top of his head, in the way of cats. He moves to squat at the back edge of the bench, looking down at the dog, his tail twitching back and forth, the classic pose of a cat waiting at the door of a mouse. He flicks an ear at Idea, and she understands it's her move. She squats down next to the bench and calls gently to the little dog,

"hey puppy. Hey little friend. What's up?"

The dog shivers, puts his head between his paws. From above the cat jumps down and crouches directly behind him, his whiskers stand out erect from either side of his cheeks, in his throat comes a low menacing growl. The little dog looks askance at the cat behind him and shoots forward. Idea catches him and lifts him up to her face. He licks her face and settles into her arms, cocks his head to one side. She carries him around the park, looking for his person. No-one comes forward to claim him. Idea carries a large canvas bag about with her, and though currently full of snacks and books and pens and miscellaneous knick-knacks, there's still room for the dog. She gently pours him into her bag and takes him back concealed in this way on the train, back to Tanaka's. She starts calling him Scruff-pup without much thought and hides him in her room for only half a day before Chester figures it out. Tanaka does not like pets in the house, but Chester and Scruff-pup make twin sad faces at him, and he concedes to a temporary arrangement. Scruff-pup is not allowed in the main part of the house, but each day he whines and scratches for admittance, tenacious. One day Chester takes him in his lap, sitting on the floor with his back up against the door to the main house. Scruff-pup jumps off his lap and keeps up with his whining. Idea snaps her fingers,

"There was this old movie back in the day that I watched as a kid. The main character is a fluffy dog, she's always whining and trying to get humans to understand that 'little Jimmy is stuck down the well' or whatnot."

Chester nods, purses his perfect lips,

"I remember that old show Inspector Rex."

"Oh yes that German German Shepherd?"

Chester chuckles,

"Yep, the German German shepherd."

Idea shakes her head,

"no this was really old, you know, back when Americans had sort of British accents. Or maybe it was British?"

Chester grins

"That is old."

Idea claps her hands at Scruff-pup, and he climbs reluctantly into her lap, she tickles him behind the ears, and he looks momentarily like his mind might be empty. Idea kisses the top of his head and looks at Chester.

"Anyway, don't you think it seems like ol Scruff-pup here wants to tell us something?"

Chester leaps up as he feels the door push against his back, almost tripping over Idea and Scruff-pup.

It is Tanaka, he gestures at Scruff-pup,

"I believe I know who this animal is."

He smiles, Idea is now familiar enough to the nuances of his face to know this. Chester kneels, folds his arms, and raises one beautifully arched and fulsome brow. Tanaka approaches, and looks closely at Scruff-pup, studying him very closely.

"Yes. I believe this is the small companion of our dear Varvara- sama, 'Pericles' or some ancient Greek nonsense."

Idea holds Scruff-pup up under his armpits and looks at him,

"Pericles? Old Scruff-pup?"

Tanaka brushes a microscopic lint from his crisp linen shirt, then makes eye contact with the dog. Scruff-pup's ears triangle upward in anticipation.

"At Mortech, Varvara has not been registered in the security logs for many days. It has been her custom to visit regularly until now."

He gestures for them to gather in Idea's room and closes the door behind them. Idea sits on the bed, immediately the little dog jumps off her lap and starts to whine and paw at the door. *Pericles?* Tanaka and Chester sit at Idea's little table. She hastily jumps up and begins to clear her clutter from it, mindful of Tanaka's distaste for clutter. Tanaka waves her away, "Unimportant. What is important is that none of us know where Varvara lives. She has also not responded to her work email in many days."

Idea groans in frustration,

"why are you lot such effing wierdos?"

Tanaka looks at her, his face stony. Chester smothers a boyish laugh behind Tanaka's back. Tanaka turns to him and gives him a look. Chester sobers, his naturally playful energy ebbs away. The tone in the room becomes grave.

"This is a matter of great concern. Varvara is very old. Very lonely. The presence of her dog here should be viewed not merely as some mystical serendipity, but a real and pressing cry for help."

Idea nods, her hand goes to her lower belly.

Chester taps his bottom lip, points at the dog,

"when I opened the gate to her, on the evening she came here for dinner, I noticed one of those old fashioned takushi pulled up at the curb. I didn't really take it in at the time, but is it possible she uses an untenshu to drive her about?"

Tanaka brings his hands together in a sharp and sudden clap that makes Idea jump.

"So! You are correct! She uses old Kobayashi, the retired untenshu."

Idea asks, "retired?"

"Yes, yes. He is retired but has great passion for his work. He has mainly stately old dames on his client list, I'm certain Varvara is one of them. I know one other of these ladies quite well, she continues to best me at Go. Quite infuriating."

Tanaka stands, leaves the room rapidly. Chester goes after him and the little terrier bursts also from the room. Tanaka is searching and dialing Kobayashi's client as he walks. Idea feels a little impotent, trailing after them uncertainly. Chester turns and sees her and catches her in a hug.

"You were right about the 'Timmy's down the well' thing!"

Idea pauses. "Timmy...?"

Chester chortles, his jovial demeanour restored.

"The British-American dog?"

Idea gives a lopsided smile,

"oh yeah. Timmy."

Idea sees Tanaka leave the house, with the dog shaped saviour in a large leather bag over his shoulder.

She cries out, "wait!" But it's too late.

Chester takes her arm and leads her to the kitchen, sits her down in the leather chair.

"He's unstoppable when he's like this. Don't worry."

Idea looks down, saying quietly to herself, "Scruff-pup..." Her head slumps into the shelter of her upraised shoulders,

her arms go across her chest, her fingers clasp her arms. She is suddenly angry. She looks up at Chester.

"I'm not a child. You and Tanaka. I'm riding along in your wake. I must begin to make my own life. I need Varvara."

She stands, goes to the door, and goes out of it. She is wearing house slippers and does not stop to put on her shoes from the small shelf inside the entrance foyer. She does not get her bag, just starts running.

Chester runs his hand through his thick hair, his tall frame sags for a moment. *These strong-willed individuals.* He decides to follow her at a distance, undercover. He runs to her room, grabs her bag, also grabs a croissant from the tray on her table and holds it in his mouth as he puts his wallet in his pocket, slips on his loafers at the entrance and leaves. He stops half- way down the path, then returns and grabs Idea's shoes from the shelf, shoves them in her bag slung over his shoulder and sets the house alarm. Out on the street, Idea has vanished, she left the house at a run. He stops and rapidly eats the croissant, brushes off his fingers and crosses the road, making his way randomly left and down the hill. He pauses then and goes back to the house, fetching his bicycle. She won't get too far away.

Varvara despises her weakness yet continues with her plan to die. She has decided the best way is to starve herself to death. She is no stranger to hunger. It may be an over-long process, but surely such an old body will quickly submit. *Yet, the interminable waiting.* She thinks often of Hermes and curses herself, *it had to be done. He must have some chance for survival, he need not rot here with me.*

She trusts that she will not be found. Even Kobayashi picks her up at a pre-designated place, he does not know her home address. She types an email to the Mortech Five,

"I have gone to Kyoto. Carry on without me for a time" and hits send.

She feels lighter now. Almost giddy with glee. Death will bring release, she is no longer afraid, was surprised to understand that she had been afraid of death. *Some ridiculous religious mind virus picked up in the gutters of the collective human psyche. Death will be the final nothing. Sweet obliteration.* She puts her finger inside the screw down nutcracker she found in the bottom of one of her drawers. Painfully she screws it down with her other hand, pausing to rest now and again. Then she stops. It will not work. The rings are very high quality, antiques. Varvara remembers. She stole them from the Russian drug dealer in Berlin. She shot him in the back as he pissed with the door open. She did not go to prison, he was a notorious criminal. She was treated as the victim, she hated this, but it was very convenient to not go to prison. *I shot him because he deserved to be shot, I will not insult animals by naming him one.* She has worn these rings of his since, her private trophies of victory. She has understood that she must allow her memories to surface now, knows that she will never be free of them by holding them captive within. *They have been buried in shallow graves and begun to rot, I must be rid of their stench.* She schemes for a time on how to remove the rings. Then she takes her heavy good quality scissors from a drawer and hacks off her hair to the scalp instead. She runs her hand again and again across the surface of her newly born skull. She begins to mutter, it does not matter. She may allow the madness to claim her now.

Kobayashi does not know where Varvara lives. He is upset to hear she may be in trouble. Tanaka has arranged to meet him at her customary pick up place in one hour, then the plan is to search in an outward ring from this starting point. He cannot take the little dog into the lab and calls Chester, but he does not answer. Idea also does not answer. He sits in his private self-driving car with the dog confined to the far seat across from him, his attempts at incursion having been settled with a stern look. He logs in to the private Mortech Five email on his phone, patiently typing in the encryptions. There is a message from Varvara, sent but an hour ago. *So. She is alive yet. The email states that she has gone to Kyoto. Perhaps she simply left the little dog behind?* Something does not feel right in his stomach however, Tanaka is keenly attuned to any notes of disharmony he encounters. He does not reply, though she will see that it has been read. *How to best her at her own game, for her own good? Is it right to interfere further in her private affairs?* Tanaka gestures at the vehicle interface and soothing jazz begins to play. He closes his eyes momentarily and holds his fingers to his temples, then looks down at his feet, the dog has placed himself there. Tanaka simply nods. *No matter.* He programs the car to continue to the location with Kobayashi. *Asakusa?* Very odd. Takushi like Kobayashi are still allowed to operate in a limited fashion due to preservation of Japanese culture laws in Japan. Private non AI vehicles are still in a slow process of being phased out. Japan does not resist the self-drive technology as the Americans do. Tanaka shakes his head, *America, an absolute mess.*

8.

Missing

V ance Janssen spends much of his waking consciousness embroiled in dreams. Although given to dark obsessions as a youth, he was secretly a Pokemon guy, making yearly pilgrimages to anime mecca Japan until the pandemic years saw him locked down in Europe. His work with Mortech Lab provided the opportunity to abscond more permanently from the Netherlands and it has been a dream come true for Vance. The bulk of his work is done, this phase one trial period leaves him free to think nothing more of Mortech except whether there's a collective noun for narcissists. Vance's own genius lays in his particular skill in AI, VR, AR, and game design. His position in the Mortech Five is known as The Gamer. Back in the day his early encounters with VR left him nauseous, but repeated dosing over the years sees him currently simmering in a VR sauce. His origins are soundly middle-class white boy and this means he's eminently suited to fabricating the generally dark and hedonist reveries of the VR world. *Same old filthy rich pervs the world over, my work is booming. Whatever gets you off, friend.* He sees the email from 'Baba Yaga' Varvara pop up in the notes corner of his peripheral vision and gives zero fucks. *Oh, one fuck, turn off fucking notifications. I was forced to work closely with the witch queen for far too long. Oh she's a genius, no question, but ACTUAL dark, some motha skeletons in that closet, reals.* He pauses and does a few token stretches in his chair to stop his body atrophy. *Damn. Nothing but to ride this beast till it drop. I'm messing around these days with some even more fringe-tech neural link shit than Mortech and its the bomb digs.* Then it drops into his gut, and he feels sick. *The emptiness.* Vance's chattering mind skates over the sludgy film curdling in the penumbra of this beckoning portal to nothingness. He is in the business of creating the most cutting edge dream distractions for the very real collective horror of emptiness of the citizens of planet Earth, it's his bread and butter. He is a hollow man, obese with content to mask his pervasive discontent. Vance is gaunt and almost translucently white. He never sees the Sun that still creates (and destroys) all life, even on Earth 2038. It is very hard for him to remember to eat, he's also currently applying his intellect to potential ways of rendering shitting and pissing obsolete. Truth is he's dehydrated, constipated and ill. No one has physically touched him for some time, though he's done *everything* in VR, to the extent that *truth tell I'm just really fucking bored.* He is known most commonly now by his gamer tag: ghost_eat. He has come to think that this is his true name, *Vance Janssen is some bullshit my parents came up with.* His mind registers a kind of dull interest as his hands slowly heat the metal end of a cigarette lighter. These hands pull up his sleeves, press the metal into the flesh of his forearm. Momentarily he registers the pain and feels a surge of dopamine to his brain. His arms are riddled with burn scars in various states of healing and inflammation. He does not register the dull fever his body burns with. In his time with Mortech, Vance has never seen The Mathematician. He has always assumed Hades was the fifth member of the Mortech Five. He thinks now of Hades. *Now there's some actual creepy shit right there.*

In truth he is a clinically depressed, anorexic man in a filthy apartment in Tokyo, but he does not know this.

Idea runs until she notices the flapping of her house slippers against her soles, then loses one and stops to go back for it. She pauses. *What am I doing?* She looks around, *same well-to- do neighbourhood, only where am I?* Her body ran before her mind came online. *Well. At least I am programmed into the house retina scan. Good.* She begins to walk. *Everything in these neighbourhoods looks the same. Fuck.* A very well-kept looking older woman whispers by, and she can't help but cast a very judgemental glance down at Idea's house slippers.

Idea does not realise that she mutters out loud,

"the woman is dewy with privilege for chrissakes, and she's on me for these? I must get out of this bubble. I don't know who I am."

The woman is offended, but Idea is too absorbed in her madness to notice, and she moves along. Idea is still spooked by the thought of resuming her old identity, or what scraps may remain of it.

"What if I don't like me? What if that's really why I consented to the whole SS Solipsist delusion? Also, I can't go around with a name like Idea now there's *others.*"

She stops again. *I'm talking out loud aren't I?* There were at least some pros to life on board the SS.Solipsist. Idea thinks of Chester and Tanaka, *they are actually so cute. I'm grateful. But I must begin my own life. Real life, whatever that may be.* She walks until she gets that cramp in her feet that you get when you are out of practice with flip flops. *huh so I'm usually a flipflop pro eh?* Suddenly Idea begins to enjoy herself.

Understanding who she really is is like an Easter egg hunt. She finds that suddenly, she actually very desperately desires the scraps of her identity from Varvara, *from this what's his name? The Hypnotist?* Idea puts her hands on her hips and rotates 360 degrees. *If I wasn't lost where would I be?* It occurs to her that this is an old saying of her Father's. *I can't quite recall who he might be. Was he always giving what he considered to be pithy observations? Is that just a Dad thing?* She remembers the trick though, you just forget that you are lost and move purposefully in the direction that you are going. Idea turns to walk backwards and sees Chester on his bicycle coming towards her. He pulls up, all sweaty curls and dishevelment. *Naturally he looks even more handsome. If that's possible.* Chester has one of those faces that looks adorable when he's mad at you. Idea slumps a little and feels embarrassed.

"Sorry!"

Chester forgives her immediately and holds her bag aloft. He roots around in there and pulls out her shoes. Idea takes them, exchanges them for the house slippers, and slings her bag across her chest, grinning a small lopsided grin.

"Man of my dreams."

Chester runs a hand through his hair and stands with his long legs splayed out. An amusing image strikes Idea; *he's kind of like a Disney horse.* Chester gets his phone out and looks for messages from Tanaka, "Damn. Ok. We missed a call from T. But he probably just wants us to dog-sit, no?"

Idea nods, "Totally."

"Hey. Let's form our own detective team?"

Idea agrees enthusiastically.

"T has dropped me a pin."

He quickly looks in maps,

"we can actually make it pretty quickly on the train. Jump on?"

"I'll sit in your basket like E.T?"

Chester guffaws. He sees she is kind of like E.T actually, currently practically bald, brown coloured and big eyed. Idea cocks her head, she's picked that up from Scruff-pup. Chester pats the middle bar of the bike, she jumps on side saddle, and they careen down the hill to the station.

Varvara has spoiled Haruki's visits to Hoboneko park. He needs new haunts. *The untethered life. I need to trust. Ok. I'm deep in the flow... aaand nothing. No clue. Sweet FA. What I need is $$$.* Haruki makes a list in his head. *Clams. Moolah. Dosh. Dough. Pocket Lollies. Pocket lollies? Pretty sure that's not a thing.* Haruki has had notions all his life about making a living as an artist. *Or an animator? Or a writer? Or a film maker?* In fact, he's done all these things, except make a living. He feels he is at the bottom level of skill in this mecca of supreme artistic talent. He's always relied on IT work to keep him flush. When he was married he had almost tightroped across to the corporate scene, but Haruki just doesn't have the heart to be ambitious. Despite notions of masculinity regularly updating in the new century, left over toxic assumptions about masculinity still haunt him. *My father is super masc, even now. Very traditional. Kind of hyper old school Japanese. It's super weird how he's with my mum. Some balancing factor?* Then Haruki stops. Notices. *These are the same old thoughts I always think about my Dad. His relationship with Mum. Are these thoughts even true?* A memory of his Dad wearing a paper hat from a Christmas cracker floats into his mind. It's as though his minds' eye zooms in, *is that a MOCK*

serious expression on his face? For years Haruki has believed his father never laughed. *But it's just not true.* This hits him like a revelation. Like freedom. *What if life is never what you think it is? What if we are all busy just making shit up?* Haruki remembers the time his Dad told him about pachinko. At the time he could not picture his father playing pachinko. Haruki decides to go play pachinko. He shakes his head at himself, so far he has avoided things like pachinko and karaoke, thought of them as tacky. He sees that actually this is what his mother would say and roll her eyes. Haruki realises that he does not know what his own opinion of pachinko and karaoke really is. He leaves his apartment, clatters downstairs and jumps on his bicycle. He remembers a few pachinko parlours he noticed in Asakusa. *Damn, maybe I'll even visit some kind of pet cafe.*

By the time he gets to Asakusa it's that odd time in the life of urban humans between the home commute and the concurrent emergence back onto the streets for evening activities. *It always makes me feel kind of lonely, like why aren't I doing what everyone else is doing? I wonder if us humans aren't just some sort of algorithms ourselves? Busy investing meaning into our little hamster patterns?* As he walks Haruki notes it still feels warm despite it getting on to evening. *I dig Asakusa, maybe I should drop in on Cho and Felipe? No. This is actually one of those weird days where I try to put two puzzle pieces together and they look like they fit together but then it's totally obvious they don't fit at all.* This kind of thinking makes his mood begin to droop. *What's that thing Felipe says? 'Stop riffing on only the minor chords?' It just feels quite farcical to be going to play pachinko. What am I thinking?* Haruki wanders the streets with his hands in his pockets. Almost doing things. His hair sticks up a little at the back where he's been ruffling it. Finally, he sits on a complimentary shoppers' bench by a four storey discount store. He can see a pachinko parlour down in the mall beside the department store. He doesn't go in, and contents himself with a little people watching instead. Over the road he can see one of those old fashioned takushis, and he gets out his little pocket sketch journal and does a quick sketch of it. *That untenshu is a pretty ancient looking dude. Shouldn't he be retired?* There's a bit of traffic although it's after the rush, mainly self-drives. A beautiful example of a real gentrified looking self-drive pulls up next to the takushi. *Maybe a custom make?* A short, stately and straight backed older Japanese man emerges from the vehicle, fully suited in a three piece despite the warm evening air, and his silver hair is immaculate. The self-drive whooshes off to park itself or *whatever it is these AIs do to while away the time.* He's carrying a little terrier, one of those standard issue old lady pets. *Wait a sec, isn't that little Odysseus?* Haruki feels himself stand and crane his neck toward the tableaux of the man and the dog and the untenshu. Whatever is happening for the trio, it all seems urgent and tense. Haruki trots over the road and bows to the man, speaking in Japanese as well as he can,

"Sumimasen. Gomen nasai. It's just, I know that little guy."

The dog notices Haruki and starts wagging his tail, jumps down suddenly from the man's arms and comes over to sit on Haruki's shoes. *The man has one of the most classically inscrutable faces I've yet seen. But he's evidently currently scrutinising me, nonetheless.* There's a mutual pause all round. Then, they hear the sound of running feet and turn as one. Approaching them is a tall curly-haired Euro guy and a kind of Asian looking woman but with brown skin, her hair is very short, but seems brown also. The little dog runs barking toward the woman. Haruki notices before she stoops to scoop him up that her eyes are also brown. An unusual light brown. The group stands together on the street, question marks all round. Haruki chuckles and snaps his fingers, saying in English

"Hey! You know this is kind of a meet cute. Like a group meet cute."

The Euro guy looks amused, but the woman just buries her face in the pups fur. The old untenshu guy chuckles aloud and says,

"meeto cute, ne?"

Haruki notes that the straight-backed Japanese gentleman's eyes raise ever so slightly heavenward. The woman jerks a thumb at Haruki, and asks rudely in English "who's this guy?"

The gent turns to her, and switching to English, tells her

"he says he knows Pericles."

Haruki says, "Pericles? I thought his name was Odysseus?"

He hears the woman quietly mutter into the dogs' ear,

"Scruff-pup."

Tanaka addresses Haruki,

"If you know this dog, you will know that he belongs to Varvara Kuznetsov? "

Haruki nods yes, says, "Hai! Varvara-sama."

Tanaka continues,

"Idea came across her dog wandering on his own. We believe she may be missing, we are looking for her." *'Idea'? What?* The hound in question whines and struggles in the brown woman's arms. The untenshu gestures at him with a gloved hand,

"Maybe he knows where Varvara lives?"

Euro guy shrugs, "Its worth a shot."

Tentatively the brown woman places the dog on the footpath, holding him gently around the chest for a moment, then releases him. The pup trots to the centre of the group and sits down. His little back legs splay out a bit around his round tummy and he looks up at each of them in turn, head cocked to one side, his small eyebrows raised in concern. Haruki can't help himself, he starts laughing, tears coming out of his eyes, slapping his thighs.

"Well, I guess that old chestnut doesn't work!"

The dog whines and stands up on his back legs in a begging posture, then cowers as though he's done the wrong thing. The others look more serious and Haruki simmers down. He squats and encourages the dog toward himself, saying,

"Varvara-sama always had him on a tight leash. He's a follower..."

The older Japanese gentleman now bows formally towards Haruki, "Hajimemashite."[35] He points to his chest, "Namae wa Tanaka."[36]

Haruki bows and points to himself, forgetting for a moment to give his surname first to this traditional looking man.

"Haruki."

There's a domino effect. Euro guy points to himself,

"Chester Kask" *Chester?*

The untenshu bows military style, bringing his heels together, "Kobayashi, konbanwa."

They all look towards the brown woman who looks stricken and then looks down, mumbling in English

"No Idea."

Haruki feels nonplussed and sees Chester pull the woman into a side hug, telling Haruki,

"Long story."

Haruki smiles at her and says in English,

"First name Long? Or is it Japanese style, First name Story?"

The woman points at him and says

---

35 *"pleased to meet you"*

36 *"my name is Tanaka"*

"First name Dad, last name Joke?"

The dog goes now over to Kobayashi and sits on his feet. Tanaka is still in thoughtful pose. Everyone stills. Tanaka looks at Haruki and speaks in English,

"You referred to Varvara as 'Varvara-sama'. May I ask how you know her?"

The leftover energy of secrecy from his time at Mortech still has Haruki feeling cagey.

"Well, she was my boss."

Tanaka nods, his hand goes to his chin, then he points to Haruki,

"Then you are Haruki Mori."

Tanaka gives him a deep bow.

"Gomen-nasai.[37] It was unfortunate yet necessary to terminate your employment at Mortech."

Haruki feels kind of pissed.

"That was you?"

"Hai. But perhaps I was too harsh, too hasty. We can work out a suitable compensation?"

Haruki bows, "For Fujioka-san also? Doumo arigato gozaimasu,"[38]

Tanaka looks to the woman who doesn't know her own name. For Haruki his expression is unreadable. The woman shakes her head 'no' very slightly. *What's that about?* Tanaka brings his hands together in a single definitive clap.

"So. Mori-san. We have reason to believe Varvara may be in need of assistance. I believe she does not know how to ask for it, yet I sense she needs our help."

'No Idea' gestures at the dog,

---

37   *Sorry*

38   *thank you very much (respectful form)*

"He showed up at a park I was visiting the other day and came home with me. Tanaka figured out his identity. I'm not sure about this whole 'Pericles' thing though."

Haruki says, "is there a hobo cat at this park? Got his own little sheet of newspaper?"

She laughs,

"hobo cat? I always called him 'Sarareman'."

Haruki chuckles.

"Classic! That's the park then. I met Varvara there a few times, it's not far from the lab."

Ms. No Idea looks at Tanaka, "Really?"

Tanaka says, "You have all been frequenting the same park? Interesting."

Haruki speaks up,

"I haven't wanted to go back there. Actually, I had a confrontation with Varvara-sama there recently."

A few passers-by gawk at the group as they go past, and Tanaka makes a decision in that moment.

"We must put our heads together and make a plan, but it is no good standing around in the street like this."

He pulls out his phone and swipes and types with perfunctory gestures. There's a chime from Kobayashi's pocket.

"Kobayashi-san. I have sent you the address for a little place we can go to conference. Mori-san, if you will ride with Kobayashi?"

Kobayashi bows, and opens the passenger side door of the old takushi for Haruki. The custom self-drive pulls up silently not long after, and the other three plus dog climb aboard and whisk away.

Haruki looks around inside the takushi,

"I've never been in one of these. Good quality doilies."

Kobayashi chuckles. *Huh. The old fella appears to be enjoying all this.*

Idea cuddles Scruff-pup as she sits opposite Tanaka and Chester. *I feel super embarrassed. 'No Idea'! I can't keep telling people that's my name. It just keeps popping out of my mouth. Haruki is the first person I've met since waking up that is unaware of my situation. But wait, not really unaware, he worked for Varvara. Probably read my 'readouts'.* She squirms in her seat, feeling hot and embarrassed. *I need a better working title.*

"Guys."

Tanaka raises an eyebrow ever so slightly at 'guys'.

"I need a real person's name."

Chester appears to almost visibly put on his thinking cap. Tanaka's face is Tanaka's face. *Reading his face is like trying to translate Hieroglyphics without the Rosetta stone. How does Chester do it?*

Chester waves a finger at her.

"Diana!"

Some blonde, white woman in an overly large peter pan collar comes to mind. She rolls her eyes at Chester,

"No."

Tanaka offers one,

"Samantha."

Chester looks and him and stifles a chuckle. Tanaka turns to him, smooths down his immaculate trouser legs and crosses one knee over the other.

"Samantha is a very good name."

Idea racks her brain, then stops.

"What country am I even from? Is there a land of brown English speaking kind-of-Asians?"

Chester winks at her, says,

"You have a sort-of-British- American accent?"

Tanaka very slightly dips the end of his good quality shoe,

"No. You are from Singapore."

Both Scruff-pup and Idea give twin head-cocks to the side.

"This is something that you already knew?"

Tanaka gives one shake of his head,

"No. However I have already privately surmised your accent is that of Singapore. I have had many work associates from this country."

Idea plays with Scruff-pup's ears and winks at Chester,

"So. Samantha is a typical Singaporean name?"

Tanaka very slowly tips his foot in the other direction.

"Samantha is a very nice name."

Chester puts his hand on Tanaka's shoulder and gives it a squeeze.

"You could even be a mix of both Indian and Chinese? Maybe you are actually Malaysian?"

Tanaka nods,

"Chester is correct. This is a good premise. However, I have known no Malaysian women. I do not know their names."

Chester leans forward and clasps his hands together between his open knees,

"nor I."

Idea groans,

"Is it even appropriate to name me based solely on my theoretical ethnicity? Maybe we should go with Samantha? But that just feels very not right."

The self-drive swishes to a stop and slides open its side door. Tanaka puts both hands to his thighs and stoops to leave the vehicle,

"we have arrived. Come."

The takushi has arrived first and Tanaka bows in acknowledgement of the superiority of Kobayashi's traffic mastery over the self-drive.

Kobayashi takes off his gloves and hat and then puts his gloves very precisely inside his hat. He places this neat bundle very reverently on the front seat of the takushi and locks it manually. They stand outside a nondescript office building in a pretty much featureless office area of Tokyo, it is now on the late end of twilight, and the night air has finally started to turn fresh. Tanaka leads them inside and they approach a wall of lifts. At the same time both Idea and Haruki blurt out

"I'm not good with lifts." and then look curiously at each other.

Tanaka gestures towards the door to the stairs off to one side and looks subtly to Kobayashi. Kobayashi simply follows in affirmation. The building has many flights of stairs, and Idea begins to get weary. *Was I always this unfit?*

Chester notices and moves to help her,

"you've lost a lot of muscle tone in the pod no doubt."

Haruki stops on the stair above her, turns and folds his arms across his chest. His face goes through a rapid gradient of expression from shock to understanding,

"you're Occupant XE!"

Chester curses.

"Idea. I'm sorry. The cat has climbed out of his box."

Sometimes Chester's versions of English aphorisms are a little odd.

Haruki stands stock still just staring at her open mouthed. She taps her lips,

"Careful. A fly might get in."

Haruki recovers.

"I'm sorry. It's just, this is a big shock for me. I had this really odd urge to bust you out of that pod! Varvara-sama was totally gaslighting me on it though. Kind of auto- suggesting that's what I should do at the same time as letting me know I was her lab rat. I was super torn, I couldn't figure out what was my intuition and what was manipulation."

He's jabbering. Tanaka is at the next landing above them and calls down, "Come. We have much to discuss."

Eventually they reach the correct floor. Kobayashi takes out a white cloth from his pocket and wipes his face of its sheen of sweat. The group follow Tanaka through the lift foyer and up to a glass door, through which a spacious lounge is visible. Tanaka allows the retina scan and ushers all inside. There is a large picture window covering one wall. Leather armchairs and sofas cluster in groups about the room. The place is empty of human life. Tanaka gestures for them to sit in the luxurious lounge seating over by the window. He attends to his phone, making brisk taps

"Please. Douzuo.[39] I will organise refreshments."

Idea can't help putting her face close to the cold glass and looking down. The street below looks quite far away. She looks out across the city now visible to her from above. It is an amazing view of Tokyo. Scruff-pup stands beside her, he's been passed around the company and predominantly carried up the stairs. A service-bot approaches. This one has been created to be reminiscent of an old fashioned art deco refreshment trolley. Idea scoops up Scruff-pup and holds up the little dog as a question to Tanaka.

Tanaka gestures at the floor with one finger pointing down, "pets are not allowed. But it seems Pericles is an integral part of our company."

He addresses the dog, "please, Inu-san,[40] come this way."

Tanaka walks away and the little dog follows obediently at his heels to the restroom.

---

39 *"go ahead"*
40 *Mr. Dog*

Haruki looks after them.

"Cute. He needs to go."

Kobayashi wipes the back of his neck with his folded cloth and then puts it in his pocket,

"Kawaii, ne?"[41]

Haruki has learned Kobayashi is in fact fluent in English but prefers to speak in Japanese.

There's a comfortable silence now between the company. Chester folds a napkin into an origami crane and says,

"Look at us, at a loose end without Tanaka driving us."

Everyone chuckles happily at this, and Tanaka returns with Scruff-pup trotting at his heels.

He pours himself a little neat whiskey from the drinks-bot and then turns to them,

"a good joke?"

Chester gestures at the empty chair opposite him and smiles up at him winsomely,

"I'll tell you later sensei."

Tanaka sits neatly and crosses one leg over the other, revealing one plain business sock. Idea looks down at her own already scruffy shoes, she had bought these for herself in a 100 yen store. These wonderful shops rarely carried items actually priced 100 yen anymore, but they retained the name as a symbol of the bargains within. Tanaka's typical Japanese preppy concept of women's fashion just feels wrong for herself, however it has to do, for now. She has no clothes she has chosen for herself. No money of her own. The scruffy shoes make her feel somehow more like herself. *Whoever that is.* As the others chat amongst themselves Idea does a slow scan of all the shoes. Chester's' beautifully fashioned brown

---

41   "Cute, eh"

brogues, Tanaka's business shoes plain, yet clearly excellent, custom made for him by Chester. Kobayashi's shoes are extremely shiny, Haruki sports beat up old gym sneakers with the name 'Volleys' on them. She decides to sit on the floor with Scruff-pup, and he allows her to gently stroke his little paws. He looks up at her with shiny eyes and licks her hand. She looks then at each face in turn and asks the question on everyone's lips.

"How do we find her?"

In the silence that ensues there is a low phone vibration. Tanaka withdraws his phone from his pocket and reads the screen,

"there's a problem at the lab."

He stands swiftly.

"I will have to leave you. This is urgent."

Haruki also stands "Varvara?"

Tanaka shakes his head 'no',

"I'm sorry. Varvara must wait. I booked this room until 9pm."

He looks pointedly at Scruff- pup,

"You must leave before this. Just pull the door closed when you leave, it will lock itself. Again, my apologies."

Tanaka leaves, and Kobayashi coughs a deep rumbling cough, taps his chest with one hand,

"Sumimasen, in this life I smoked for as long as I could. Now this. My karma."

Haruki goes over to the window and gazes down at the Tokyo night below him. He turns back to the remaining members of the company and shrugs with his hands still in his pockets.

"I really want to have a great idea right now..."

Idea slips off her shoes and draws her feet up under her, cross legged, her skirt forms a hammock for Scruff-pup. Kobayashi looks a little perturbed at her discarded shoes, then appears to decide to turn a blind eye.

At Mortech lab, there waits a short, slender man of late middle age. He is very well turned out, his style eclectic. He sports a perfectly waxed 1920's moustache, the latest mania among fashionable men. This excellently groomed man is Lennox, aka 'The Hypnotist'. None but his closest confidantes know that Lennox was once (long ago now) a girl child. He began his hormonal transition treatment in his pre-pubescence. His devoted French mother quietly and privately arranged for him to receive the treatment in America, the only place then with underground gender reassignment treatment for pre-pubescents. They retained their legal names but assumed new ones while in the USA. Lennox was born Marie Lesceux. The name 'Lennox' had occurred to him as a small child one night as he lay in bed listening to his parents argue. *My true name.* His father moved away soon after this argument, and his mother refused to speak of him from that point. Sometimes Lennox can almost remember his father, there's a few impressions left, but he rarely thinks of him now. Lennox keeps up his hormone treatments at a low dose these days, just enough to keep his beautifully formed moustache looking luxuriant. It has been some time since he spent time speaking French, and for years he has dreamed only in English. Despite this he retains a strong French accent and ramping up the French schtick is one of his favourite hobbies. Lennox waits now at Mortech in room 7, he is the first to arrive. Occupant SN has been found dead in his pod, apparent massive cardiac arrest. The staff

member on duty awaits questioning in room 9. Of the Five, Lennox'
role is the most contentious, he is responsible for the 'narrative identity
adjustment', and is thus known among the Five as The Hypnotist.
The adjustment process is reversible, it is all clear and concise in the
paperwork, though the clients were so greedy to live their ideal lives that
they eagerly signed away all legal responsibility of Mortech should the
process prove irreversible. The process is a type of 'hypno-tech' Lennox
has developed himself, he holds the keys to return each client to his
old identity. *If they want their moldy old narratives back, voila, they
shall have them.* His methods are still experimental, his research not
yet fully vetted by academia. Lennox does not mind, he considers all
human knowledge as a never ending experiment and he is intrigued to
study the results of this first pod batch. A man enters the room and sits
behind Lennox, but Lennox immediately forgets he is there. Soon after
follows the skeletal white haired hedonist Vance, his eyes covered in a
seamless band of dark glass and his mouth covered by a black rubber
mask. He is very tall and very gaunt. He wears a long, black shapeless
robe. His lobes droop as though they once sported very large spacers.
Lennox entertains himself with musing on Vance's aesthetic, *it's like the
grim reaper got together with someone from Tron and raised this one as a
little foster kid in the suburbs, with death metal for lullabies. Really. Too
much.* This reaper sits across from Lennox, but between the dark VR
glass and the black rubber mask is visible only his fine Dutch nose, so
he dismisses him as a conversational companion. Tanaka enters, *and of
course now the ball will start to roll. Tanaka takes charge of all scenarios,
so completely enamored with the clarity of his own equanimous mind is he.*
Lennox inclines his head in greeting, and calmly strokes his moustache.
"The Russian is in Kyoto? I have seen no response from her on this
urgent matter."

Tanaka remains standing.

" Varvara will appear as she chooses. We must talk to the staff member on duty. He is one of yours?"

Each of the Five has two hand-picked staff members. Lennox gestures with his open palm at Vance,

"one of his, I believe."

Vance says nothing. *It is a marvel that he is even physically here, that speaks volumes in itself.* The man sitting at the back of the room stands up and goes out the door. Tanaka notices him for the first time and turns to watch his back as he leaves, saying aloud,

"The Mathematician."

Lennox is fascinated by this little scenario for the blink of an eye, and in the next blink forgets it. Tanaka leaves and precedes to room 9. Lennox and Vance follow him at a well contained personal distance from each other and Tanaka. *How did the Mortech project ever come to be? It is laughable to call us a 'team', or even colleagues.* Inside room 9 is a chubby Chinese man. When he speaks it is revealed that he is an American. Then Lennox reconsiders, *No. Canadian.* The man looks to Vance for support. *He will find none of that there.* Tanaka looks at Vance,

"You will facilitate this meeting?"

Vance shakes his head once in the negative. Lennox considers Tanaka more closely, *his tone betrays just the teensiest droplet of anxiety. Why, it could even be called curt. Here was I, thinking Tanaka was imperturbable.* The chubby man speaks,

"Sumimasen sensei. Gomen nasai. Gomen gomen."[42]

The man is quite probably about to poop his pants with fear. It is very likely he has worked under zero supervision thus far. Of course, Vance has not been here since the occupants entered their pods. And he insisted

---

42   *"Please excuse me. I'm so sorry. Sorry sorry"*

*on naming the pod occupants himself. All but Varvara's pet project, XE.
Tanaka is barely taller than the man standing up.* Lennox hides a small
smile behind his moustache, *but he has tall vibes.* Tanaka raises his
hand, placating the man,

"Please. English is fine."

The man looks relieved. He looks as though he is cursing himself
inwardly, stands and bows to each of them. *Huzzah! Gaijin. We are so
funny.* Tanaka gestures him back into his seat,

"enough. Your name? The details of the incident? Keep in mind that we
will also go over the security footage most attentively."

The man nods several times in rapid succession. *Where did Vance get
this chump?*

"My name is Gareth Chin. Everything in the lab was completely
textbook for most of the night. I checked Occupant SN's readouts
and saw that he was showing signs of physical distress. I initiated the
emergency protocol as per my training. The medical team were on site
in no time. As I understand it by the time they opened the pod he was
in the midst of massive cardiac failure. They zipped him up in a bag and
took him away."

The man is sweating, dark circles are visible on his shirt under his
armpits. Vance goes to the wall panel, and with his back to the rest of
them tips down his face glass and allows the retina scan. He swipes
and types into the interface revealed, then the wall panel slides further
across to reveal a full plasma screen. He replaces his face glass and takes
a seat. They silently watch the security footage. Vance has programmed
the AI to select and display only movement that is out of the ordinary
pattern of a lab shift. Events are as the man has stated. Lennox glances
over and notes that he wrings his hands with anxiety. *Why do these
schmucks continue to live their lives as employees?* Tanaka looks to the

others of the Five and receiving no specific feedback gestures at the door for Gareth Chin,

"you may leave. I will escort you out."

While Tanaka is gone Lennox puts his feet up on the back of a chair and admires his custom kicks. *I love this word. Keecks.* Vance gestures at the screen and brings up the report from the medical team. *Massive cardiac arrest. Dead as soon as they opened the pod.*

"Vance. What reverie did you have old occupant SN marinating in? I can see from the footage that he was a big sack of fat."

Vance stares straight ahead.

"You know I can't reveal the reveries. Client privacy."

From the side Lennox catches a small reflection on the dark face glass that reveals Vance is immersed in some gaming or other such distraction on the inside of the glass. Lennox takes a deck of cards from his pocket and begins to shuffle like a casino pro, and teases Vance, saying

"I thought these VR glasses were considered lame."

Vance does not respond. Last time Lennox saw Vance he had sported a pair of pure white contacts over his irises. *Skinny weeaboo boy.* Tanaka returns. This time he draws a chair up to the screen and leans back to read from the top. *So courteous. Tanaka would never stand to block a screen. Ever the gentleman.* Lennox continues to shuffle, hoping the repetitive shlupping sound of the cards irritates Tanaka, *even just a teeny bit, no?* Tanaka completes reading the report, takes his phone from his pocket and glances briefly at the screen. He replaces it in his pocket and turns to face them.

"We knew there was a chance this could happen. As you are aware, legally we are covered by the extensive paperwork the clients signed before embarking on the experiment. However, for me this is a thing of great shame. Great sadness. I recall, though morbidly obese, SN's medical showed his heart to be in good health. There is the strong possibility these health reports were fabricated. I had them triple checked, but it is now very important to go through the reports of all the other occupants."

Tanaka closes the wall panel and moves to leave the room.

"This is not the end of this matter. Please remain available for further conference. Goodnight."

Lennox follows, replacing the deck of cards in his pocket. He speaks to Tanaka's perfect-postured back,

"What about Hades?"

Tanaka turns, pauses, then asks Lennox,

"Will you perform this task? I have much to do."

Lennox shrugs elaborately *Awesome. Ok Dad.*

"Sure. Why not?"

He tucks the task away for later. *May as well check out how the other vampires are faring while I'm here.* He doesn't bother to bid goodnight to Vance. *Pointless.* He briefly recalls there was a fourth presence in the room. *The Other One. Also pointless.* A sweet young woman has clocked on to take over the pod shift. Lennox puts on his 'French/artistic/gay' act.

"Charmed to meet you mademoiselle." He puts his hand over his heart. "I am Lennox. One of the Five you know."

The girl bows and speaks softly, "Nakamura."

Then she bows a second time and moves to go about her work. *So professional. Little minx.* In the midst of each character he dons Lennox becomes almost convinced of the act himself. It can take him a moment to 'take off the wig'. He recalls occupant XE, and swishes over to check out her interface. The pod is not active. *Fascinating. But why was I not informed? I have her identity adjustment 'keys' after all.* Lennox looks over at Nakamura checking methodically through the pod interfaces. *Getting anything useful out of that one will doubtless be like squeezing the proverbial blood from the stone. One of Tanaka's I must assume. Naturellement.*

Haruki reflects, *It's the funniest thing.* They've all ended up at a karaoke joint that Kobayashi frequents. Somehow the topic came up and Kobayashi learned that none of them had ever been to karaoke before. They've even snuck in little Odysseus in XE's bag. All are quite drunk by now, and the playlist has been eclectic to say the least. Haruki glances surreptitiously at OccXE. *I still don't know what to call OccXE. 'OccXE' seems really wrong. Chester seems to actually call her 'Idea'.* He has to admit that he is still fascinated with her, even more so now that she's out of the pod. *She's kinda nutty.* Haruki finds this very endearing. He feels the crush taking him over, and winces internally. *I promised myself never to crush on anyone again. Ever. She's being pretty cagey with me still, but I guess she's really been through something, is going through something.* He looks over at Chester. Haruki thinks the guy is probably a bit older than him, but very handsome and boyishly playful. Haruki has noted the warmth between him and XE. *I wonder if they are a thing...* He looks over at the old untenshu, Kobayashi is singing his little heart out. *I feel fond of the man. It's not just the sake.* Odysseus is fast asleep inside the bag on the floor at their feet. Haruki can see his little lips twitching as though he's yapping in his sleep. *What a day it's turned out to be.* Haruki feels like the thin membrane of a bubble will burst when this night ends, and this makes him begin to dip into melancholy.

Haruki shakes himself out of it. *It's a habit, a hiding place; this tendency to the morose.* Chester looks at his phone, leans over to XE and whispers something to her. They allow Kobayashi to finish his song, then gesture at him to turn the music down.

Chester says, "I'm sad to say, we need to wrap this up. Tanaka is back home and would like us to return also."

Kobayashi is too drunk now to drive them home.

Chester assures him, "don't worry, he's sent the self-drive over, it'll be here in 15 or so."

The karaoke joint is back in Asakusa. Haruki will catch the train and pick up his bicycle. Now everyone looks sad. Chester holds out a hand to Kobayashi and they shake. He fist bumps Haruki with a chuckle.

Chester says, "We'll reconvene. This Varvara thing still needs solving..."

Rosy cheeked with drink, Kobayashi holds up a finger,

"It is somehow possible to trace her through the money she deposits in my bank account?"

Then he shakes his head,

"I don't know, privacy laws."

The company part ways outside the karaoke bar. The self-drive will also drop Kobayashi home. Haruki refuses, he's happy to catch the train. The little dog looks at him from out of the bag slung over XE's shoulder and gives a little yap. Haruki waves at him and making a pretend phone with his hand he says

"Call me?"

Haruki notices that, instead of bursting as they drive away, the membrane of their shared bubble stretches to accommodate the new distance. *This thing is far from over.*

9.

The Pattern

Lennox adjusts his microphone, smooths down his moustache and admits Hades entrance to the chat room. He mutters to himself internally, *everything's in the email report, but the man needs a personal handhold.* 'Here, hold my penis while I piss'. *What's his actual name again?* Of course Lennox knows what his name is, *he is that disgusting species, the celebrity.*

Lennox enjoys playing as though he has never heard of him. Hades does not notice this game. In his mind, Lennox points to himself and exaggerates his own accent, *Narcisseest? Moi? Hades of course always makes one wait. A VIP. Very Important Penis.* Lennox has never had an interest in full surgical transition. *My own masculinity is something pure.* He checks the chat box, Hades enters. His face fills the screen, The man of the moment, Vish Bakshi. *Didn't he run for senate at one stage? A paragon of Capitalism. A winner. He has that radiance of the tech elite. It is as though an invisible laurel wreath adorns his brow, a gold coin slowly turns above his head.* The man exudes permanent ketosis and the Silva method. Hades is obscenely famous, his title in the press is 'Celebrity Tech Guru'. Lennox congratulates Vance again on the nickname Hades. *Perfect! He glows with righteousness. Reverse ironic. It is quite likely the man is literally Satan himself.*

Lennox has looked up the meanings behind his name.

'Vish' meaning poison. Bakshi meaning 'payroll master'. It is ridiculously apt. I may never stop enjoying this. La! I am forgetting to listen to what the man is droning on about.

Instead, he pictures him in an overly large chair, his right hand stroking a hairless cat. *mwahahaha! The main thing is that my head nods and my face is bland, receptive. Hades is the money in this Mortech debacle, and one must genuflect at the money. Oh, the clients pay a pretty penny. But what a pity venture capitalism renders itself so all pervasive. They drive up their own market. It's like real estate. A pissing contest.* Lennox never thinks of money. *Oh, I have it. Enough to never think of it. This is as it should be. It is 2038 and capitalism still flails about like a dying Kraken. Consumes power juices like it doesn't have stage four cancer. The Age of Aquarians are dancing around celebrating 'the return of the Christ Energy' or some such drivel, but 90% of human beings on Earth still can't afford to eat. Yummy! This body of Christ really fills the belly, I'll get a chakra cleanse for dessert. Shit. He's waiting for me to say something.*

"Lesceux? Are you hearing me? Let's get this cleaned up pronto. My feelings for Mortech haven't changed, I'm still VERY on board, but this doesn't look good. I know this tech has wings. I had a clear vision on this one, I'm feeling the future, I'm tapped in Lesceux, deep in the flow. Don't make me question myself."

"Bon, Mr Bakshi, I love that you can ally us on this. At Mortech we all implicitly trust the Vision will keep us flying true. We are going through all the health reports even more thoroughly of course. Old fatty must have bought himself a quack, no?"

"I wish I'd had the opportunity to meet him, maybe give him some mentoring; I've followed the Keytone Mastery protocol for a decade myself. Well, I'm sure he went down hitting all his money shots 'inside pod'. Godspeed him to the great beyond. Ok must rush, Elon's got me on a short leash these days...but I'll check in soon. Ciao."

Hades clicks out of the chat, and his pure white teeth linger as a dazzle in Lennox' eye for a moment. Lennox scoffs to himself, *I'll wager he's off to midwife The Singularity. Byeee.*

Tanaka struggles to sleep. For him sleep is sacred, he will not go to bed until his mind is clear. Chester reeks of alcohol. He sleeps face down, a thread of drool spills from his mouth.

Tanaka rolls onto his side to face him. *He is so beautiful, the heart of my heart.* Tanaka considers Chester's physical beauty as merely the radiance of his good nature. *A gift.*

Tanaka rolls backs to his own side of the bed, swings his feet directly into the slippers arranged perfectly next to his bed, puts on his robe, and ties the cord at just the right tightness about his waist. He leaves the bedroom and goes out into the garden. The temperature is ambient, the night sky is velvet dark, the moon has, on this night, shut her luminous eye. He can still see stars in the sky above Tokyo. *Arigato gozaimasu.* Tanaka stands firmly with his two feet exactly shoulder width apart. There is no excess fat on his body, his stomach is a flat board. His posture is elegantly erect. Tanaka is now in his late sixties, but he feels as vigorous in his body as in the days of his youth. He notes however some quality of 'softening' of his mind as he ages. *It is good. 'The inflexible reed must break'.* He nods twice with conviction. *I must end my tenure at Mortech. I will clean up this mess , once that is done, I will be done.*

Chester has often spoken of his desire to live for a time in Kyoto. Tokyo has a way of sinking its teeth into you. Tanaka was born in Hokkaido, his parents both University professors travelling regularly to Tokyo for work. He spent most of his childhood with his Obaachan and his grandmother inhabited an older Japan that he fears no longer exists. Her understanding of social graces was perfect, exquisite. But she was not rigid. Her mind was clear, ringing like a zen bell. His parents were quite bohemian, smoking pot and listening to the latest jazz, expounding philosophically with the artists and intelligentsia of Tokyo. *Beatoniku.* As he reminisces on his parents he has that nostalgic urge to smoke. He gave up smoking long ago of course, it is at odds with his love of perfect health. *It is true that the urge never dies, but merely lays dormant.* He has no plan on how to find Varvara. He knows he must clear his mind, sleep well and let it give birth to the solution unimpeded. Tanaka takes one last look at the sky then moves to drink a glass of water and go back to bed.

In the morning he feels restored. Chester shuffles about, quite theatrically haggard, his chin already showing the beginnings of a luxuriant new beard overnight and Tanaka marvels anew at his abundant hairiness. He prepares a healthy, and more importantly, hangover appropriate breakfast for all, including the dog, who enters yawning hugely. He sips slowly at his perfectly brewed green tea and waits for Chester and Idea to join him at table.

Idea enters and stoops to tousle the dog behind the ears.

He asks her "You have given this hound sake last night also?"

Idea smiles, she is beginning to slowly understand when he is making a joke. Chester enters in a rich butter yellow silk robe, his ivory cotton pajama pants and brown leather house slippers form the perfect complement to his robe. Tanaka is already fully dressed in his customary suit. Idea seems a little stiff in the very nice clothes he has provided her. *I will give her a little more spending money, let her expand more fully into her slowly emerging sense of identity post-reverie.* The three eat amicably together for a time. Idea expertly eats her egg with chopsticks, sips at her coffee and then speaks.

"I want to talk about the reverie I experienced..."

She looks inquiringly at Tanaka.

He asks her, "You feel revealing it may assist us with our Varvara conundrum?"

"Yes. Maybe? It's the oddest thing really. Varvara designed herself a sci-fi reverie."

Tanaka feels nonplussed.

"Sci-fi? With lasers, space battles?"

Chester chuckles and wipes his mouth with his napkin. Idea grins and shakes her head.

"No lasers. No spaceship battles. It was less Star Wars, a little more Kubrick. I was drifting, absolutely alone through space in a self-cleaning ship with a possibly (but not certainly) AI database for 'company' and an observation deck showing an unchanging view of the depths of space."

Idea makes a sick face,

"dear gods! The food..."

Tanaka, repose restored, leans back in his chair very slightly.

"So. The ultimate fantasy of a lonely woman who is incapable of love. An AI you say?"

"Well, it was more of a library database. I called it Library, with a capital L. I'm not sure why I did that, it seems odd now. There was no means of piloting the ship, nor even an engine room. There was some holo-functioning, but nothing outlandish. It could be called peaceful, except

I had the sneaking suspicion I was actually dead, perhaps in purgatory or something. Strange thing is, I got a real bee in my bonnet about figuring it out. Eventually I actually knew I was in a box."

Tanaka pauses for a moment to read her face quite searchingly.

"I was very careful, seamlessly lowering your doses of the unique balance of drugs I dose the occupants with. It had to be done just so, yes? I did not agree with the plan Varvara concocted in regard to your 'plight'. She painted it as compassion, but she is too complex a woman to be motivated purely by compassion."

Tanaka notices Idea's hand go to her lower belly.

She tells him, "I figured out in there that I must have lost a child. I think my child died. Before."

Chester reaches out his hand and takes hers into his.

Tanaka tells her, "I am sorry. I who am childless, cannot understand your loss, but maybe I can come close in my way. My wife wanted children. I agreed heartily. It was not possible for her."

Idea looks surprised.

"Your wife?"

She looks at Chester.

"Tanaka. I thought you were gay?"

Chester reaches out his other hand palm up for Tanaka and Tanaka turns it over, squeezes it very gently once, and returns both of his own hands to his lap.

"I loved my wife very deeply. She knew all along of my romantic interest in men. We had an arrangement...She is my first love. Chester is the love of my life."

Hermes waddles over and lies on his feet. Tanaka submits. Idea looks over at his Tamaya[43], visible in the foyer near the door and nods in

---

43 *Ancestor shrine*

understanding.

"She died?"

"Bowel Cancer. It was this difficult journey with my wife that shifted my path to focus more totally on anesthetics, on pain relief. I was already qualified in this, but I spent more time in the past focusing on my early training as a surgeon only."

Idea is looking at him as though she is burning to ask a question but is also equally reluctant to ask it.

"Please. Ask this question. I see it in your face."

She pauses, clearly seeking the right words.

"Tanaka, It's just. Well. Why did you get involved with the Mortech thing? Now that I've spent a bit of time with you I consider you to be a man of integrity..."

Tanaka inclines his head,

"and you judge Mortech as a project with its roots in hedonism, narcissistic impulse and avoidance of responsibility?"

Idea raises her eyebrows, bites her lip, then simply nods. Tanaka expands on his theme,

"These pod occupants at Mortech. If you peel it all away, what they seek is pain relief. They want to avoid this life. I do not approve of this in and of itself, but there is the question of the tool. Can it be used for good? Is it right to allow these wealthy clients to trial this technology for the wrong reasons? I have believed so. I am using them; to understand whether a person can be ultimately relieved of the burden of a 'problematic identity'. Perhaps I am also as guilty of this faux compassion as Varvara. As for you, Idea-chan, I had some nagging doubts I could not find peace with."

He sees that Idea will tuck the nugget of this away in her pocket, to take out and scrutinise in private.

Idea says, "It's funny. I really, really wanted out of there. Bless your nagging doubts."

He brings his hands together in his customary way, this time soundlessly, tilting them slightly upward in prayer.

"This is very good. Very healthy. But it gives us no clues on where Varvara lives."

A petite Indian woman dressed all in black expertly cracks the security on the door to Vance's apartment. She knows him. She enters, puts her hands around his throat from behind, and begins to squeeze in just the right place. She is medically trained. Vance appears not to register her soft fingers around his throat until his body successfully delivers the urgent message that he is asphyxiating to his chronically distracted brain. His body now begins to instinctively fight for its life. Then, she tears the VR glass from his eyes and draws a hammer from her backpack. There is the crackle of electricity, the sharp cracking of plastic shattering under force as she smashes his CPU, then his custom built GPU, she adds his VR glass to the pile of what is now nothing but detritus, and then smashes it easily. Vance does nothing, the fight or flight seems to have drained from his body. She studies him. He looks hollow, empty, a ghoul barely tied to the earthly plane. She shouts at him,

"Vance! It's Rav. It's Ravenna."

She punches him in the gut, tears the rubber mask from his face. Vance crumples, defeated. He drops to his knees, then curls into a ball on the tide of filth that litters his floor, an abandoned and empty piece of human trash.

Ravenna mourns. Vance was once a passionate activist for an ideal Earth. He lived and breathed the advocacy of freedom, was at the writhing centre of the anti-surveillance capitalism protests in Berlin. He burned with a hot fury, made elaborate schemes to serially assassinate the shadowy puppet-masters pulling the strings of the world. He lived in anarchist squats around the world, nodded patiently while fervent believers in alien rescuer gods listed the evidence of the manifestations in their lives that proved the acceleration of their vibratory fields. He called Rav his 'furious goddess'. He had been ready to set fire to the 1% and watch them burn in hell. He said he needed to infiltrate the shadowy worlds of the elite, to become one of them, become the ghost in the machine. He would destroy them like a cancer from within. Rav has been looking for him for three years. *Looks like the cancer got to him before he got to it.*

Rav drags him by the arm, kicks the debris from the mildewing futon in the corner of his one bedroom apartment and tosses him onto it like a garbage bag thrown at the foot of a brimming dumpster. She is sobbing, and slaps at his face repeatedly, screaming
"wake up! wake up! wake up!" over and over and over again.
He does not fight her, he seems to register her presence and then slink away inside himself. *Slinking back to the dirty alleyways of his festering mind.* Finally, she knees him in the chest, tightens a strap around his arm, slaps the delta of his veins visible through his translucent skin and plunges a syringe into one. He submits easily to her tranquiliser, and the emptiness finally claims him authentically.

The old woman lays sprawled face down on the floor of the hallway leading to her bathroom. The memories hold her down, down deep as though in the pool at the bottom of an implacable waterfall; its thunder is silenced down here in the deep. She registers these memories as a turmoil above, but she is safe down here in the deep peace of the quiet depths beneath. She watches them play out as though they are a silent movie, she floats suspended, held in the palm of an ineffable hand. She hears a voice calling a name: Jana. Over and over. *Jana is hiding.*

There is a noise now at the fringes of her awareness, a dull pounding. Her mind dismisses it, *just your heart pumping blood. Clinging to its purpose. But not much longer now, not very much longer.* Her eyes come suddenly open. There is a face above her. This face is unspeakably kind and seems to glow with a nimbus of light.

"Obaachan? Ah no... grandmother?"

A small hand clasps hers, so gently. Varvara's voice croaks, her throat dry,

"my rings... so painful."

The face nods, shows concerned eyes. *The eyes. So sweet.* Varvara registers it as the face of her mother, murdered so long ago now. *So, so long ago.* Varvara understands. *Finally. I am dying.* Then, the face is gone, and Varvara feels abandoned anew. *Of course. Grace was never for one such as I.* She curses her tears as they make their slow tracks down her soft parchment cheeks, and she closes her eyes again. *Defeated. Weak.* She feels her hands taken up and her eyes flutter open. Small but able hands hold the bolt cutters, they cut the thinnest parts of the bands of her rings now, efficiently, deftly, methodically, one by one. Blood rushes into her fingers, sharp and painful, a constellation of pins and needles shocks her numb hands into wakefulness. Now she weeps freely, openly. *Why answer my prayers only now?* Her disowned sense of Presence is briefly revealed, a page turns and reveals two words. 'I AM'. Varvara is shocked; she backs away from this light. The voice belonging to the hands speaks again, warm and with a heart breaking kindness. Varvara's eyes clear and she sees a small and sturdy Japanese woman. The woman touches her shoulder, looks again in her eyes saying

"It's Michiko. Your neighbour. Ah no, sumimasen, I never caught your name?"

Varvara feels something for another human being she has not felt since she was four years old. *Trust.* She perceives that the kindness in this person's face is not a mask. *No, this face is wrought from kindness.* The woman bobs her head, her eyes are grave. Before she understands what is happening Varvara hears her own voice say

"Jana".

The woman gives a small apologetic bow,

"ah no... sumimasen, I am your neighbour."

Varvara suddenly recalls her. When she first moved into her house, this small silver haired woman had come to her door with a gift of one beautifully presented fresh peach. She recalls her impatience at the time over Japanese social protocols. *Of course, this woman is my neighbour. I have seen her many, many times, greeted her unthinkingly, forgotten her instantly after each greeting.* She remembers now that she had failed to offer her own name when they first met. Of course, the woman did not press her for it; she was too kind. Michiko sits quietly, allowing Varvara; *Jana* to register all this. Then she speaks,

"Forgive me. I see that you are in need of recuperation? Will you allow me to help you?"

Michiko pauses again and looks around,

"the little dog...?"

Jana thinks of Hermes with the understanding she must lie to Michiko. *One last little lie.*

"He ran away..."

Michiko squeezes her hand very gently and places her other hand to her heart.

"Oh. I am so sorry."

Michiko hesitates, then speaks

"Ah no. This may sound a strange suggestion. Sumimasen. In my family we have a home in the mountains, near a little town called Komoro, not so far from Nagano. It is very beautiful. Very peaceful. Would you perhaps... ah no..."

Jana waits, and simply bathes in the warmth of Michiko's face, asking "A beautiful place?"

"Hai. Well, I have a very strong feeling to ask you if I may take you there? This is very forward, please forgive me."

She points again at her heart

"I have a very strong feeling. This feeling urges me to trust it, no?"

Jana feels a sense of wonder, she also trusts this strange feeling. She nods simply. Michiko looks very pleased.

"Is there anything I can collect for you from your home?"

Jana shakes her head once.

"There is nothing for me here."

Michiko nods, her eyes momentarily look unfathomably sad. Jana feels a kinship with this woman that shocks her, *in this moment I would go anywhere with her.* Wonderingly she allows the small woman to help her to her feet and accepts her cane into her somewhat re-awakened hands. She sees that the small person calling her 'Grandmother' is an ancient grandmother herself. This woman is neat and self-contained. Whole with self-trust. This woman leads her now patiently to her own front door. Varvara sees with surprise that it is open, its elaborate old fashioned lock unforced. At the curb of her house waits a self-drive. She allows the woman to settle her solicitously within the vehicle, to sit beside her, to clasp her painful hand very gently. She looks again at the woman's face and sees that inside the depth of her black eyes is the quiet strength of trauma unresisted, transmuted, a deep peace Jana has never known. She feels her heart hurt her and knows with it that she mourns Hermes very genuinely. Jana allows herself to cry for her small and loyal friend. Michiko passes her a handkerchief, it is embroidered with tiny fat hedgehogs and strawberries. Somehow this cracks Varvara further open, the little hedgehogs remind her of her dog. Michiko allows Jana to cry as she needs. Finally, Jana nods and gestures that she is ready to leave. As they drive away from the house Jana looks back at it, mentally strikes a match and throws it into its centre, and nods with satisfaction as it kindles instantly. She sees the corpse of Varvara rapidly consumed by tongues of fire. She experiences the heat of this fire as the dawning of a radiant sun of gratitude and allows herself to bask in its warmth.

Ravenna waits. Vance comes awake softly at first. As he surfaces more fully he seems to become cognisant that he is in hospital, and he sees that his arms are bandaged, that his wrist is attached to a drip. He surges to his feet, makes to tear away the canula from his vein. Rav puts her hand against his chest, and pushes him gently but firmly to the bed. He looks up at her face; is startled when he sees who she is.

"Rav! What the fuck?"

Rav leaves her hand against his chest and taps it slowly and rhythmically. "Vance. You lost yourself. You are not this 'ghost_eat' character. This was merely the mask you donned to play out your scheme, your master plan. It is not you. I *know* you."

She looks searchingly in his eyes, sees that the love he sees in her eyes terrifies him. He surges again to his feet, shoves past her, and runs from the room. Outside his door he is captured easily by two nurses, they maneuver him expertly back through the door. She shakes her head, *his body is so weak.* Vance crumbles to the ground and begins to rock, muttering over and over,

"nononononono."

Rav squats in front of him and tries to take his hand,

"Vance. This is withdrawal. You are an addict. We are helping you. Please see this."

Vance turns liquid eyes to her, then covers them with his hand and starts to sob. It sounds hollow to her, contrived, she has seen this before. Rav signals to the nurses behind him, pulls his hands away from his eyes and looks at him silently. He moves to hit her, she catches his wrist swiftly and nods to the nurse. The nurse jabs his buttock with the syringe, and he lets out an animal howl, fixing Rav with a look of utter betrayal.

"Vance. We must clear your mind. I am so sorry about the tranquilisers. You'll come to understand it. Come back to us. You've been lost."

Vance is not thinking at all, his autonomic nervous system follows its protocols to the letter, he droops, swiftly knocked out. Rav assists the nurses to carry him back to the bed, then sits by him and tenderly presses his hand to her face.

As he potters about in his kitchen, Haruki hears his phone chime from his bedroom. Generally, he tries to keep up a semblance of distance from his phone, and he pauses at the sink to imagine himself making a a sort of nonchalant stroll by his phone, whistling, hands in his pockets. He shakes his head at himself, then pauses again, tapping his chin with one finger, then makes an elaborate show of casually sauntering into his bedroom, looking at his phone with seeming innocence, then diving on it, laughing at himself, *Rancho relaxo mate, no need to be desperate.* He looks at the message notification before opening it, it's from a number he doesn't recognise. He shrugs, opens it, and reads:

"Want to come on an adventure to find me a better name?"

Of course, this can only be one person.

He types, "What's in a name?" adds the thoughtful face emoji, then hits send.

She does not reply. Haruki can't help but feel sorry, and he overthinks what was wrong with his essentially 'off the cuff' reply. Finally, he goes about his life in a kind of faux equanimity, but in truth it is a pregnant pause. After a day and a half his faux equanimity begins to become a genuine surrender, and naturally, only then he receives a reply. He pauses before opening the message and can't help but curse his beating heart. In the same breath he is able to shift his perspective and feel grateful he is alive, that his heart beats. *Open the bloody message mate.* He takes his phone to his couch and sits down to read the message. Totoro appears like magic and jumps up into his lap, swats at the phone, bumps his head on Haruki's hand, then settles, his belly fluff moving in and out with the fierceness of his purring. He opens the message,

"Where would a lost name go?"

Haruki can feel his heart pumping blood to his fingers. *Damn feels.* He allows his fingers to type

"to the mountain?" and add a Fujisan emoji.

Thanks fingers, having a little trouble here with my brain. He throws the phone across the couch. *What's with the romantic nerves? I hate this shit. I'm too old to have a bloody crush.* He feels Totoro's claws sink into his thighs and shouts,

"Buddy! Ow!"

The look Totoro gives him is fierce with love, his claws remain in Haruki's tender flesh.

"ow, ow, ow!"

Haruki taps on the paws and they finally contract. Totoro reaches one paw towards Haruki now, his purrs rumbling even more deeply. He closes his eyes and stretches all his paws to meet in one paw pile, the fur of his belly fluffing up in a tussock, his ears flattened out by his now upside down head. Haruki buries his hands into this fluffy tussock, and he can't help exclaiming

"Toto buddy. I love you!"

The purring intensifies and then drops off, Totoro appears to have fallen asleep. Haruki hears his phone vibrate, and he curses to himself that he has thrown it just out of reach. He attempts to scooch across to the phone, without disturbing the sleeping cat, and of course Totoro sinks in his claws. Holding the considerable bulk of the cat steady with one hand, the questing fingers of his other hand finally make contact with the phone. He brings it to him, then lays it face down next to his thigh for a moment. He closes his eyes and breaths slowly in and out. *Let it all go, let go of letting go, let go of letting go of letting go.* He chuckles to himself, *cool*. He opens the message.

"Planning party? Meet you at the swan boats? I've just now learned they exist."

Haruki smiles, texts back "yeps. 11ish?"

That gives them a couple of hours. She replies right away.

"Come anytime, I learned they exist because I'm currently messaging you on board a swan that is lolly pink. Message when you arrive."

Haruki sits still for a bit, feeling a little torn, he doesn't want the cuddle with Toto to end. He falls into a sort of timeless state until finally Totoro jumps off and goes to his food bowl. Haruki instantly leaps up and grabs his bag, yelling "seeya buddy!" as he races downstairs to his bike.

He knows the swans in question are in Ueno park, a huge park in Tokyo that houses the zoo, it also features a pond brimming with giant lotus. It's a real family park, and many people Haruki sees there today still wear masks. Though the pandemic years are long over, they have left the world permanently altered. New viruses are announced regulalry and the citizens simmer in fear. He walks by the pond, *considering the lilies,* messaging with one hand,

"Here."

The day is hot now, his back sweats under his cotton shirt. He feels a little embarrassed by the outdated style of his sun hat. He sees her on the banks of the smaller pond at the further end of the park, giant brightly coloured swan shaped paddle boats polka dot its waters. She's laying back with a sketchbook over her eyes, and he drops down beside her quietly. She lifts the book, turns her head toward him and squints one eye.

"Hey."

Haruki taps his lips, mock serious, points at her,

"Brownie McBrown?"

She punches him in the arm and scoffs.

"Dork."

She's merry though, and sits up cross legged, tucking her sketch book away in her voluminous bag. A cute little face with pointy ears pops out. Haruki greets him warmly,

"Odysseus! Hey there buddy."

The dog gives a joyful bark and runs over to give an OTT greeting, in the way of dogs.

She smiles at the two of them, saying

"This guy has so many names, maybe he can sniff mine out?"

Haruki tousles the dog and looks thoughtful.

"We need to give him something to catch the scent."

She nods, "So. You had some mountain lark in mind?"

He shrugs, telling her "I'll take any notion to get out of Tokyo for a bit."

He feels a bit embarrassed, *we don't even know each other*. He huffs out a breath quietly, counselling himself, *go with the flow mate*. She pulls at blades of grass and then tosses them aside in a small pile.

"After spending time trapped in outer space, I'm so down for an Earth style adventure."

Haruki raises his eyebrows with curiousity.

She makes a gesture vaguely above her head,

"The pod reverie had sci-fi vibes, but not like Star Wars, more like Kubrick."

"Wah! Lonely?"

She nods, "I had my little vacuum cleaner buddies, a very nice AI called Hal."

Haruki asks her, "for reals?"

"Well, not really, I called the AI 'Library', because it was. A library."

Haruki feels a bit tight in the chest, he feels awkward and insecure with her. He presses forward regardless,

"Um. You know, I kinda had a thing for you, back at the lab. I had this weird feeling I needed to rescue you."

He feels immediately embarrassed. *Fuck! I am a massive, massive dork.* He covers it by becoming extremely attentive to the dog. She looks down, also seems embarrassed, muttering

"my prince."

Haruki winces, crosses his eyes at himself. She picks up the pile of grass blades she has pulled out and tosses them up in the air.

"I am actually so fucking grateful people wanted to rescue me. I wanted out."

Haruki feels the dog squirm in his grasp and allows him to waddle across to sit in her lap. He tells her,

"the spooky thing was that Varvara-sama acted like she put the idea in my head. Sort of gaslighted me. I had this kind of internal battle about whether it was an intuitive feeling, or whether I was actually just being manipulated"

Oh. I think I told her that already? She purses her lips

"We still can't figure out how to find her. Varvara."

Haruki's hand goes to the back of his head and rubs his hair.

"Do you really want to find her?"

She stretches out her legs and the dog wanders away to sniff at this and that.

"She hinted that she knows my previous name. But... I don't know if I want that one."

She breaks off some new tufts of grass,

"I feel oddly grateful to her, even though it appears I consented for her to lock me up in the Kubrick Koffin, back when I supposedly knew who I was."

Haruki begins to build a small series of sculptures from the plant debris around them. She joins in and they quietly and seriously build a small sculpture village together, for a time not speaking, but starting to feel more relaxed with each other in the process.

Haruki tells her, "Tanaka put two weeks' pay in my account. He didn't have to, I was casual staff."

Idea tells him, "Tanaka is a peach."

Haruki laughs, surprised,

"a peach?"

"Yeah. But I need to begin to make my own way, now I'm back in the big wide world. Now I know there still *is* a world."

Haruki fusses a little with the sculptures, altering things here and there.

"I kinda need a working title for you. I've been sheepishly calling you XE in my mind, but it feels really wrong."

She looks pained,

"It *is* really wrong. *Inside*, I was calling myself Idea. It's actually short for No idea. Like I blurted out weirdly, the other day."

"I heard Chester calling you that. *Idea.* Are you and he...?"

She gives him an unreadable look, Tanaka style.

"Chester is a very beautiful man..."

Haruki feels his heart sag.

"Who is totally besotted with Tanaka."

Haruki's eyes open very wide.

"Ooooh. God I'm kind of an idiot, aren't I?"

She laughs, "Only kind of?"

He starts to dismantle his sculptures one by one, piling the materials into subcategories.

Idea says "I didn't mean it. Just jokes."

He looks up at her face, she looks a bit stricken.

Haruki says quickly, "Aw no! It's just. Tanaka. I thought he was a kind of self-existing entity. Like zero needy. Above it all. I can't imagine him, you know, 'in love'."

She nods, "He is above it all. But he's still human; has a fine heart beating in his chest. He says Chester is the love of his life."

She joins in on the sorting, and tells Haruki,

"I'm cottoning on that it's just his poker face. It's so hard to read that everyone projects that he has no feelings. Chester just *gets* him, *loves* him."

Haruki begins to slowly and happily to let go of his insecurities around his feelings for this woman. An invisible knot loosens, and it all starts to feel more natural. *Like we've known each other for a while already.* He allows himself to receive all her little ways into his heart. They spend the day together, pottering here and there as the whim takes them, and soon he starts calling Odysseus Scruff-pup instead as she does. *It suits him.* As twilight begins to tip over into night they see that Scruff-pup is pooped. Idea holds him up by the front paws and his head droops,

"I need to get this baby home."

Haruki picks up a Gingko leaf that lays at their feet and drapes it across his eyes. Scruff-pup sneezes and the leaf floats back down to the path. They chuckle together at this small nonsense. Haruki tries to flip another leaf at his feet onto his shoe, then shrugs ironically,

"You know; I've got a little time off work..."

She takes his hand quite suddenly while flicking her own leaf onto his shoe with her foot. Her hand is warm and soft. *How long has it been since I've held someone's hand?*

"We still don't know my name. Shall we go to the mountains? Tomorrow?"

She's like a child, sweet and excited. Haruki's heartbeat begins to speed up. *My neighbour will feed Toto.*

"To Fujisan?"

"Why not? It's a start."

She squeezes his hand. They catch the train home together in comfortable silence, still holding hands, watching the patterns of light shift as they travel. She gets out at her station, and gives him a little wave, "Tomorrow."

Something is not right. Tanaka feels it at first like a stone in his shoe, then the sensation moves to his chest area, a feeling of tightness. He is sitting in his private office going through the medical paperwork for the pod occupants. Everything appears to be in order, as he had already determined before commencing with the first batch of clients entering the pods. Tanaka clicks the file he has been reading on screen closed and leans back in his swivel chair, steepling his hands and crossing one leg over the other. *It's Vance. The boy has never felt right.* Tanaka's mind recalls The Mathematician. Tanaka seems to be able to focus on The Mathematician much longer than anyone else. On this occasion the thought does not step aside swiftly as is customary. *There.* He sees a small snapshot in his mind of the man during the interview in room 9. While the others (including himself) focus on Gareth Chin, The Mathematician is focused intently on Vance. *Intriguing.* It is very hard to get a grip on exactly who The Mathematician is. All notions slink away when he attempts to pin them down. Tanaka grabs at this little scrap of memory and perceives that The Mathematician has allowed this to be seen. He telephones Nakamura to check on the lab. *She's taking a lot of shifts over her university holidays.* All is well at the lab. He swivels to take in the large artwork that adorns his office wall. It is a zen ink painting by a famous Japanese contemporary artist, a traditional theme but rendered in an almost abstract style. He witnessed its creation himself. It depicts a solitary man making his way up a mountain path. Its markings are spare, barely recognisable individually, but as a whole the piece has a striking poetry to it. *It lives.* Tanaka often sits in repose with this piece, allowing his mind to step away from its chatter. Into the space created around his pattern of thought comes an image of Varvara's hands. In the image her fingers are empty, free of the rings that customarily adorn them. Tanaka allows this piece of data to transform into a black pebble; he places it mentally onto an empty Go board, then he waits for the white player to make his move. In this mental game of Go he does not play to win territory, but to fall into The Pattern. For Tanaka 'The Pattern' is his conception of the bigger picture, that place where his own narrow point of view expands to take in new possibilities. He takes the position of spectator as well as of both players and allows the game to play out with as little interference from his conscious mind as possible. To all outward appearances he sleeps. His experience of time ceases. Tanaka's eyes eventually open. He knows what he must set in motion, he is still not absolutely sure of the correct timing, but he telephones Nakamura. *It begins.*

In the morning Tanaka sees a couple of news notifications on his phone that perturb him. He goes to the living room, gestures at the blank wall opposite his lounge suite and a large screen appears there. Chester looks up mid-coffee with surprise, Tanaka is religious about never interrupting breakfast with media. The news is part way through a report on mass worldwide closures of train networks, including Tokyo. Some kind of infrastructural network virus attack. This is not new news. 'Terrorist' activity is at an all-time high. Fanatic groups are organised and mobilised like never before. The Tokyo train system has back-ups on its back-ups, and usually remains stable through these attacks, but this one has won through. The report wraps up and a new report begins on a man found dead in his Colorado compound. It is Vish Bakshi. Tanaka is shocked. *Hades!*

"American celebrity tech guru Vish Bakshi has been found dead in his Colorado compound, to all appearances the cause of death is erotic self-asphyxiation. He was found wearing the latest in Mitech VR Glass technology, official sources indicate the data immediately preceding his death has been wiped from the device. It is the tenth in a spate of deaths involving the device around the world , Mitech stocks have plummeted to an all time low."

Tanaka gestures at the screen and it blanks, falls silent. Idea looks questioningly at him, goes to say something, but Chester intercepts her with a quelling look. They both remain silent. Tanaka returns to the breakfast table and takes up his green tea. *It is the same VR glass Vance was wearing last time I saw him.* He checks his phone, there is a message from Lennox on the Mortech Five email.

"Room 7?"

Tanaka sets his ceramic cup down gently then stands and goes to the bathroom, washes his face and brushes his teeth. Chester follows him; his face is an open question. Tanaka dries his hands, replaces the neatly folded towel over the rack. He pulls his cuffs into place as he puts on his suit jacket. Chester trails after him like a child. Finally, he sits on the bed, his yellow robe spilling open to reveal the curly hair on his chest. Tanaka faces him.

"I cannot speak of these matters at this time."

Chester nods. "Can I do anything for you?".

Tanaka withdraws the slim control card for the self-drive from his pocket and holds it out.

"You have said you would like some time away? Idea plans to go to the mountains? Take her. I will message my friends Martin and Michiko for you to stay with them. I will stay in contact."

Tanaka leaves their bedroom swiftly and does not look back at Chester.

Haruki waits at the curb below his apartment and waves as the self-drive pulls up beside him. He has a duffel bag slung over one shoulder. Idea's eye is drawn to the walkway beside the apartment block, she sees a fat grey cat leap onto the high wall beside it in one fluid motion. Haruki climbs in beside her smiling broadly, picks up Scruff-pup's paw and makes a mini high five with it. Then he notices their subdued faces and becomes more serious. He looks a little surprised at Chester's presence. "Chester? Um. Hi."

Chester leans forward with his hands clasped together between his knees. "Things are going down at Mortech. Maybe something to do with this Vish Bakshi, you saw the news? Tanaka suggested we leave town for a bit."

Haruki looks a little embarrassed and tells them,

"I kinda skimp on watching the news as much as possible. These days it's..."

he shrugs, Idea guesses he's not certain of Chester's 'political' persuasion as yet.

Idea lets Scruff-pup down to sit on the floor and Chester continues,

"There's been system attacks on the Tokyo train networks, and on different infrastructures around the world. No-one's putting their hands up yet, cult activities are getting more and more effective all the time. That Big Tech celebrity Vish Bakshi was found dead, and Tanaka quietly wigged out. He's co-opted your trip with Idea to the mountains. Sorry for intruding."

He looks at Idea for help explaining and she can't help looking away out the window beside her. *Embarrassing.*

Chester continues, "But we can stay with some of Tanaka's friends, so it should be very nice."

Haruki just nods quietly then, accepting it. Idea feels a bit anxious, the sweet spell of yesterday felt a little flat in the morning. *He likes me.* She's been actively *not* thinking about him since she got up. But when Chester let her know Tanaka's wishes she found herself calling him before thinking, telling him to get ready for a pickup, neglecting to give him the details. *Yesterday was sweet, like a first date. Feelings like this make me panic. Gain is loss.* She doesn't consciously remember her romantic past but there's a tightness in her chest, almost a nausea in her stomach. *Clearly my body remembers some things.* As she wrestles inwardly she sees his face properly, had been looking *through* him.

It's so open. So sweet. Full of concern. He's my friend. She takes his hand, "Are you still down for a trip to the mountains, or up north at least?"

He nods yes, "North? Not Fujisan?"

Chester speaks up, she sees him noting the chemistry between them, *Chester! Was that a wink?*

"Tanaka has some old friends, an ex-pat Swiss-German guy and his Japanese wife. They live outside some tiny town in Nagano province called Komoro. I haven't met them. It's a couple of hours or so to get there. We can take it easy, stop for snacks. Something's really got to Tanaka though. That's rare. So, we'll stay on the alert. Ok?"

They all settle in for the drive, Chester uses the interface to signal the vehicle to begin, Tanaka has messaged the vehicle the travel coordinates from his phone so it pulls smoothly away from the curb and into a traffic made up predominantly of its own kind.

Lennox looks expectantly at the open door. So far it's just Tanaka and himself in room 9. *Oh, and that one.* Tanaka emanates a vibe that's hard to read. *That's not unusual, but this feels different.* Lennox is wearing an ensemble that he considers may possibly be his best yet. *Not that present company has two fucks to rub together. The world is in a flap. Seems even old T's got his knickers in a twist. Oh, maybe just a leetle further up his crack than he prefers. Me, I find it hard to know when the world is in more of a flap than the usual flap. According to the popular psyche, we humans have been in imminent doom since old Prometheus did the deed. What do they expect? Every third kid these days runs a VR brothel in their spare time. You can't fire up the panopticon and expect ALL of them to take it up ze arse. Most people in this world are still waiting for their dinner, and they didn't even get breakfast. Eat the fucking rich! Yes, let them strangle themselves with their own belts, why not?* Lennox has a sneaking suspicion about Vance, who is notably absent. *Had a feeling the ol' death goth schtick was a little frayed around the edges.* He shuffles his cards, today it's the Crowley classic tarot deck. He does not believe in the tarot, just enjoys the aesthetic it adds to today's ensemble. He observes that Tanaka is giving 'waiting for Vance' it's due and he scoffs inwardly. *I know that he knows that I knows etc etc.* He draws a scarlet silk handkerchief from the pocket of his embroidered waistcoat and blows his nose theatrically, making sure it makes a satisfying hoot. No one has noticed that embroidered on his waistcoat among the flowers are little words like 'fuck' and 'cunt'. *Boohoo, wrong audience.* Now he sees that Tanaka is about to come directly to the point. *My favourite thing about the man.* He brings his hands together in his customary gesture, *sensei delivers his truth nugget.*

"I have set in motion the awakening protocol of our clients, ahead of schedule. The experiment. It must be finished as quickly as possible, but too quick is very dangerous. Very reckless. The loss of Hades. Mr Bakshi is, as you know, very serious indeed for Mortech's future."

Lennox mimes looking around the room as though to a judge and jury, his shoulders raised, palms up at the ceiling.

"Did I miss the brainstorm session? The conference where we discussed this?"

As he looks around his eyes skim over *that one* and he feels a momentary disturbance in *ze force.*

Tanaka bows formally to Lennox. " Sumimasen."

Lennox gives him a sharp gaze,

"Well? You know something else about this that I don't?"

Tanaka appears to look unruffled, *but oh! He IS ruffled. Fascinating.* Lennox puts on his best (albeit still French accented) Sir David Attenborough impression inside his head *His glistening summit glimpsed for but a moment, Fujisan's clouds gather about his face once more.* Lennox goes into his casino shuffle act and ramps up the French accent,

"Naturellement. It is Vance. The Mitech Glass. 'E has hacked the world, no?"

Tanaka says, "Presently my own concern is for our clients."

"And 'Ades?"

Tanaka remains silent.

"Bon. E has met his natural end."

He pretends to look around once more,

"where is our little h'emo keed?"

Abruptly he tires of his own schtick and reels it in. He stands gracefully,

"Enough play. This house of cards falls in the first breeze. Together we wrap up this Mortech folly, yes?"

Suddenly The Mathematician speaks. Lennox looks at him with a double take. The man appears to be mild looking, bespectacled, wearing a brown hand knitted sweater vest. *Really?*

"Look to The Pattern."

Lennox nods, taking it in, mock serious, *yes, yes. The Pattern, the fractals, the mutual masturbation of wave particles no?* He gets distracted for a moment picturing himself wearing this 'Mode a la Mathematique' *It is a lewk.* He looks again at the apparent space the man had filled, *The Mathematician dissolves back into his event horizon.* He waits for Tanaka to speak. Tanaka remains silent. The Mathematician does not re-emerge from the deep. Tanaka leaves the room abruptly without a backward glance at Lennox. Lennox hastens his short legs to catch up and walk as an equal beside him, *he whose legs are equally short, but impelled by a will force greater than my own.* He feels a prickle of the hairs on the back of his neck rising, signifying the accompaniment of *ze elephant in ze room.* Lennox slows down momentarily, enjoying the irony of this new quip. They proceed to what Lennox has dubbed The Pod Bay. *Open the pod bay door Hal. I'm sorry Dave, I'm afraid I can't do that.* Nakamura bows as they enter, Tanaka begins to go over the real-time data of the pod occupants, looking for some clue about 'The Pattern' spoken of by The Mathematician. Lennox signals that he'll 'lend an oar' and he starts to go over the readouts of the pods at the further end of the room. For a time, silence reigns. He allows himself to become absorbed in the moment, ceases the arch banter of his mind and hangs it up like a costume on a rack. Under the mask of jester, Lennox possesses a gravity of mind most rare. In the pod bay there is no way of accounting the passing of time, the pod occupants follow carefully manufactured circadian rhythms of their own, unhooked from either the diurnal or nocturnal rhythms of the planet housing their coffins. Each vampire slumbers in an eternal dreamscape, *not knowing if he is the butterfly or the man, so to speak.* Silence reigns, each figure in the lab held in the spell of their own intense focus. Eventually the process is complete. Lennox finds himself bowing to Tanaka, *this bowing, she is a virus.*

He tells him, "I find nothing out of the ordinary."

Tanaka blinks slowly, seems frozen in place. *La! Perhaps he actually trusts me enough not to double check my assessment?* In fact, it is Lennox who trusts Tanaka implicitly. Eventually Tanaka gives a penetrating look, just to the left of Lennox' shoulder. Lennox looks around, perceiving the bespectacled man behind him. *Ah. The fucking Pattern.*

As they drive closer to the mountainous North of Japan Idea feels the crossing of a sort of invisible boundary inside her. A veil lifts, and to dwell in Tokyo from this new vantage point seems like madness to her, a fugue. *It's as though this is MY planet Earth, this sweet smell of green things growing.* Her skin drinks this smell in and funnels it directly to her heart. *I did not realise that I was so thirsty for this.* Idea feels burdens lift from her back and feels the dawning of a new lightness of being. She looks at Scruff-pup, his head at the air vent, Chester has switched the air cycle to take in the oxygen from outside. Self-drives don't have opening windows and Idea feels nostalgic for dogs with their heads out car windows, their tongues streaming like fluttering victory flags. *Scruff-pup was used to riding in Kobayashi's ancient takushi, but would Varvara have allowed him to put his head outside? The woman is an enigma, way*

more of a true dark glass than what people assume about Tanaka. In her opinion Tanaka was transparent, direct, a polished lens. Everyone has been very quiet on this journey, each mulling over their private thoughts. There's a sense of respect somehow for the change of air they now share. Like a cocoon, she feels the self-drive will release them as butterflies on arrival. Then she stops her reverie. *I'm making assumptions about others again.* She holds Haruki's hand. *It's the sweetest thing. Just this.* She gently studies Chester's face while he looks out the window. *Chester does look more relaxed though, I'm certain. There's a 'vibe in the room', for sure.* Chester catches her eye and twinkles his own at her,

"sweet mountain air, nothing like it."

He gestures at the interface screen to light up, then looks at the livemap readout, "Not far now."

He looks at his phone.

"Nothing from Tanaka."

He sighs, scrolls. Idea notices now the strain at the corner of his lips, she grows serious, and crouch-walks across the small lounge room of the self-drive to tuck herself in under Chester's arm. She puts her hand on his heart and looks up at him with warm and sorry eyes,

"Tanaka will call as soon as he can. He's got this. He's always got this."

Chester just nods, and the self-drive lets out a chime, speaking with a polite British accent,

"15 minutes from your destination."

Chester looks at the interface, puzzled,

"I thought Tanaka had that function turned off?"

Idea puts a hand over the screen.

"oh! Can we leave it on? She's ever so polite."

Haruki puts a hand up, "Can we have Italian mode please?"

They spend the rest of the journey toggling the voice on the AI, for some reason this never gets old. Eventually the car turns into the driveway of their destination, the house is further up a short steep climb. Chester intercepts the control and programs it to park below.

"These little city self-drives struggle with a steep incline."

None of them has much luggage, so they collect what they have and begin to walk up the incline. Scuff-pup barks like a maniac; his whole body quivers with excitement. Haruki points at him with his chin, "Old Scruffles can't decide what to sniff first!"

A Chiba inu appears at the crest of the incline, barking at them from above. Appearing next is a very tall man in his seventies with white hair and a two tone beard, then beside him a small, comfortably plump Japanese woman in her late sixties at least, her long silver hair done up in an untidy pile on top of her head. They both wear what appear to be rather eccentric hand knitted cardigans; the air is so much cooler and fresher here in summer than in the stultifying humidity of Tokyo. Idea sighs happily to herself, *it smells so green out here.* The man shouts to the dog in English with a Swiss-German accent,

"Asterix! Come, come, yes you've done your good security man work. Let us greet our guests."

When they reach the top of the incline, puffing, the two dogs walk round and round in a circle sniffing each other's bottoms, and Scuff-pup falls to the ground belly up. The tall man laughs,

"Yes you can still eat him Asterix, 5 second rule you know"

The Japanese woman punches him in the arm, then looks up at him with fondness. She bows deeply at the guests, and they bow back.

"Hajimemashite, namae wa Michiko desu."[44]

The man holds out a hand to shake, offering it as a question, in some circles hand shaking has fallen out of popular use.

---

44   *"Pleased to meet you, my name is Michiko"*

"Martin. Welcome, welcome. Michiko plans to feed you until you pop, come come."

Greetings exchanged, the group make their way up to the house. Idea stops at the front. A climber vine has almost engulfed the house. Chester chuckles,

"Did you know that you live in a shrub?"

Martin looks mock offended then holds out a hand in dramatic presentation,

"Of course, Chateau Shrubbe!"

Inside Idea sees that it is built from hand rendered clay earth, everything in the space is round, natural and organic. Idea is euphoric, *this feels like home.* There are two large wooden tables with long bench seats taking up most of the room. Martin tells them,

"we have many guests actually. Musicians, artists, etc. Michiko buries them all out the back herself after she kills them with feeding them too much food. Don't worry! They die happy."

Michiko ignores this quip. The table is set out with many different kinds of intriguing foods, contained in ceramic bowls of all types and hues. Chester admires the ceramics,

"so beautiful!"

Michiko beams very sweetly and Martin draws her into a side hug,

"Our Michiko is a potter of some distinction, famous even in Tokyo!"

Michiko waves him away and gestures at the table, "dozou, dozou. Please go ahead."

The company eat to their hearts content. There is a dizzying variety of seasonal dishes, all hand prepared by Michiko, largely from vegetables grown in her own garden. Michiko keeps gesturing and offering more. Idea holds up a hand, rubs her belly and looks mock seriously at Martin.

"She really is trying to kill us!"

A little cat enters the room, a tiny kitten only, yet with a large presence. Michiko picks up the kitten and brings it over to Haruki, she has spotted easily the principal cat lover among them. Idea looks over at him fondly, *not hard to discern, look at him, he's instantly besotted.*
Michiko hands him the little bundle,
"Namae wa Ko-chan, ne?"
The kittens' fat little tummy rumbles with purrs. Mother cat enters next, she gives a little trill and jumps up beside Haruki, then licks the kitten all over its face. Haruki looks almost cross- eyed with joy.
Michiko holds her small hands clasped together over her heart.
"kawaii ne? Ko-chan is Neko-chan's last baby."
She looks over at Martin, who rolls his eyes, saying,
"It appears our dear Ko-chan may be here to stay."
The group take a tour about the property, it is a bohemian enclave, dotted with handmade buildings of different types of experimental eco-engineering. Martin has a local friend who loves to experiment with eco-architecture, and the couple run the place as a sometime inn. Evidently Idea and company will be staying in the large Mongolian-style yurt. It is cosy inside, lit with a warm ambience, traditional Japanese futons and bedding are stacked against the wall. The property also features a handmade wooden Japanese bathhouse and Scandinavian sauna. Before Idea knows what's happening, she finds herself immersed, naked among the entire group, in piping hot water up to her neck. Michiko provides each of them with cotton yukata[45]. Idea's is a beautiful deep pink, patterned with small rabbits, cherry blossoms and moons. She decides to wear only yukata from now on. *Is that allowed?* Finally, they bid goodnight to their hosts, and roll out a futon each in a little row in the centre of the yurt. Haruki holds his stomach and his heart at once,

---

45   *traditional cotton bathing kimono*

"I don't know which of these is more full."

Chester, laying on his back under his blanket, hands behind his head, comments wryly,

"I didn't know my beloved was friends with hippies."

Idea sits cross-legged on top of her futon and holds up a hand "Confession. I think I might be a hippy."

Haruki holds up one finger, says, "I think a more accurate title would be Bohemian."

Idea claps her hands together like a small child.

"Yes! I'm a bohemian. I never want to leave."

Chester rotates one finger next to his temple,

"Chica es loco."

She throws a pillow at him,

"Chester! I thought you were a Bohemian!"

He shakes his head no,

"That's Czechoslovakia," then stifles a yawn.

"It looks like it's goodnight from me."

He rolls over in his bed, drawing the covers up around his chin. Up on one elbow, Haruki gives her a lingering gaze, his head resting in his palm. Idea realises she is too excited to sleep, smiles at him, and holds her hands together in a gentle prayer shape, hoping he doesn't feel rejected. He winks at her, rolls over, is soon emitting the slow and steady breathing of sleep. As silence dawns in the room, she hears the crescendo of the frogs and cicadas outside. She goes out into the night, just breathing it in. *To think, I only recently believed that the earth was utterly destroyed.* Scruff-pup ambles tiredly out of the yurt to stand beside her, looking up, his eyes shiny. They share a moment. *He gets it.*

Ravenna watches Vance use a custom built phone to tune into various news sources he has hand selected, he has never trusted the algorithms of the mainstream media, then asks herself, *these days, who really does? It is the age of confirmation bias.* But Ravenna feels heartened, *this is classic Vance, he still seems largely disoriented, but it appears he has begun to recognise the fugue state that was ghost_eat.*

She has explained this was his plan, to infiltrate the world of the elite, beat them at their own game. Instead, he lost himself. She has told him that she has been searching for him for three years. She knew he would go like a homing pigeon to Japan; his personal mecca, but his trail was cold and dark. Dr. Ravenna Gupta honed her skills in India during the pandemic years, but she has shifted her medical focus, and works now in this Tokyo hospice for recovering hikikomori, in the VR addiction recovery program subsection. Ravenna perceives Earth 2038 as two Earths, she calls them Capitalism A and Capitalism B. In the world of Capitalism, A, the free market reigns, Tech Giants have become nation states, specialising in 'augmented' realities. They literally make their own money. If one builds an empire within a VR environment this holds true out in the so called RL, Real Life. Blockchain currency used within any AR or VR environment is coin accepted also in RL. Those Earth citizens floating just below the cream that floats to the top of the economy suffer through their RL experiences, distracted by dreams of making it big in VR realms. Her own country of origin, India, provides the bulk of the massive IT workforce propping up Capitalism A. Cap. A wears a thin moral veneer co-opted from Cap. B.

The marketing departments of these tech giants are careful to propagate content demonstrating balanced use of their tech, they 'care', they are 'transparent'. VR is presented as eco- responsible, humans are now free to run locust in virtual realms, the planet will be able to recover from the collective fever dream of the industrial age. *Apocalypse averted*. The reality is infinitely more squalid. VR tech giants began mining the moon 5 years ago, this is old news, practically archaic, no one thinks of it, backyard poets still gaze starry eyed up at this moon, definitely not incorporating the mining bots busy on its surface into their sense of connection with the universe. Then there's Capitalism B. The heroic attempt to forge a Golden Age from bio-tech. Humans, doing their very best, yet still worshipping at the altar of their own false idol: technology. Cap B is presented as a benign dictatorship, it is more like a controlling parent. *They know best, and we are their little tin soldiers, packed away into our safe little boxes for our own good*. Ravenna sees herself as one of the fast disappearing 'real' humans holding out against the zombie apocalypse, *the zombie apocalypse where they eat their own brains for dinner; all the while complimenting the chef*. In truth the masses are in survival mode, as ever. *This VR scourge is available only to those rich enough to indulge in it, but they hold the rest of humanity ransom to their addiction. Of course, addiction to pain relief is an old story, there's nothing new under the sun, round and round it goes, where it stops nobody knows. My Earth could be called Earth C, that one invisible to Earths' A and B, the one most humans now inhabit. It is difficult for those who inhabit the vast realms inside the VR universe to remember that their bodies still reside in this other Earth, this Earth of those left behind to pick up their dirty underpants, and breath in the rank stench of assholes at the same time.* 'Tako' glides into the room. He is a medi-bot, named after the Japanese octopus for his multipurpose arms. Rav can't help but find him cute but also curses her easily activated susceptibility to emotional design signifiers. She pats him on the head regardless and his little retro-digi eyes make the shape of love-hearts. She looks up to see Vance regarding her with a sardonic grin. She takes in his beautiful blue eyes, relieved now of their goth-core white lenses. He does a little mock kpop dance routine from the hospital bed, then laughs at his own joke. At his crown she can see the stripe of his blonde regrowth. His hand goes to his head. "Let's shave this?"

She nods, silent, but pleased. He takes a chair, and she programs Tako to do the deed.

Tanaka finds himself walking out of the lab, providing no explanation to those he leaves in his wake. *The Pattern. My pattern. All this, what I'm doing, it is my pattern. This is what The Mathematician was pointing to. Not some background universal grinding of gears, not some nefarious plot, but the machinations of my own ego. My need to be right. My need to be the saviour. My mania for balance. My habit of doing everything on my own, always superior. 'The inflexible reed must break.' I quote this to myself often yet understand it intellectually only. The Pattern? In truth, nothing is certain, only change, and this time, it is I who must change. The Mathematician does not point out some dark plot at work in Vance, but the obvious need to offer the boy some genuine help.* Tanaka tears off his suit coat as he walks, unbuttons his collar and finds himself longing to smoke a cigarette. *So. What WOULDN'T Tanaka do now? He wouldn't go get drunk in a dirty bar.* He finds himself dialing Kobayashi.

At the bar, Tanaka ignores the messages piling up on his phone, but feels a pang thinking of Chester. *Chester is safe, daijoubu desu.*[46] Then he stops. *Chester wants to know I am safe. I never see this.* He takes another sip of sake, empties the cup, and continues to resist calling Chester. *Chester, right now I don't know who I am.*

Kobayashi sits across from him, very clearly in his happy place, his cheeks are rosy with drink. He pours himself and Tanaka another cup of sake, then offers Tanaka a smoke with a gravelly cough. *Old Kobayashi looks very happy; very peaceful.* Tanaka takes the cigarette, lights it, and feels a rush of pleasant nostalgia as he pulls the smoke into his lungs. This little bar is one of the few left where you can still smoke real cigarettes. He looks around, the bar is an old fashioned jazz den, found down a set of grimy stairs. The air is thick with smoke and Tanaka pauses to blow a perfect smoke ring to add to the atmosphere. *This cigarette is redundant, the bar smokes itself.* Kobayashi holds up his finger and pulls a joint from his pocket with his other hand. He puts it on the table between them, then starts quietly tinkering with the coasters. Tanaka throws back his cup of sake and stands, draping his suit coat over one arm. Kobayashi chuckles and moves to pay their tab, Tanaka allows it, he is following his newfound creed, *what wouldn't I do?* The two then climb the stairs to the street and stroll toward the nearby river. Kobayashi starts to whistle that old song, 'minna yume no naka' (*Into a dream*) Tanaka finds himself singing along, marveling at how apt it is.

What is it you're looking for?
Are you still going to search for it?
Don't you want to try
going into a dream, into a dream?

---

46   *it is ok*

They sit on the bank of the river passing the joint back and forth, reminiscing on times past, and eventually just sitting in companionable silence together. Finally, Kobayashi stands, takes Tanaka's hand in his two and bows rather unsteadily. Tanaka waves him away cheerily.

"I'll stay for a bit longer, ne?"

As he walks away Kobayashi holds up a hand,

"ja,ne?"

Tanaka replies, "mata, ne?"

Tanaka feels at peace. He sits in a quiet space just below his mind, the better to observe it's pattern. *I do not know what to do. I do not know what is right. This is ok.* He takes his phone from his pocket and messages Chester "Daijoubu desu."

He does not add any emoji, this would only cause Chester concern.

Jana sits by herself on the back patio of Michiko's mountain home, enjoying the verdant tumble of garden in view. Michiko is a passionate gardener and Jana feels just like the bees buzzing about it. *The nectar is all here. There's nowhere to go. It is not so easy to put the ghost of Varvara to rest, that bad habit of a lifetime. Michiko is so kind.* She feels tears leak from her eyes. *I have become feeble minded. Sentimental. No, that's Varvara again; Varvara is dead, she got her wish. I want to die now in this peace, in this acceptance. Varvara was endlessly at war with life; Jana wants to slip seamlessly into oneness with it. Michiko is my angel of grace.* Jana has not yet entirely abandoned Varvara's extremely well thought out atheism. *Though Grace is perhaps behind the greater pattern all*

along. It is simply a mistake to blot it out. Jana sees into the anti-grace campaign Varvara was obsessed with. *This type of control is simply the mask of fear, unskilled and short sighted.* Jana has finally found the courage to feel her fears, *after only a lifetime of pain. The ironic pain of holding back pain.* Jana has learned that Michiko herself experienced a similar legacy of war, that she was orphaned and abandoned in the conflagration of Hiroshima, only she was somehow able to bend, where Jana became rigid. *What a difference it made to the aftermath.* Jana is beginning to understand that this somehow was also grace, the way it went for her. Michiko has demonstrated to Jana the understanding that some things, most things, are ultimately beyond ones control. *There's a much bigger picture of course. Varvara in her arrogance believed she knew this bigger picture. What a joy to learn she knew nothing all along.* The newly rescued Jana herself feels like she is still a child, but this seems a fitting state in which to spend one's final hours. She thinks again of Hermes. Varvara concedes that she misses him. Michiko has a cat. This arch creature steadfastly ignores her; the feeling is mutual. Michiko brings out a steaming teapot of green tea and two small cups. These two Obaachan sit peaceably together, simply receiving the beauty of Michiko's rambling garden. *There's something about this mountain air.* Jana thinks not of Mortech, she has added her work to the bonfire of Varvara. *Tanaka will sort it out, of course.*

10.

Fireflies

*V*ance allows Rav to nurse him back to health, *to doctor him.* He carries out an internal condemnation of himself as he sits bored in his hospital bed. *Somehow I've shaken off the whole ghost_eat thing like a bad case of scabies. Let her believe that. I'm actually pissed I DIDN'T engineer the Hades thing, or the spate of VR deaths. When it comes down to it, I'm essentially just a poser. An empty facade. Some people never change. Trouble is, Vance Janssen is apparently also an act. Rav always had beliefs about me, her own projections. I was never the hero idealist she believed me to be, I didn't lose myself. Ghost_eat was more like letting go, sinking more deeply into the hollow man under the mask. I ditched the hero act, embraced the fucking shadow or whatever. But I won't be sharing all this stinking introspection with Rav, leave her to her world views, she's got it all neatly summarised. The hero act was a useful social passport, it always worked on the ladies.* Vance despises himself and craves his own destruction.

Too much of a fucking coward to end it for real. He clings to the nausea his own personality creates in himself. *Which one is me? The one who is sickened, or the one who is sick? Both. I'm a stain. I'm the discount version of Hades. I'm scum. I'm the chewing gum stuck under the shoe of Satan. Fuck! I'm enjoying this. Self-flagellation is my hobby, my kink.*

In fact, Vance craves the dream. *The essential distraction that VR provides from this fucking faux self-aware bullshit.* He sees Tako enter the room and summons him over. As the medi-bot approaches he trips it over with a foot, then reaches into the place where he knows he can turn it off. He enters the control panel with an easy set of codes and tinkers with the bot, thinking, *see if I can program him to sniff underpants or whatnot.* While he tinkers, his mind coughs up a thought of Mortech. Vance registers his position as observer to this thought. *It's like a juicy snot, right out of the nose and onto the street.* He pictures himself looking down at it, *thick and green, kinda chewy. Huh, looks a lot like me. Self-portrait in mucous. Mortech can fuck right off. Let Tanaka handle it, after all the man believes in his own status as a benevolent god.*

As Vance continues to tinker with Tako, he watches a documentary on the activity of cults that characterises the current age. *Aw. Believing in fucked up shit together. Cults are community building!* His current favourite is the neo hunter- gatherers called 'Paleos'. *They potter about in their self-built zoological gardens, weaving friendship bracelets and macrame hammocks to sell to tweens going through their ethno phase. Admiring each other's taut buttocks, listening to shamanic story- telling, warming their hands by the glow of their own radiant health. Fuck no wonder Jesus came again and no one noticed, this shits' pure gold. Oh no, here's the 'Christ consciousness' nut-jobs. Christ has shacked up in the heart of all mankind apparently. Hello Jesus? It's your old buddy, Vance. What's that? Oh -'Fuck off Vance. Coolcoolcool.'* He mentally fist bumps the inner Christ, in Vance's mind he looks a lot like Snoop Dog. *Then there's the Space Brothers. These guys believe that alien space bros vibrating at higher frequencies are visible to humans who have started to vibrate at matching higher frequencies. Jesus is just another Space Bro. So much happy clappy.*

Sad little abandoned Earth, needing wiser beings from beyond to sort out our pathologies for us. Rav comes in and sees him messing with Tako. She raises an eyebrow at him and folds her hands across her chest. *Fuck she's a goddess. Devour me my goddess. Please, eat my slimy soul.*

Right after breakfast, Haruki excuses himself. He sees the question in Idea's face as he leaves and dodges it. *I can't help it, I'm all churned up in my stomach; tied tightly in knots I know I created.* He walks quickly down the road, shooing Asterix and Scruff-pup back home. Asterix follows him, barking at him until he reaches some border line visible only to Asterix. They are in a region of Japan brimming with rice paddies. He sees an eagle aloft overhead and his insecurities are briefly muted by its magnificence. *These feelings for Idea have really got me freaking out.* He comes up to a little bridge over a river and sees down the side of it that there's a walkway beside the river down below. He turns and makes his way down the path. As he walks he starts to feel somewhat soothed by the deeper quiet and cover of green foliage. It's so quiet he can hear the susurration of the wind in the leaves. *I can't remember the last time I heard that? Down here nature simply lives out its life, intrinsic notes of the greater pattern, not consumed by anxieties like my own species, not setting themselves apart. All One. But I am human, and I am anxious. Falling in love is so beautiful; so bloody deadly. I'm not ready. Maybe we should just be friends?* Haruki is tired of himself. *Same old shit.* He wants so desperately to be Present. Apt. Clear. *Wanting to be present so hard prevents me from being present.* There's a little bubbling stream running parallel to the river, so he sits down to meditate by the stream. He gets bitten immediately and mercilessly on the butt by mosquitos. *Yeah the bloody Tao brought you my juicy butt guys. Enjoy.* He sits for a time, and slowly lets it all unravel. He hears a scuff up the path, and Idea comes into view. Feeling quite sheepish Haruki greets her gently,

"Hey."

She lays on her stomach with her back to him and dips one hand in the little creek, swishes it slowly back and forth, feeling the flow of the water. Haruki talks to her back,

"Hey friend. I'm grateful, you are bringing a fresh butt for the little vampire friends to feast on."

He rolls inner eyes at himself *Fresh butt, nice one mate.* Then he stops, decides to quit policing his own behaviour. He laughs gently at himself, *but don't overthink overthinking.* She sits up and moves to sit cross legged across from him, taking his hand in hers. He looks at her face and sees now that she is crying.

"Haruki. I'm all messed up in my heart. I'm freaking out, I'm afraid. I'm sorry"

She holds up their entwined hands,

"this is so sweet. Just this. Can we just do this for a bit?"

Haruki feels a new tenderness for her squeeze his heart. He shuffles a little closer to touch their knees together, then realises he is maybe steeping immediately over the line.

"Oh. Um. Is this ok?"

She nods, wipes the tears from her cheeks with the back of her hand. *It doesn't matter.* They are both crying now. He looks in her eyes and attempts to really open up to her; telling her,

"I'm janky at love."

She nods and replies,

"I'm pretty sure I'm janky at it too. But I can't really remember."

She laughs softly and he wants to hold her close. Her spare hand goes to her stomach and her face crumples inward as she tells him,

"my child died."

She's really crying now, and he does move to hold her. He lets her wet his shoulder with tears and snot. He hears the profound loss deep in her sobbing. There's no time here, he just holds her until she empties. Eventually she surfaces and tucks herself in beside him. They simultaneously stretch out their legs in front of them towards the stream, then both scooch forward to dangle their legs in its coolness. They sit quietly together for a time like this. Haruki throws little leaves into the flow, watching them spin and drift away, all with their own unique fates. He looks at her and says

"my wife left me. For a dominatrix."

Idea covers her mouth with her hand, lets out a little snort. He keeps up with the play, mock serious.

"I should have disciplined her more regularly, evidently."

They both laugh now, and an intimate dance of two conjoined dragonflies appears over the stream. Haruki rolls his eyes.

"Guys. Get a room."

Idea laughs even more loudly.

"This *is* their room."

They both laugh as loudly and as comfortably as they want. They feel at peace with each other. Idea tells Haruki,

"Chester is bathing *again*. Damn he looks fine in his yukata."

Haruki stands up, sticks out his little middle-aged paunch, striking a pose. She splashes him with water, laughing,

"dork!"

Haruki does an even dorkier pose, pulls his pants up very high, giving himself a fine wedgie. He puts on a snooty voice,

"In Osstralia we say 'dag'."

"Ooohh, that's what's wrong with your accent. I thought you'd just smoked waay too much 420 back in the day."

She takes a pretend toke ,

"permanent mellow."

"Heh. Yep it's so hot back in Oz, we're all pretty baked."

She smiles.

"It's obvious you aren't a real Japanese, but I thought you might have just grown up somewhere Western."

"My mum's white. Named me after the famous Japanese author. My dad gifted me the Japanese bits."

She looks sad.

"I did a fair bit of reading while Lost in Space."

Haruki sits back down next to her.

"What a weird chapter of your life."

She stands up, dusts off her butt.

"Our lives. Whoever I used to be would never had seen it coming in a million years I'll bet. This life is kooky." She holds out a hand for him, "take a walk?"

They walk together, an easy amble. Their hands each make their way into a little embrace of their own. Haruki and Idea pretend not to notice. *But it's so nice.*

"Maybe you'll find your name here, in the north?" Haruki says.

She stops.

"I think maybe I never wanted us to find Varvara. I'm not sure I need to know the person who signed her consent forms. I think maybe I'm learning how to grieve. Letting me be. Do we need to drag around our pasts so tightly?"

Haruki says, "I hope the old badger's ok. I didn't think I'd care, but it turns out I do. Wonder where she is? Wonder how Tanaka's doing?"

"Shall we turn back? Michiko was whipping up a frenzy in the kitchen when I left. She's like the food version of holiday marketing. Christmas, hot on the heels of Halloween."

Haruki laughs. *She's witty. Witty and pretty.*

She stops and puts both hands over her face while groaning with embarrassment.

"I can't believe I ever bought the space reverie. It took a while for my logical mind to bust it up."

Haruki snaps his fingers,

"We all believe in our dreams while we're in the midst of them. I think it's cool you figured it out. Got lucid."

She still looks sheepish,

"I think it was Tanaka weening me off the drugs."

Haruki smirks,

"I'll bet Tanaka's back in Tokyo kissing all the vampire princesses awake. The gay prince charming. It's kind of a good anime plot."

She looks a bit put out.

"We can't be friends. Anime is mainly terrible."

Haruki takes mock umbrage, stalks away, then puts his hands in his pockets and waits for her to catch up, telling her,

"I don't like ALL anime! How can you say that anyway? You are currently in Japan! What about Miyazaki?"

She looks puzzled

"Miyazaki?"

He feels himself about to launch into a rant, then stops. *She's teasing me.*

◇◇◇◇◇◇◇◇◇◇◇◇◇

Vance wakes. A pair of finely tooled cherry red brogues rest on the corner of his pillow, filling his field of vision. The brogues are accompanied by a pair of lilac socks, featuring tiny amanita mushrooms wearing sunglasses. The shoes are abruptly removed from his pillow, in the meantime 'accidently' kicking him in the face. *It's Lennox. The little French fucker.*

"Bon. The princess, she awakes. Or was it the toad? I always get those two mixed up."

Vance rolls his eyes,

"how did you find me?"

Lennox stands, gestures to the pearlescent sheen of his three piece suit. He turns about and Vance sees that from this angle the cloth appears to turn invisible. Lennox has always been a nerd for textile tech.

Lennox quips, "I am not just the jenioos for fashion."

He walks over to the bed and puts his face right up against Vance's. Vance can smell his sour coffee breath coupled with his heady cologne. He hisses quietly "also what was it...hmmmm? Oh yes. Fuck you."

He slaps Vance, once, sharply on the cheek. He looks deadly serious. *I have never seen Lennox look genuinely serious.*

"Selfish little child. Tell me now what the fuck you've done to the vampires?"

Vance is confused, "*done* to them?"

Lennox throws his hands in the air and starts to pace. Stops. He is enraged. "Don't play coy with me, leetle goth hacker fuckwit bullshit. We cannot wake them up. Tanaka's weaning them off the drugs and it makes zero difference."

Vance gets out of bed and slumps in the chair.

"Weaning them off the drugs? What the fuck? He's started the awakening protocols already?"

Lennox kicks the drip stand across the room; it wheels across and hits the bedside table, teeters, then settles upright.

"Hades is dead. You know this. Varvara is missing. After OccSN had his heart attack Tanaka started the process of weaning the babies off their meds. He neglected to consult us, as you'd expect from Tanaka. The important thing to note is: It hasn't worked. We don't know what to do."

Lennox pounds a fist into his palm,

"Tanaka! Suddenly 'Mr. Decisive' doesn't know what to do."

Then he grows deadly calm and fixes Vance with an ice cold stare.

"I suspect you. You, the filthy suburban parasite fake."

Vance takes this in, becoming silent for an extended moment. Then he looks up quizzically at Lennox.

"Wait. What? Tanaka 'doesn't know what to do'?"

"Oui. He is having... what to call this? An Heepy episode."

Vance laughs aloud, his eyes wide open with glee, tears spring to his eyes. Lennox looks pleased despite himself. Vance looks him straight in the eye and tells him,

"Lennox. I did nothing to the podlings. I created them their sick little dreamscapes only. I'm a poser, a hollow man. You are correct, I AM a parasite fake."

Lennox nods slowly. Evidently he believes him.

"Well. Put on your big girl pants, no? Tell Dr. 'Mummy knows best' that you are needed down at the lab. You need to excuse yourself and come help clean up the mess you had a hand in creating."

Vance looks callow.

"I did the fucking job I was asked to do. I'm done."

Lennox indicates the leather lawyer's satchel beside the chair.

"I brought you your contract. Old fashioned style. I thought you might forget the terms. Your contract runs until the *completion* of the first trial."

Vance eyes the satchel for a moment, then goes to the chair and calmly sits in it, crossing one leg over the other, relaxed now, he's realised something about Lennox, *I get it*. Lennox waits for him to speak. He draws an elaborate stopwatch from his vest pocket and begins to swing it idly back and forth. Vance points to the watch,

"this! All this is just another one of your elaborate performances, designed to deflect attention from who is really culpable here. You swore by your confidence in the efficacy of the identity 'adjustment'. That's what to blame here, and you know it. It's you who is to blame! It's you who is the fake."

He leans back, satisfied that he has hit it bang on.

I've got him by his little balls now. Lennox goes to the window and appears to be looking out. He speaks quietly without turning to face Vance; almost speaking just to himself,

"I retain the keys to the old identities. This is a non-issue."

He turns to face Vance now, leaning back against the window, one foot crossed over the other. It takes Vance a moment to read this new face. It seems curiously authentic. This is a face Vance has never before witnessed on Lennox. Lennox is always on stage, always seems on the threshold of an elaborate bow. *But is this just the ace up his sleeve?* Vance looks away and the silence becomes awkward. Then, he gets it, this time for real. He perceives in Lennox the twin of himself. *Is it possible for either of us to actually ever just be real?* They share an unspoken moment, information signals travel across the room, inner servers communicate, packages of unspoken data are exchanged. Lennox replaces the watch in his pocket.

"Tanaka reports Occupant XE is recovering quite well. I have not yet activated her keys, she is apparently not yet ready to remember her old identity."

Vance rises from the chair and begins to change out of his hospital pajamas. He collects his essentials and messages Rav. Lennox waits, subdued.

"Within her pod, XE apparently had a strong desire to awaken from the reverie. She became lucid within it..."

He walks towards Vance and reaches only about chest height on him. He looks up into Vance's face with a fierce expression.

"We *can* resolve this. We *Will* resolve this. We behave here like whining toddlers. I see that you have seen this. We must prove that we are the genius' that we say we are. We must prove we are not just a pack of rampant narcissists, empty shells only."

Vance summons a self-drive and they go directly to Mortech, messaging Tanaka en route using the Five email. *Perhaps Varvara will be flushed out of her baba yaga hut in the woods, or wherever she is.* By the time they convene in room 9, Vance has at least the beginnings of an idea.

"What if we shift up the reveries, insert a few glitches here and there. Phase it out in the same way that Tanaka has approached the drugs? Kind of like a sunset."

He ignores Lennox' little sardonic grin at his metaphor. Lennox removes his suit jacket and rolls up his shirt sleeves,.

"Bon. This makes sense. Each of us must apply this technique to his own expertise. I myself will attempt to slowly re- incorporate some of the more... uncomfortable aspects of their former identities BEFORE they wake instead of after as planned. If they wanted so badly to escape their former lives, this could be like the pin in the arse that wakes them up. The mosquito spoiling the ambience so to speak, haha. We must actually collaborate, quell surprise!"

Vance wonders, not for the first time, whether Lennox is actually even French, the schtick is so thick. Tanaka enters the room, wearing a simple linen shirt rather than the full stiff get-up. Vance double takes. *Is that a smile? He really has gone Hippy.* Lennox fills Tanaka in on their current insights. Tanaka brings his hands together and Vance thinks, *some things will never change.*

"So. We act finally like a team. We have been islands with vast tracts of ocean between them. This is good. Very good. Perhaps we shall no longer have to work to navigate our disconnection."

He looks at each of them in turn, and then seemingly at a blank space behind them. Vance turns and is astonished to see a man with wild hair, spectacles and a drab shirt. He nudges Lennox and whispers,

"who is that?"

Lennox laughs uproariously at this.

"You say you are the genius! Yet you cannot count to five?"

Then he whispers, "he is hard to remember, yes? It is 'The Mathematician'. This is the first time you see him?"

Vance nods.

"Who did you think was the fifth member?"

Vance is defensive,

"I thought it was Hades!"

Lennox leans even further in, conspiratorial now, he whispers,

"I myself see him rarely. Tanaka seems to be able to focus longest on him. The other day, he spoke! he said only four words, 'Look to the pattern'."

Vance takes this on board and drops it into his subconscious mind to work on like a koan.

Tanaka speaks, "If you are finished? So. Let us begin."

Idea has become somewhat obsessed with outfitting herself more suitably. *I can't wear Tanaka's preppy get-up one second longer.* She goes to Michiko to ask about what shops there are in the tiny town centre. *Only I wonder if all the local women are as miniature as her?* Michiko claps her little hands together. She loves an excuse to go shopping as they rarely leave their isolated paradise.

"Idea-san! There is a small festival, a market on over in Ueda tomorrow! Maybe we will find something there."

Martin excuses himself from the adventure citing the need to work on some 'research'. Michiko nudges Idea at this and whispers to her

"this research, it is a detailed investigation of napping."

Then she laughs and Martin looks at her so fondly, Idea is reminded with a little pang of how Haruki looks at herself. *I can't really believe it. What does he see in me? It's definitely not my looks, all shades of brown, and lumpy in the wrong places.* Then she drops it. *My eyes are not his eyes. Thank goodness.*

Next day they climb into Michiko and Martin's 4WD and road trip into Ueda, taking Scruff-pup along with them. Asterix stays home with Martin, he is not good with cities. Nagano prefecture is like a beautiful postcard from the past, a portrait of simpler times. Idea begins to think of Tokyo as of a difficult ex. When they arrive at the market, Idea finds it is delightfully Bohemian. She is also grateful Japanese women prefer their clothes on the voluminous side and is able to find a few pieces that delight her as well as fit her. Later in the day there will be a mini concert; there are apparently a few quite famous musicians who live in the region. At the concert they manage to find seats together at the back. For some reason Idea notices two ancient grandmothers seated in front of them, two rows down. One of the woman is white, and one Japanese. Michiko waves at the Japanese one and Idea notices Scruff-pup is agitated. He jumps off Ideas' lap and runs under the white woman's seat. He stands up with his feet on her knees, barking joyfully. Idea stands to go and retrieve him, apologising her way out of the row she was seated in. The old woman takes Scruff-pup into her lap and turns around to face Idea, she is weeping. Idea freezes in place, astonished. *Varvara. Isn't it?* Haruki also stands, then Chester, polite Japanese voices object behind them. The Japanese grandmother next to Varvara signals that they should all move aside. Michiko ushers them as a group into the shade of trees beyond the seating area. For a while no-one speaks but Scruff-pup, now making little urgent groans, his backside looking as though it will be wiggled off completely by his tail. It can no longer be called wagging, having become more like a circular propellor. Idea feels pain in her heart. *Scruff-pup! I don't want to say goodbye to you.* Varvara holds out a regal hand to quell Scruff-pup and he is shushed immediately with this one gesture. She holds out the other arthritic hand towards Idea; oddly introducing herself as "Jana."

Haruki speaks up now, asking "Jana?"

The old woman nods.

"Varvara is dead, was never a real person. She was a mask of protection only. I had forgotten this. I was born Jana Zmolek. I am from Czechoslovakia, I was orphaned in the war. This seemed to destroy me. Yet here I am. Michiko rescued me."

She drops these bombs rapid-fire and turns to the small Japanese grandmother beside her, evidently also a Michiko. These two Michikos bow solemnly to one another, then giggle, holding their hands over their mouths as they laugh. Apparently they already know each other very well, In fact Michiko number 2 is a some-time neighbour of theirs in Komoro. The group move away to sit at the side of the river nearby where there is a bench for the two grandmothers to sit. Jana pats the space left beside her for Idea. She takes her hand, it is cool to the touch. "I will not take Hermes from you. This would be selfish, I can see he has both found his new family and drawn us together. Hermes, truly the messenger! I would like him to come and visit with me for a time however?"

Idea just nods. She feels like hugging her; she feels awkward, and she feels strange. They sit quietly together. Chester and Haruki withdraw to give them space and go to sit on the banks of the river, out of earshot, but not far away. Idea takes a few slow breaths to soothe herself. She feels shaken and claustrophobic and can't think what to say. Then she blurts out,

"I don't want to know who I was. Before."

Jana simply nods, serene. She turns to face Idea and says

"Despite your grief when I met you and despite Varvara's self- centred mania, I could see that you were possessed of a rare and quiet strength. I reflect now that it was the strength of one in fact not self-possessed; one perhaps free of the possessiveness many of us feel over our identities. Perhaps you were shocked out of it by the strength of a pain unendurable. I saw you as one in fact willing to be broken. One surrendered. I will admit at the time Varvara read this with contempt. Now that I am remembered to myself as Jana, I can see the strength in it... the wisdom." Idea shakes her head no,

"you said that I wanted to commit suicide. This does not fit with what you say about me."

Jana now looks her full in the face, her expression is open and guileless

"you were ready to kill the suffering self, yes. To end her suffering. I understand this."

Scruff-pup, *Hermes*, sits at Jana's feet, Idea perceives an invisible leash tethering him to her.

Michiko speaks, "you say your name is Idea? This is very cute, ne?"

Idea squirms a little and asks Michiko,

"has Jana told you about Mortech?"

Michiko nods, "Hai."

Idea turns to Jana and can't help revealing a little pity for her;

"It was so lonely. In the reverie..."

Jana looks her in the eye,

"the fantasy of a broken woman, one so frightened of loss that she was unable to love."

Idea pauses to reflect,

"when I think about it, it was strangely helpful in there. To have the space to really feel the grief; free of all judgements save my own."

They sit peacefully together for a time, each in her own thoughts.

Michiko lifts her head and watches a majestic purple butterfly float by, gesturing excitedly to it with her tiny hand.

"O-Murasaki! There are still butterflies in Japan. For this I am very grateful, ne?"

Idea points at Haruki and Chester,

"I'm grateful friends still exist."

She looks sideways at Jana,

"Grateful *the Earth* still exists. God! Varvara!"

Jana tells Idea, "Varvara longed for destruction. She wanted to break everything. Her heart was broken, she sought the immensity of its reflection out in the world."

She points with one finger to her heart and her eyes are both bright and fierce,

"I have learned somehow that in fact The Heart cannot break. It is boundless."

Idea begins to cry now. Hermes transfers himself to sit on her feet. Jana places her hand softly on Idea's back,

"Idea. I want to offer you your old name. You will be amazed at how it suits you. You do not have to take it up again, you still have the choice."

Idea draws in a long breath, then slowly lets it ebb away.

"Ok. Perhaps I'm ready as I can be."

Jana looks for a moment at Michiko, then joins her hands together and flutters them simply like a butterfly.

"Your name was Bianhua. This is a Mandarin word from the Tao meaning 'Transformation'; like that of a caterpillar to a butterfly."

Idea is stunned; speechless. Eventually Jana speaks.

"I wonder who your parents were... or perhaps still are?"

Idea is very quiet on the ride home from their day trip into Ueda. Haruki wonders what passed between her and Varvara, *Or should I say: Jana; oof! I know she'll talk about it when and if she wants to. Scruff-pup has reclaimed his role as Hermes for a bit, but Jana assures Idea that he will return to her.* Haruki looks out the window for a while; his mind ticks over details of the day, until he suddenly receives a psychic email from Totoro. It is eloquent, simply a picture of his empty food bowl, followed up rapidly with an image of his miffed face. *Buddy, I'm kinda*

busy here. There's this girl... In response to this thought Haruki sees the cheeks on Toto's miffed face become even more square, the whiskers now perfectly horizontal. Chester looks up from his phone, "Tanaka needs me back home."

Idea looks stricken, horrified. Chester smiles at her kindly "Perhaps Martin and Michiko?"

Haruki feels torn. He looks at Idea.

"This will sound super 'woo', but I get these psychic emails from my cat." Her face quickly changes from very upset to very amused, and she cocks her head at him in a classic Scruffles pose.

Haruki tells her, "I'm serious! Anyway, he's not happy with the food situation back home."

Chester laughs heartily, going so far as to slap his thigh "this is the best thing I've heard in a while. Psychic emails from your cat! Bahahaha!"

Haruki slumps down into his chair muttering "well, it's always the same email."

This makes them laugh even harder. Idea takes his hand, but the corners of her lips still twitch a little.

"Go to him. I'll come join you in a bit. I promise. I feel like the mountains aren't quite done with me."

Martin and Michiko are pleased to have Idea stay longer with them. Haruki and Chester drag their feet through the process of leaving and decide to stay one more night. Haruki sends Toto an email in his mind, *Be there tomorrow buddy, promise.* There's no reply, meaning *step on it, human.* Haruki lingers outside the yurt with Idea before bed. Chester has retired early.

Haruki asks her, "Want to go for a little walk?"

As they walk through the grass, seemingly hundreds of tiny frogs scatter in their wake. They come to a grove of trees, and Haruki is horrified to see them swarming with large insects. He stops in his tracks. Idea puts her hand on his shoulder and leans in a little against him.

"Wait. H. Michiko showed me these. Come."

She leads him over to the trees and he sees that the insects are in fact just empty shells; abandoned husks.

Idea tells him, "they're cicadas, recently hatched."

They both tune in now to the loud music of cicadas in the night. Haruki widens his eyes.

"Huh. Kind of beautiful. Kind of gross."

Idea takes his arm in hers and they decide to stroll down the road to the creek, enjoying the warm summer night, balanced perfectly by the freshness of the mountain air. On the way Haruki gives space to let Idea tell her story.

"Jana gave me my old name. It's incredible actually."

Haruki waits patiently, though he's bursting to know, but she looks away. "I'm not ready to talk about it. I want to write about it; to let it sit inside me for a bit. Is that ok?"

Haruki grabs her by the hand, they run down the little slope to the creek and Idea gasps. The night is alive with fireflies. Haruki and Idea walk bedside the creek, enchanted. She holds out her hand and a firefly lands on it. Before it can fly away, Haruki makes a little dome over her hand with one of his, and he squints at the firefly through a crack in his fingers, then leans back to give her a turn. She grins and spies on the firefly, then they both let it go, releasing it to its important business. Haruki gently turns her to face him and moves in, so the tips of their bare toes are just touching. *She's actually quite tall. I didn't realise. We are exactly the same height.* He takes both her hands in his. *It's so romantic, the fireflies. Would it be too much?* He swallows a little nervous breath, almost hiccups, and asks her,

"do you like nose kissing?"

She blushes, asking "nose kissing? Sounds a bit... gross somehow?"

He shakes his head no, his lips are softly parted, his breathing speeds up a little.

"It's not. It's definitely really nice."

She closes her eyes, stills; waits for him. He moves in slowly, so gently, first putting his arms around her waist, then tenderly holding her back. He touches the tip of her nose with his, so lightly. He nuzzles her so softly. He makes his way to her neck and nuzzles her behind the ear, whispering to her huskily,

"Now it's your turn."

He feels her hands press into his back, pulling them even closer together. He can feel her heart beating against his chest, then she nuzzles him in return. He opens his eyes, she's watching him, he tells her,

"hey, you *do* know about nose kissing, you nose about it."

She playfully squeezes one of his butt cheeks and whispers in his ear, "you dag."

He finds that he has let himself grow hard, wanting her. But it's not urgent. *There's no need to be impatient, everything will unfold as it should.* They lay down together beside the creek, fireflies drift about them like fairy folk at a ball. They lay together just like this, nose to nose, breathing in each other's breath, feeling each other's heartbeats. Timeless. The sky suddenly opens, and it starts to rain, hot summer rain, but a little bit shivery in the night. They let it rain, soaking them to the skin, and then they kiss. They kiss urgently, like there will never be enough time to tell each other absolutely everything, but also languorously, like there's all the time in all the world. *Her lips are so beautifully shaped, so clever.*

Her scent... He stops to just breath her in. *She's so, so beautiful.* As they part in the morning, it's very hard to leave. Haruki cannot believe he's going home just to feed his cat. *Preposterous.* They hug. Chester winks at them and gets in the self-drive. Idea pushes him back slightly to look in his eyes;

"meet me in Kyoto? I just remembered that I always wanted to go there."
Haruki smiles and his voice catches on the way out,
"I love Kyoto."
then leaves a gap, lets it be unspoken for now, knowing that his eyes speak volumes.

Haruki and Chester are driven back to Tokyo by the self-drive. They hang out companionably together for the ride. *Ol' Chester Kask. He feels like family now.*
Chester speaks up, "we left the cutest ones behind."
Haruki chuckles,
"we are going to meet up in Kyoto, Idea and I. Hopefully little Scruffs will come along too."
Chester looks misty eyed and tells him,
"I've been trying to persuade Tanaka for a while for us to live in Kyoto."
Haruki leans forward a little in his seat,
"you two really love each other, huh?"
Chester smiles warmly and points his chin at Haruki, spreading his hands out wide, saying
"Love? My friend this crazy life is given to us, simply so that we can love. To lose love, then find it again. Make love. Pretend it doesn't exist. Fight over it. Surrender to it..."
Haruki smiles to himself *Chester has the most beautiful voice, like warm honey. Maybe I'm in love with HIM too?* He stores this away to share

with Idea and imagines she would say,
"We're all of us a little in love with Chester Kask."

11.

Symbiosis

Vance sneaks a look at the message on his phone; it's Rav, she is furious; worried sick. Vance is relieved she's got no clue where to find him, but he messages her that he'll return when he's done. It's late in the night, or more apt; early in the morning. He's in room 3 at Mortech, the fabrication lab, and he is deep in the reveries. It's dangerous for him, the sweet loss of himself into fantasy, but he feels something has returned to him, some sort of long lost 'substance.' *Am I re-materialising?* He feels a new type of engagement with his work. He is still shy of putting a finger on exactly what it is, so he holds it close to his chest, hiding it from the searchlight of his critical mind. He senses that it is precious. *New.*

Tanaka enters the lab, bearing a load, a stack of bedding. Vance can't help slumping in his chair, sinking down behind the giant monitor he had been staring through. Tanaka places his burden against the wall at the far side of the lab and comes over to Vance. He leans against the desk opposite him, then draws a small wooden puzzle from his pocket, and tinkers with it. His shirt is open at the collar. *Who is this guy? And what have you done with Tanaka?*

"Janssen-san. Sumimasen,"

he gestures at the stack he laid against the wall,

"I bring you a futon, bedding..."

Vance looks at Tanaka's face and sees that it is open. Clear. He had always seen it as narrow, unreadable. He offers what he hopes is a respectful smile,

"Thanks."

Tanaka turns to leave, and he feels himself stand up, bowing like Tanaka himself would bow,

"Tanaka Sensei. I mean it... Thank you."

Tanaka smiles with his eyes then leaves quietly. Lennox comes in soon after with konbini style bento boxes and tall cans of coffee for the both of them and he's changed into something nondescript. *Never seen that before.* Lennox looks down at his clothes, gives a cheeky grin and smooths down his elegant moustache, telling Vance

"I realised I shouldn't be so relentlessly distracting. We have work to do."

They banter over their food for a while, then Vance feels a third presence in the room. His eyes are drawn over to the computer he was working on earlier. *It's him. The Mathematician.* Vance feels a little like he's witnessing Santa delivering the presents, then feels the tide of his attention receding until finally he forgets and turns back to Lennox. Lennox winks, makes a kind of wibbly wobbly sign with his hand. Vance is mystified, but mirrors the sign, sniggering and rolling his eyes. He realises he enjoys Lennox. *What a fucking kook.*

"Hey L. Take me through the details on the adjusted identities once more."

He closes his eyes and lets his mind settle as he listens to Lennox going through the identities one by one. He sees himself within himself climbing down a metal ladder rung by rung until he reaches the bottom of a dark well. Slowly the bottom of the well dissolves and he is floating in nothingness. Phantoms appear around him, bringing a kind of phosphorescence to the gloom. In this place his mind goes over the reveries he actualised from Varvara's instruction. He is searching for loose threads, scanning for data matches with the ego narratives he is concurrently listening to Lennox repeat. *Smoke and mirrors.* The narratives he listens to become symbols only, sounds. The identity construction that is Vance begins to abate, to cease the activity of anxious self-justification. Vance thins out, becomes translucent, and yet there is Someone here. *Who?* This feels like peace, a rare spaciousness Vance seldom drops into. It adds to the process his mind is submerged within, widens the lens, loosens biases, lays down weapons. He opens his eyes. Lennox also has closed eyes; is far away and yet he feels more present. He looks brighter to Vance, like a candle flame illuminates his face in a dark room. Lennox senses his gaze, ceases speaking and opens his eyes to look at Vance. Vance feels it, there is trust between them. Vance scribbles his encryption codes on his notepad then slides it across to Lennox,

"go over the reveries. Please."

Lennox looks genuinely surprised. Vance stops, something occurs to him. He asks Lennox,

"Hey, did you ever read about mycelium?"

Lennox grins softly.

"You are also becoming the hippy?"

Vance feels the receptivity in Lennox despite this small barb.

"Mycelium is the network of fungi that webs a forest. It turns out that millennia ago, plants and fungi co-evolved. This played out not as the typical human assumption of a battle for supremacy, but as a symbiosis. It was an interweaving; a mutual benefit."

He feels a little uncomfortable now. His customary armour against vulnerability begins to re-assert its programs. Vance feels this in his body as a kind of universal tightening. *But wait.* This time, he feels resolute, he expands instead into simple curiosity, then observes his body and mind from the same receptive state he slipped into before. He notices peripherally that The Mathematician has joined them now, but he decides not to make a big deal of it, just lets it be. Instead, Vance and Lennox open to entrain themselves to the intriguing energy field that is the consistent emanation of The Mathematician. Their conscious minds drop away; memory creation ceases.

There is only The Pattern, Observed. It is timeless, this place that is not a place.

Vance returns to his conscious mind as though he merely blinked. There is no record within him of what transpired, yet the fingerprint of understanding is felt within him. Lennox stands and goes to read the reveries. Vance allows his body to take him to the futon in the corner, to lay it out, to submit to a sleep that is the deepest he has surrendered to since childhood.

Tanaka curls into the warmth of Chester's long body and allows himself to be completely held. He notices the strength in this softness. He can feel how much this softening of his nourishes Chester in turn. Chester feels to him like a hearth fire, glowing faithfully in the silence of a sleeping home, Tanaka, just a small kitten asleep by its embers with a belly full of warm milk. His mind turns to the work in progress at the lab. He feels in his body the new symbiosis of knowledge between the remaining four members of the Mortech project. *This is very good.* Chester has told him about Varvara. *She is dead, in her place a sweet*

and stately grandmother called Jana. She wants nothing more of Mortech. So. Let her spend her twilight years in peace. Tanaka mentally lights an incense stick to Varvara, *a battle scarred warrior finally able to lay down her weapons and return home.* He pictures her evanescence and gives thanks for grace finally allowed entrance to work its healing on a wounded heart. He notices the new absence of anxiety in his body in regard to his work. He notices Chester looking into his face, he gently touches the tip of Tanaka's nose with his finger, then transfers it to point to the Japanese maple in the garden visible through their bedroom window. *It is kouyou⁴⁷, the first leaves of aki⁴⁸ adorn her.* They sit up in bed together, then move as one to go out and visit her; *Momiji-sama⁴⁹.* Tanaka stands in the garden with Chester and feels a rumble in his stomach. He chuckles and pats it, saying,

"Shokuyoku no aki"

Chester winks back,

"the autumn appetite? I think mine might be year round."

Chester now leads him by the hand and sits him at the breakfast table. He takes off his pajama shirt, revealing his glorious, luxuriant chest hair.

"I'm going to make you Mulgipuder⁵⁰, please do absolutely nothing."

Tanaka leans back, obedient, relaxing into simple admiration of Chester. *I'm home.*

Haruki sits on his couch with Totoro sprawled in his lap. Every now and

---

47   *Autumn leaves changing colours*

48   *Autumn*

49   *an affectionate and respectful title for the Japanese Maple*

50   *traditional Estonian savoury breakfast pudding*

then Toto sinks a possessive claw into Haruki's thighs. Haruki endures it. Totoro has let his disdain over the situation of appalling neglect be known, and now rests, sated, suitably appeased. Haruki barely registers Toto's ample weight, his phone lays at some distance from his hand, very recently tossed aside. Idea has messaged him.

"H. I'm understanding that to be together, we must first be apart. I'm asking for a period of no contact. I want us to meet in Kyoto as agreed, but let's meet fresh, as though we've never met. I hope you understand. I'm working myself out. With love, I."

Of course, this is probably wise, probably reasonable, but what Haruki really feels is rejection. Spread atop the rejection is a deep shame that he feels rejected. These two are but the icing. Beneath these lurks an emptiness, a dark crevasse. Haruki knows this crevasse, it is the guardian at the gate of that most painful place, abandonment. He has been here before. *I can't feel that again. Not ever again.* His mind adds to this the shame of being incapable of learning from his mistakes. His tears slip down his cheeks silently, their composition is bitter, highly acidic. Totoro is oblivious to this playing out of inner tragedy, he is whole, replete. Haruki finds himself craving the crevasse. This empty place can provide a relief from the shame, the rejection. When he enters the crevasse, shame and rejection become concepts only, he sees that they are the same thing. He feels a kind of relief, breaths out a long sigh. He has no feelings here. Nothing touches him. Abandonment roils like a leviathan beneath, but he merely notes its presence, it is not relevant to him.

Haruki goes about his days now from the empty place. He has not understood that this is a semblance of detachment only. His mind is only too happy to fabricate whatever it thinks he needs. Haruki does not see that he play acts. That he is hollow, hijacked, going through the motions.

There's a mantra looping in his mind. *Love never works out. Love is an illusion. Egos just consume each other and leave nothing but empty shells.* This mantra seems not to touch him. *I'm cool. I'm Fine.*

He meets Hiro and Felipe down at Tsuki. Felipe leaves his hand on Haruki's back overly long and looks at him too closely in the eye. Haruki laughs too loud, drinks too much, craves a smoke.

He rides his bike about. He logs in and makes some coin in the VR arenas. He eats many bags of salty snacks on the floor of his kitchen. He keeps his phone at a distance, he watches anime he has seen many times before. Totoro orbits him like a moon, always close, but self-contained and enigmatic.

He plays pachinko for the first time and wins a frying pan. He lingers overly long in bakeries, his paunch swells in complement.

He avoids Hoboneko park.

One morning Totoro vomits on his bed. Haruki is enraged. He chases Totoro from the house, wielding the pachinko frying pan aloft. Totoro disappears. Haruki cleans his food and water bowls and leaves out biscuits each day. Hoping. There's evidence Toto is eating the food, but he no longer chooses to spend time at the apartment when Haruki is present.

Haruki walks around bent slightly forward, his head seeming to confidently lead his slumping body, like they've had a disagreement.

He is tired. Exhausted. He does not want to leave his apartment. He spends more and more time in VR watching his different blockchains grow. He does not notice the vibrant colours of autumn about him. This is not like him.

Deep in the night Haruki comes awake. The light of the full moon silhouettes Totoro on his windowsill. Totoro leaps from the sill to his bed and pins him down by coming to stand upright on his chest. His four paws feel hard and painful. The plume of his tail weaves back and forth like a snake emerging from a basket. Then he leaves Haruki's chest as abruptly as he arrived, returns to the windowsill and sits like a sentinel in the light of the moon. He regards Haruki with an unreadable face, then licks his paw, cleans his whiskers, and leaves without a backward glance. In that moment Haruki feels Totoro's exit like a body blow, it leaves him bereft. He feels himself cracked open like an egg and he crumples to the floor beside his bed. Tears spill from his eyes, he moans like a wounded animal, over and over again. Snot drips from his nose freely into the clothes piled across his floor in drifts, he drools, he gnashes, he thrashes about. He begins to smack himself in the face, to punch his own arms, his face is a rictus of pain. He slumps face down and his fingers grip his stinking socks white knuckled. After a time, Haruki is emptied fully, what felt overwhelming now recedes, abates. The tide carries his stories of abandonment out to sea and dissipates them into salt. True emptiness rides the returning waves and claims him now. There is only the sound of his breathing, the rhythm of his heart beating. Grace dawns over this sea like the returning sun.
There is no more story of Haruki, only *this*, as close as close.

Lennox lingers at the lab. He lurks. He pictures himself as an anxious mid-century father at the hospital waiting for his child to be born, chain smoking, a circle of sweat staining the back of his shirt. Everything has been set in motion, the awakening protocol not just amended, but metamorphosed. *I await my butterflies to dream they are men once more.* The Four, as he thinks of them now, mirror their proteges, also amended and surrendered to their metamorphoses. *Tanaka has softened, learned to bend, to accept help, to concede to other points of view. Vance has discovered he has a soul, has re-united it with his living body. Myself? Bon. It is discovered that I truly care. That I actually enjoy collaboration. And The other one?*

He raises mental hands, palms up to the ceiling. *Poff. How should I know?* They share staff members now, Gareth Chin taps quietly in the corner at the staff interface, make believing Lennox is simply furniture, *just the desk lamp.* Lennox sinks fluidly now to the floor, a cross-legged sprite, it would not seem amiss if he pulled a wooden flute from his pocket. A figure emerges from the gloom. It is a tiny old woman, a grandmother. She seems to bring her own light with her into the lab, it is an ambience, a soft glow. Lennox does not stir, simply watches as though she is a ghost he does not wish to disturb at her rituals. *It cannot be her?* Gareth Chin sees her, stands hurriedly and brings the swivel chair over to her. She sinks gratefully into it. She is like a tiny glow worm, wrinkled and luminous. *Or perhaps numinous is more apt?* She nods peaceably at him. Sucks her teeth. She folds her misshapen hands in her lap. *It IS her.* Lennox stands and sweeps her his most eloquent bow,

"Madam?"

She smiles beatifically at him and answers with simply

"Jana."

Lennox folds his arms and leans back against the nearest pod. She lifts a hand to indicate the lab occupants,

"how fare they?"

Lennox smiles gently and says to her,

"they 'ave been kissed, but awaken more slowly than the legends make out."

She burrows somewhere beneath her wrap, draws out a small rustling bag and proffers it toward him,

"Lemon drop?"

He takes one, pops it in his mouth. They exist in companionable lemony silence for a time. Finally, her lemon drop apparently dissolved, she speaks, gesturing at the pods with her chin.

"They'll need me. When they wake."

Gareth has drawn near, like a small boy to a campfire, his marshmallow ready on its twig. Lennox stands to study the pod interface, *it seems the pod occupants don't want to miss their cue, OccupantGA appears to be surfacing.* He straightens up, waves Gareth to attend to OccupantNI, draws his phone from his pocket and sends private messages to Tanaka, to Vance. Jana rises slowly, it is clear her body is in some pain. She shuffles to OccupantTY. Lennox sees *that one* enter the lab, then make his way to the pod of OccupantAB. Lennox hastens to the staff interface and messages,

"all hands on deck."

OccupantTY awakes. Jana stands over him like a grandmother waiting at the end of that long tunnel to the other side. He's fighting it and has awakened enraged. Jana says nothing, only looks down at him with infinite patience, then abruptly Lennox can hear the man sobbing, disoriented, she reaches toward him, and holds her cool hand across his brow. Tanaka enters with Nakamura close behind, was apparently already waiting nearby in room 7. He hastens to the final pod, OccupantLU. Medical staff enter, Lennox ushers them to assist Jana. She leaves with OccTY to go to the medical hospice facility ready and waiting to receive the awakened occupants. Then, it's a waiting game. At some point Vance enters and takes charge of OccupantNI with Gareth to assist him. The next 24 hours see the occupants gradually awakening and being whisked away for recovery. Occupant GA, though first to show signs of awakening, takes longest to surface. Lennox stays by his side, Nakamura waits backup with Lennox, she's gone to get them each a can of coffee from the vending machine down the street. Then, in the silence of the empty lab, it happens. The pod hatch opens, Lennox leans in. GA is silent, staring with incomprehension at Lennox. Then his eyes clear, he reaches out his hand and Lennox takes it, and tells him, "welcome back."

12.

Body memory

Idea considers her reflection in the mirror. Her hair is sticking up like a brush, growing back in earnest. *It's strange that I saw myself with long hair in the reverie. I still don't really want to see this 'Hypnotist'. I don't want to simply resume my old identity. But what's stopping me? The truth is I feel reborn. I feel free. Who was this Bianhua? Was she just a caterpillar?*

Idea scoffs, laughs at herself in the mirror, speaks aloud to her reflection, "caterpillar? So that makes you some kind of big brown butterfly?"

Later that day she fossicks about in Martin's shed and comes across a silver bicycle. The vinyl name stuck on the cross bar is Pegasus. She wheels it out to show him.

"Ah! Pegasus! Once my trusty steed. My beloved."

He comes over to kneel beside the bicycle and wipes the seat with his hand, "now you are dusty. Abandoned."

He looks up at Idea and tells her,

"She was a custom build. I was once very much the nerd for all things bicycle. Now? Have I grown old?"

He goes into the shed and comes out with a large spanner.

"You want to take her for a spin? We can adjust the seat."

Idea pauses to reflect, *do I even know how to ride a bicycle?* She feels some kind of reply to this question in her body, *I think I do.* Martin adjusts the seat, and they take Pegasus down to the road. Idea stands with her legs either side of the cross bar for a moment, then takes the leap. She rides, a little wobbly, but she definitely knows how to do it. *A body memory.* Idea rides the bicycle down the road and begins to feel a surge of pure joy. *This is something that I love.* She returns to Martin radiant, and he holds up a hand for a high five, laughing and exclaiming "you are also a nerd for this? Marvellous!"

From then on Idea's horizons are able to expand. She rides out every day and begins to build her own map of the area. One day she rides into Komoro town and spontaneously decides to take the train to Nagano city. A man enters from another carriage and takes the seat opposite her. She can't help but stare, for he is a man something like herself- a 'sort-of-Asian', painted in shades of brown. He notices her staring, and to her embarrassment he comes to sit beside her.

He says, "I don't see many folk who look like me around. Where are you from?" Idea winces. *Awkward, um. No Idea.* She deflects him with a friendly, "you first."

He leans back, folds his arms across his chest.

"Well, I'm a little bit Sri Lankan, a little bit Chinese. There are some white colonialist throwbacks mixed in there too apparently. I was born in Sri Lanka but grew up in Singapore."

Idea feels a bell chime inside her. *Me too. Apparently.* She looks more closely at his face. *He reminds me of someone. Someone other than myself.* She realises she is staring again. She smiles and says

"Sorry. Wow. It's not often I come across someone with a similar origin story to myself."

The next station is announced, and the man stands, looks a little torn, then tells her "That's my station."

He holds his hand up in a wave and goes to the door. He smiles at her as

224

he leaves the train. Idea closes her eyes after he leaves, and a scene enters her mind. She's running through a field of sugar cane. A boy runs ahead of her, laughing. He dodges to one side, and it takes her a moment to change direction in her momentum to chase after him. She's holding a plastic water pistol in her hand. She knows this boy, he is many shades of brown, like her. Her eyes fly open, her heart thumps within her chest, *I know this boy.* For the rest of the train ride, she feels agitated, her mind careens about, finding no purchase. Every time her face becomes visible in the train window opposite her, she can't help staring at it over long, looking for the boy as though she'll locate him in her own face. Then she tries to block the memory out. She is scattered, at odds. When she reaches Nagano, she has an internal epiphany. She had refused the smart phone Tanaka offered her, preferring just a basic method of contact, *just a phone phone.* There was apparently a strong retro trend in 2038 to use these old 'basics' and Tanaka had not questioned her. She realises now she has been steadfastly avoiding the internet since waking from the reverie. *Library, you old monster.* She realises she can simply go to the library in Nagano and use the internet; image search herself and potentially get actual answers, unlike those provided by Library. *This is terrifying.* She leaves the train and finds that she strolls aimlessly about. She does not go to the library. She goes to a bakery instead and eats an incredibly delicious croissant. She walks in a random direction and finds herself at the famous Zenkoji shrine. As she lights an incense stick inside the shrine the little brown boy enters her mind again. In this memory he wears only cheap cotton shorts, is about nine years old. He holds a sparkler aloft and writes his name in the air, *Max.* She remembers him then, *my little brother, Max.* She holds the incense stick and writes with it as though it's a sparkler and with this gesture she remembers what her brother always called her, *Bibi.* In a rush the face of her little son comes to her now. Also, a little brown boy. She sees him on the shore of the sea. He's about four years old. There's a chocolate brown dog, his tongue lolls from the side of his mouth as he runs, he is wet and covered in sand. The little boy is giggling so hard that he staggers about. The dog barks joyfully. Idea's hand goes to her lower belly. *His name was Lim. My little boy. My baby.* She does not recall who Lim's father was. Idea makes her decision. *It will be ok to remember who I was. It's not a trap. I'll hold it lightly. Maybe Max is wondering where I am? And my parents? Are they still alive?* She dials Tanaka's number, *Time to talk to The Hypnotist.*

Lennox waits in his little salon. It is beautifully appointed, boasts velvet armchairs, tasteful ornaments. cushions done in tsutsugaki style. The space has a finely curated palette. He waits for XE to arrive, *Bianhua. Bon. A lovely name. Very apt.* He closes his eyes and allows his sense of boundaries to expand for a moment, unfurling his senses to probe beyond his self-narrative. As he leaves the domain of his identity, he doffs his cap, *This Lennox, he is a funny guy, no?* Bianhua enters the room, her hair is short, like a fluffy brown crown. She is accompanied by Jana. She offers him her hand and introduces herself,

"Call me Bibi. I have started to remember things already... organically."
Lennox steeples his fingers,
"Interesting. Yes, yes. The adjustments could certainly unravel on their own over time I believe, now that you are out of the thrall of the constructed reverie. But you want the keys I have already prepared for you? They are yours to claim."

He gestures to her to take a seat in the armchair opposite himself. Jana sits unobtrusively to one side on the sofa.

"It's just. I remembered my brother. I've got a strong feeling he might be looking for me... my parents also?"

"Ah. Naturellement. Your family. These threads are strong. Now. This process. It might feel like a bit of a bumpy ride. I had to turn some keys in the locks of the other pod occupants to bring them awake. They were not so lucid as yourself. Still, many of them are as yet reluctant to have their old stories returned completely."

Bianhua nods and opens her hands out to the side,

"I feel open to it now. Like my old self is not a trap. Like I can choose how to hold my memories. Hold them lightly. I don't know if this is false confidence." she pauses, "I have this sense of trust. beyond my small self."

Lennox looks over at Jana, she still has that glow. *Trust. There's something in this. I find that I understand. The Self beyond the self.*

He beams at the two women then claps his hands and says

"Bon. Then let us begin. Now, I will let you in on a little secret, the name given to this technique, 'hypnotech', please know this name is merely jargon, mumbo-jumbo to ease the opening of wallets. In fact, the process is not elaborate. I simply hold small keys that perfectly fit waiting locks."

He places headphones over her ears, starts the rhythmic toning that assists his work, then he takes his pocket watch from his vest and puts her under easily. The process includes words linked to corresponding light pressures on certain key points on the body, a pre-programmed map of awakening that lays dormant, waiting for his touch, his input of the correct sequence. He does not hurry Bianhua. He trusts his intuition. *Not everything now. Not yet. Just some things. Important things.*

After the process with Lennox is complete Bianhua sits with Jana in an old fashioned Japanese tearoom, overlooking a garden. Exquisite sweets glisten on a small wooden tray, Jana pours green tea into two small cups. Bibi is surprised to feel that the return to herself feels comfortable, like she has woken from a dream yet again. *But what is dreaming? What is waking? Who am I when I am neither awake nor dreaming? There's something I still need to speak with Jana about, the thing with the spheres.*
"Jana. There's something I want to ask you. About the reverie."
Jana folds her hands in her lap and waits patiently for Bibi to continue.
"Inside. In the reverie. There was a...phenomenon. I experienced, um, sort of archetypal symbols emerging from my chest. It was like I created them, but also as though I sort of 'midwifed' them, like they were born from me. I encapsulated them in spheres and fed the spheres into a receptacle inside the library. Library received this as 'input' and created an infographic about it, about me, about my internal 'thought-scape' so to speak. But you know all this? You wrote it?"
Jana takes a sip from her tea and sitting back, she appears to fall asleep.
She is very, very old after all. I struggle to relate this beatific woman with Varvara. I wonder what transformed her?
Jana opens her eyes, sees Bibi studying her. She smiles.
"I was not asleep. For me presence and absence have become one. No inside, no outside. Do you understand?"
Bianhua recalls her time back on the observation deck, before she 'woke up',
"um. Maybe?"

Jana nods, seems satisfied, takes another sip of tea, gazes out onto the garden. Bibi tries again,

"Jana. The spheres, can you tell me more about this?"

Jana looks into her eyes, then tells Bibi,

"I did not write this thing, this phenomena as you say, into the reverie. It is unique to your own experience. It is your own creation. Intriguing, no?"

She closes her eyes again and subsides. Bibi is stunned. She closes her eyes, as though to search within herself for an answer. *My own creation?* The uncanny feeling of the reverie comes over her once more. She begins to feel claustrophobic, her heart begins to beat more quickly and her throat constricts. She feels *that feeling* in her chest. Then she opens her eyes and looks at Jana. She is napping peacefully, this time Bibi is certain of it. Bianhua looks out at the garden and as she listens to the clink of teacups in the room and the low murmur of voices she feels how she recieves this experiencing inside her. *No inside, no outside... maybe I do understand after all.*

Haruki is surprised to receive a message from Idea letting him know that she's in Tokyo. He's been feeling good, has seen that he has held the persona of Lover a bit too tightly for much of his life. *Time to let go of Romeo and Juliet; the tragedy and the drama.* He sees how he had subconsciously held his ex-wife captive in his mind as a love object. It felt so sweet, so nourishing to love, that he hadn't seen how she wasn't really free to leave him, in terms of his trauma at her departure. Even though he always blithely assured himself he wasn't possessive, there it was all along, the abandonment, a gaping pit of neediness. Haruki has braved the pit; seen that it is ultimately empty, a mirage. Abandonment was just another scary story he had told himself, he had been invested in it somehow. Believed in it. *A sad story of loss and despair.* Even so, his heart still thumps when he receives the message from Idea. She has signed it 'Bibi'. *Huh. I guess she found her name in the mountains after all.* He tickles Toto under the chin before he leaves the house. 'Bibi' wants to meet him at Hoboneko park. *Or is it Sarareman park? Classic.* He decides to cycle all the way there, he has been riding his bike further and further of late. When he arrives, he sees her sitting next to Hoboneko on his customary bench. She is scratching the cat behind the ears. *Oh, so you acknowledge HER existence? Huh. Maybe he prefers to be thought of as a working man.*

She looks different. He sits beside her, holds out his hand to shake as though they've never met,

"Haruki Mori."

She dodges the shake, turns his hand palm up and high fives it with hers instead.

"Bianhua. Bibi for short."

Haruki asks, "so you found your name?"

She smiles,

"I'm gradually being stitched back together. On my terms. I remembered some things spontaneously up in the north and decided to go see The Hypnotist. Did you hear about him?"

"He sounds like one of the Mortech Five?"

"Yes. A natty little gent. French. He gave me back a few things, not everything. Just the important things I think. My family. My origins..."

"Ah. Brownlandia. Mr and Mrs Brown miss their little girl?"

She punches him gently in the arm

"Dag."

He laughs and says to himself, *it's true. I am a dag.*

"Bianhua? Sounds mysterious... beautiful?"

"Yeah. Look it up. My parents were interesting people. I remember that now."

She puts her hand over her heart,

"it's good to have them back."

She pauses, and Haruki gives her the time to tell him whatever she wants to.

"The Hypnotist also returned the memory of what happened to my son... how he died."

Haruki moves a little closer to her, touches her hand very lightly with his fingertips and tells her,

"I'm here for you. When you want me. To listen."

She takes his hand, brings it to her lips and kisses it very softly.

"Haruki. I need to leave Japan."

He feels the loss of her in his body. But he doesn't drown.

Doggy paddles mate. You'll make it.

He looks her in the eyes,

"Ok. You need to go see your family?"

"Yes. I still want us to meet some day in Kyoto. If you still want to? But I don't know when..."

Haruki nods. Embraces not knowing.

"Ok."

She stands, points proudly to a silver bike chained up across the way,

"Pegasus. Do you have a bike?"

He admires Pegasus,

"I do. But mine doesn't have a name, weirdly enough for me. I tend to give everything a nickname, it's an Australian habit I think."

She takes him by the hand and asks him,

"Are you busy today? We could go find a name for your bike?"

They leave the park together, Haruki looks back at Hoboneko as they leave and he appears to be snoozing, laying on top of his newspaper. *Sarareman! Ha! Old friend, hard at work I see.*

Jana takes Hermes to the home of Tanaka and Chester. He is overjoyed to see them but looks up at her as she leaves and cocks his head, whining a little. *He knows. Just as I know.* She scratches him under the chin and whispers in his ear

"I love you Hermes. I always loved you little friend. Thank you."

She allows the men to escort her to the gate. Bianhua does not know when she will return to Japan, but Tanaka assures Jana that Hermes will be well cared for until her return. Jana returns north to spend her last days with Michiko. *I don't know how I know these are my last days, but I know. Curious.* As she sits in her chair overlooking the garden she reflects on her time at Mortech. She feels she has done all she can now for the awakened pod occupants. She thinks one by one of the Mortech Five, places their titles down in front of her in her mind's eye like members of the major tarot arcana.

The Architect. The Anesthetist. The Hypnotist. The Gamer.

The Mathematician.

She quietly removes her own card, snaps her fingers; it disappears in a puff of smoke. For days now she has been internally referring to the team as The Mortech Four, quietly disappearing herself. She marvels that, in the end, they could be genuinely thought of as a team. *But soon Mortech will be no more, the experiment is almost at an end, not one of us wants it to continue. But there may be new collaborations, new experiments.* She thinks of the pod occupants and snorts to herself as she recalls what Lennox told her. Apparently Vance had named the six occupants for the first two letters of his favourite Pokemon. *Ridiculous child.* She thinks of her own pod name, XE, and chuckles to herself. She did not tell Lennox that she simply made it up. *It means nothing at all. Nothing whatsoever.* She laughs at herself now. *This life! How very ridiculous.* And quietly, very simply, her heart stops beating, her old lungs draw their final breath and her tired mouth sags open in an O of awe.

So. The Pattern.

Thanks

Much thanks to my family and friends for your support
in all my creative endeavours. You know who you are.

Author Biography

Writer, artist and spiritual nerd Jessica Berry was born creative and curious. For all her multi-disciplinary creative adventuring, her favourite thing to make is the tiny tears caused by transcendent laughter.

She is the author and illustrator of two children's books and an insight card and book set. Wake is her third adventure in publishing.

Follow: @kundalinguini_